Laurie lives in Victoria, Australia with her partner and two cats (who have a mansion outside). As a Sci-Fi aficionado, she maintains an active blog of science fiction, fantasy, and flash fiction pieces (found at www.solothefirst.wordpress.com), and serves as a regular volunteer at her local theatre company. (Including several stints as Assistant Director). She has several short stories published in the Antipodean SF E-Magazine. www.antisf.com and many new books on the go.

White Fire

A Toni Delle Adventure

Laurie Bell

Dedication

White Fire is dedicated to Nana and Poppa Bell. You taught me the joy of reading, took me to the library, inspired me, read to me, read next to me, showed me just how important books could be. Look, I wrote one!

PART ONE

CHAPTER ONE

"Collision in less than one minute."

Zach's pixilated face disappeared from the screen near Toni's elbow and a large countdown clock appeared.

"Really?" she snapped at the Computer Intelligence Interface. Targeting controls moved of their own accord under her fingertips as Mate continued to fire at their attacker.

She glanced down at the canine robot. He lay in the small opening under the console in front of her knees. A hardline cable snaked from the console into the back of his head, parting the fake fur covering his metallic body. It gave him direct access to the *Blackflame*'s weaponry and cut seconds off the ship's reaction time.

"Keep shooting, Mate." Toni had never been more glad for Mate's micro-speed and predictive accuracy. *Kheghing hell, this is a disaster.* They were going to end up as floating pieces of frozen flesh and inactive chunks of metal.

"Direct impact," Zach reported. Toni didn't spare a glance at her viewer as she threw the *Blackflame* into another dive, preventing the second ship achieving target lock by mere seconds.

"We have to get out of here, Boss," Zach warned, his voice rising above the scream of the overextended generator.

Ya think? Toni put the *Blackflame* into another spin. "Mate?"

"I have completed the scans," he announced, voice steady. Toni's heart was trying to escape out of her throat and she wished she had even an ounce of her partner's robotic calm. Her hands were clenched so hard around the control stick, her fingers were cramping.

"Did you get what we need?" she shouted. The pitch of her voice rose as the *Blackflame* rocked sharply again. *Shenghi! Stay out of their targeting sensors!* Tendrils of her hair slipped across her face. She didn't have a hand free to yank the white strands away.

"I have been unable to paint either ship with a marker."

"We have entered the asteroid belt," Zach announced. Toni didn't need the CII to tell her that, she could tell from the way the small ship bounced and jolted like it was achieving orbit without a gravity stabilizer. She strengthened the deflector shield and flicked on her personally designed predictive tracking program.

"Zach?"

"The *Renegade* and the *Tigerforce* have halted outside the belt," Zach confirmed.

"That is because the pilots are not fools," Mate said.

Meaning she was. Well, he wasn't wrong. Toni cut the *Blackflame*'s speed and allowed momentum from the NSD, the Normal Space Drive, to push them further into the field. "Mate, I need you to navigate with Zach. Plot us a course through this madness." She pulled hard on the stick as a misshapen hunk of rock appeared in front of them without warning. Sweat dripped into her eyes, slicking the skin where her electronic shades sat on the bridge of her nose. She didn't dare release the controls to stop them slipping. The bridge's harsh lighting speared into her sensitive eyes, making them water and blurring her vision. *Icy.*

She couldn't initiate a Ticyon Flux Field from within the belt. Small pieces of rock no thicker than her fingernail would prevent the *Blackflame* generating a field of Ticyons solid enough. Without the field to force space to bend, there was no way the *Blackflame* was jumping. She had to get them out of the asteroid belt.

Her body jerked forward with the strength of the next hit. Her shades flew off her face as her safety belt crushed her chest. The cockpit lights immediately dimmed. *Thanks Zach.* Even in the midst of a firefight he was aware of her limitations.

"We need to get out of here. If the shields fail, we'll be mashed into pieces."

"Yes, Zach," she said, sarcasm dripping from her tone. It was that or scream in terror. "Are the two ships waiting for us?" She squinted into the display screen, the brightness of the backlight sent spears of pain into her eyeballs. Details blurred into a wash of color.

"I can no longer see the *Renegade* or the *Tigerforce* on the scanners. However, that does not mean they have left the system."

"We'll have to take the risk. Mate, have you got a path?"

"Seventy-eight percent probable."

"Seventy-eight percent probable we'll get through the belt in one piece?" The C-bot didn't answer. *Shenghi!* "What are my options, guys? More speed or less?"

"Floor it," Zach told her.

Mate contradicted him immediately. "No, greater speed will increase our chances of taking damage. Severe damage."

"Trust me," Zach said.

Toni flicked her gaze to the closest screen. Zach's digitized face blinked up at her. "Boss, trust me," he implored. *Could a CII implore?* As Zach was the first CII Toni had ever owned, she didn't know if his emotional responses were the result of the modifications she'd made to his programming or if he'd always had that ability. *Kheghing hell. Make a freaking decision already.*

She could trust Mate. Zach was an unknown. And yet …

Pulling her straps tighter, she ordered Mate to lock himself in. Taking a deep breath, she addressed the CII. "If this is a short trip, pal, I'm resetting your defaults."

Two near misses and one heart wrenching moment of indecision later, the *Blackflame* shot out of the asteroid belt at full speed. Sweat saturated Toni's silk shirt. After she peeled her hand off the stick, she clutched weakly at her stomach. Breathing through her nose, she swallowed back bile and sank into her seat.

"Great flying, Boss!" Zach whooped with electronic glee.

"Seriously, I am reprogramming you," she told him, her voice wobbling. After a moment, she lifted her head. "The two ships? The Stargazer and the Sunchaser?"

"The Stargazer designated *Renegade* and the Sunchaser designated *Tigerforce* are no longer appearing on our scanners."

"Khegh it!" Toni let the *Blackflame* drift while she recovered from the battle and the stress of flying through the asteroid belt. Luckily her shades weren't broken. Slipping them back on her nose protected her delicate eyes but not her pride. *Useless.* She laid her head against the seat rest and breathed slowly. *I'm still here.* It had been touch and go. Her hands shook—khegh it, her whole body wracked with tremors. Her skin was clammy, she was probably in shock. Mate monitored her vital signs but hadn't said anything, so she couldn't be too bad off. A lie down and a nap, or a very stiff drink, was on the cards. She'd failed to capture the pirates. Tears prickled. She was a failure as an agent and as a pilot. *What am I going to do now?* She pictured her boss's face when she told him the news. Antonio Zaambuka wouldn't say a word she was sure, but his stare would contain all his disappointment. Scratching her nails against her neck scars, her mind fell blank.

This was not the glowing start to her agent career she'd been hoping for. "How can I call Zaambuka now? I can't report I've lost our main suspect."

"So don't tell him."

Toni squinted at the CII's face on the screen near her elbow. "Zach, I have to. Look, you're new, I haven't fully explained the situation and I—"

"Perhaps a better option would be to delay your report until you have something to offer?" Mate suggested.

She smiled down at her long-time friend and scratched a hand through his fake fur. The course chestnut strands tangled beneath her fingers. "I'm so glad I have you, Mate. What would I do without you?"

"You will never need to find out. I will always be here."

There wasn't a lot she was grateful to her parents for—not that she'd ever admit to, anyway—but Mate was the exception. Mate was everything. "Good plan." She stared into the viewscreen at the empty blackness outside her ship. Plasteel and a deflector shield was all that stood between her and a nasty death. "I should get him a tie," she mused.

"Boss?"

"Do not bother to ask, Zach." Mate said dropping his head to rest on top of his paws.

Toni looked down at her friend. "Aww—he's new. We should tell him about our mission."

Zach appeared on every screen. His digital face lifted the outline of an eyebrow. "Boss? Our mission is to find the hijacked supply ships and stop the hijackers, isn't it?"

Toni grinned, well aware it made her look a little mad. The CII wouldn't notice. Kheghing hell, she loved their non-judgmental little circuits. "Do you know how we got you, Zach?"

Reaching forward, she started tapping their next course into the navigation program. All the shipments had gone missing between their pick-up point on Marn and Waystation EEXDU or Waystation Tildex. She decided to head back to EEXDU.

"I was assigned to you when you were gifted with the *Blackflame* upon your graduation."

Toni took a moment to stroke the panel beneath her fingertips at the memory. "Yes, Zach. Zaambuka, Ant—I call him Ant—gave me a ship, this ship. I thought it was a loaner, you know? But nope. Registration codes and all—in my name. I still don't know why."

"Because he believes in you, Toni," Mate said.

She shook her head. Numbers ran through massively complex calculations beneath her hands. "It still doesn't make sense. I'm sure it's a test of some sort." She watched the numbers dance. *I won't let him down.* She would solve this case. No matter what it took.

"And the tie? I still don't understand."

Toni let loose a laugh. The numbers stopped. "Let's go," she told the CII. Through the screen, space blurred and dissolved as they jumped. She leaned back and released her security belt. "Tie! Ha. Ant is pretty retro—loves old human traditions. A hang over from growing up on one of the border settlements. Well. He wears these old human clothes, suits and stuff, so I like to buy him ties—the more garish the pattern, the better. We, uh, don't have a lot of money, Zach."

Toni burst out laughing. Her hysteria was probably a result of the adrenaline release from the recent battle.

"Why do you call it your mission?" The CII still sounded confused. How could an electronic voice sound that way? Curious. She'd better check the coding she'd tweaked, she might have tagged something incorrectly.

"And our actual mission?" Mate asked, disconnecting from the ship and moving out to sit down beside her.

"Oh Mate, way to spoil the mood." Toni thought back to the rumors they'd heard on their first visit to Waystation EEXDU. "We know management suspects pirate activity in the area and we know a Sunchaser and a Stargazer are frequent visitors around both Waystations from Zach's hack into the security feeds," she mused aloud.

"Engineer Danson on Waystation EEXDU mentioned a Stargazer offloading crates of water with the Marn logo. Do you believe they will return?"

"They'll be long gone, Boss." Zach insisted. "The two pilots wouldn't dare return to the station. I think they'll disappear completely."

Toni dropped her head into her hands. Mate shuffled closer and pressed his body weight against her leg. She lowered her hands without thinking and ran her fingers through his faux fur.

"Stopping them today does not mean the next shipment will be safe from hijack," Mate told the CII.

What next? Blank. Her mind was completely blank. Failure. That's all she could see.

"Boss?"

"Just give me a minute." What had Zach said before? She straightened. Stop the hijackers. "How did the pirates find out about the shipments?"

"Boss?"

Toni glanced down at Mate. "How did they discover the shipment route?"

"We looked into that," Zach interrupted.

"Tell me again. Break it down," she ordered. "The shipments are loaded on Marn, but the route is not assigned until they arrive at the first Waystation. You spoke to the dock master and the clerk who organized the schedules. There was no time for the message to be changed or altered before the route was assigned, therefore no time for it to be discovered and intercepted."

She gazed up at the cockpit ceiling. Both the clerk and the dock master on the first Waystation were clean. "The second Waystation?"

"The control center was tight. Backgrounds checked out. No anomalies, no new staff, no sudden departures. I hacked the system and there was nothing odd." Zach told her.

"I only told you to get into the security feeds. You hacked the servers?"

"Yes."

"Did you run a check to see if anyone else hacked the servers before you?"

Zach was silent.

"And what about the first Waystation?" *Why didn't I think of this before?* Toni twitched her head to the side. How could Zaambuka trust her to handle this investigation alone when she'd forgotten some of the most basic elements of a con—distraction and misdirection. She could fix this. She *would* fix this and solve her first case. Zaambuka would see. She could do this. "What about data leaks?"

"We will have to return to both locations to run those tests, Boss."

CHAPTER TWO

The *Blackflame* arrived on Waystation EEXDU early in the Waystation's morning, or so the local time alert told her. To Toni, it felt like late evening. She should have checked the station's standard time and squeezed in a nap. Time differences always gave her a dull headache.

As the two agents stepped off the *Blackflame*'s ramp, Toni tasked the CII with the job of infiltrating the Waystation's electronic systems to search deeper after he reported finding fragmented code. She and Mate headed to the dock master's office to confirm the shipping routes again. The stolen manifests listed basic medical supplies, water, clothes, and mechanical parts. It seemed like an odd list of items to steal. She wondered if the pirates might be setting up a base somewhere.

The dock master scratched at his balding scalp as he thought about his answer. His skin, tinged aqua-green, suggested he originated from the Odeen Sector, but Toni couldn't be sure. A forked tongue darted out to lick his lips. Well, that confirmed it. "Yeah, I remember a Sunchaser. Big old mark on the stern. The pilot was hard to forget."

"Why is that?" The smell of alcohol wafting off the dock master was so strong. Toni didn't know if it came from his breath or his clothes.

"The woman stood out, you know what I'm saying? A bit like you. I mean, not see through and all, but she made an impression. Built real nice and knew how to dress. She was memorable, all right?"

Toni tugged the sleeve of her silk shirt down over her wrist. Silk was one of the only materials that didn't irritate her sensitive skin. "In what way? I need more than just an impression. I need a description."

"'Bout your height. Hair that was all colors. Purple eyes. Astril accent."

"Astrillian?" What was a Sector Two native doing all the way out here?

"Do you mind getting me a screen capture off your security vision?"

"Honey, those things don't work. They're just for show, you know? A way to deter troublemakers."

She sighed. *Of course* the security systems didn't work. Her shades vibrated against her nose. A message from Zach popped up on her glasses display.

Zach: Hey Boss.

Toni glanced up, locating Mate. He was still prowling the docking port, matching each ship to the station's database. With no signal from him, it was unlikely he and Zach had uncovered a discrepancy. *Hm. What else could Zach have found?* She asked the dock master for a copy of the delivery docket to compare it against the list Zach pulled from Marn. The dock master swayed unsteadily as he returned to the main office.

"Zach?" She barely gave voice to the utterance, knowing the small microphone in her shades would pick it up.

Zach: Boss, I think I've found something. You were right; it looks like there was another hack, a week earlier than mine. The coding was buried pretty deep. They did a decent job covering their tracks, but I have located two access points. One in the morning, and again a few hours later. They pulled the dummy route from the navigation system, but it looks like it didn't confuse them for long.

Gotcha! "Anything you can track? Can you tell me where the hack was made?"

Zach: Send Mate to access the exact terminal and I can get a better read for you. I'll flash a map of the location and request Mate head back to you now.

"Thanks." She signed off as the dock master returned, carrying a small notepad.

"This is all I could find."

"Thank you," she told him. Mate emerged from the shadows painting the rear of the bay black. The dock master's eyes widened and his tongue darted out to taste the air of the bay.

"What is that?"

Toni's lips quirked up in the corner. "My pet."

"That's a pet?" The dock master stumbled back as Mate drew near. The man let out a sharp screech and ran toward his office. He didn't take his eyes off Mate the entire way.

"Stop it," she admonished when the C-bot reached her side.

Mate looked up at her and tilted his head. "I am not sure what you mean."

"Uh huh." She rolled her eyes. "Come on. Let's find that terminal."

*

Mate backed out of the console's base. "That is all I can access."

Using the C-bot's signal, Zach had accessed the Waystation's system and discovered two more pieces of information about the unknown hacker. The attack originated from an internal connection via a booster box installed into that particular terminal, and the signal was a familiar one. Zach's text bubble appeared.

Zach: It's definitely the Stargazer. It appears he's a frequent visitor.

Toni spoke quietly, peering around to see if they were being watched. "Zach, can you leave a little gift for our Stargazer friend? Something to activate next time he lands here?"

Zach: Yes.

She smirked. There was no way she was letting the pilot escape now. Finally, she had a chance to solve this case. Those pirates were as good as captured. "It can't be noticed, Zach. Throw a timer onto it. Don't let it activate on install."

Zach: I gotcha, Boss. Are you headed back?

She shook her head. Though Zach couldn't see her, she found the behavior was instinctive. There was time to go over Marn's supply list again and check her info drop.

Zach: Boss?

"No. We'll be back soon, though."

Toni headed toward the station's meal zone. Last time here, she'd set up an informant's anonymous drop and had Zach post several reports on the holonet with hidden messages. She didn't expect anything would come from the request for information, but on the off chance there had been a response, she should empty the inbox.

With Mate covering the meal zone entrance, Toni strolled to the rear wall. Below the large holoscreen were several small ports. Eyes followed her across the floor; she ignored them through long practice and leaned back against the wall, playing with her shades. Slipping a hand behind her to feign a scratch, she slipped a fingernail-sized chip from one of the ports.

A good ten count later, she straightened and headed to one of the meal counters. Searching the boards for a meal that didn't sound too disgusting, she purchased a small bag of fried cerulean stick-leaves and wandered back out of the zone.

*

"Zach, how's that message chip coming? Anything on it?"

"Yes, Boss. There's an encoded message."

"Can you break it?"

"Working on it."

Mate raised his head. "Why encode the message?"

Toni shrugged. It did seem self-defeating. She returned to the tablet in her hand. On it were the two manifests "Mate, are you seeing what I'm seeing? There are discrepancies with the water volumes." She sunk into the three-seater, the worn red cover stretched but never seemed to tear. Mate lay at her feet. She needed mats. No, a rug—she should get a rug. The interior of the *Blackflame* was pretty bare since she hadn't had time to purchase anything personal. To do that, she needed to solve this case and get paid more than the stipend Zaambuka gave his agents at case assignment.

"Who would steal water?" Mate asked.

"Someone desperate I suppose," Toni said.

"I've been investigating the stocks. It's too expensive already. It's only going to go up. Maybe the pirates are part of a black market ring? It appears there's good coin in water supplies," Zach jumped in.

"I have a feeling we're missing something."

"Boss, I've opened the message," the CII announced a moment later.

Toni sat up. "What does it say?"

Zach projected the reply onto the nearest screen, and Toni read it quickly.

> *Supplies not what you think. The Reef, Uxt. Contact will provide further intel. Belani woman seated close to the bar, alone. Code name: Jasmine.*

"Can you ping the source?"

The CII declared negative.

Mate rose up on all fours. "This sounds like a trap, Boss."

Toni agreed. Still, she'd heard about Uxt. The planet was a water world with only five percent of its landmass located above the surface. It had become a major tourist mecca after the inhabitants of Uxt built a massive entertainment complex and casino under the planet's ocean. The Reef, Zach informed her, was a well-known bar located within the complex.

Toni knew that already. The Reef was talked about in glowing terms at the Academy. Every traveling Defender or Sentinel who addressed her small class had ended the lecture extolling the virtues of the bar on Uxt, with a suggestion to the new graduates to stop at The Reef if they were in the area. Toni had always intended to visit. "The place will be full of Defenders, Sentinels, and STCT. If this mysterious contact wants to meet us there, then let's do it."

CHAPTER THREE

Mate let out an unhappy snarl and paced in a circle when she told him to wait outside. As Toni entered the bar, she let the swinging doors catch her in the back to stop them rattling, removed her shades and peered from the top of the flight of stairs into darkness. Her eyes adjusted quickly, allowing her to make out the interior. The Reef opened out onto a rectangular floor. Along the back wall she spied a counter with two men behind it. *Shenghi!* The enormous man on the right yanked bottles from beneath the bar, throwing them up into the air from all four limbs. Somehow, the other barman, the one with the flaming red hair, avoided a crack in his skull while pouring drinks for the crowd standing three deep in front of the counter. What tables Toni could see were fully occupied. Gray STCT uniforms, Sentinel red peaked caps, and the occasional gold flash of agent badges, allowed Toni to relax—her back was covered.

Yellow and green Defender uniforms dotted the room, but were mostly gathered around a ten-seater circular booth in the far rear corner. There was a lot of laughter coming from it.

A few darkened corridors appeared to lead to washrooms and what was likely a rear exit. Why on Marn would her contact want to meet her here?

Toni approached the lone woman seated at a table close to the bar in the corner furthest from the Defenders in the rear booth. Voluminous black hair cascaded around her bare, dusky shoulders, a stark contrast to Toni's own straight white locks. The Belani woman's pointed ears twitched and pricked up, her eyes widened as they traveled up and down Toni's body. "Jasmine?" Toni enquired, taking a seat opposite.

"Love the shirt."

Toni appreciated the compliment though she didn't respond. It wasn't a style choice. Jasmine gestured to the four-armed barkeep. "Jeri, two more." Somehow her snarky voice carried above the loud chatter, or perhaps Jeri had been waiting for her, because he raised one arm almost instantly in acknowledgement.

"What do you have for me?" Toni asked. No point in wasting time.

"Hey, there, hold up a little. You're fast, hun. How about we both have a drink and get to know one another first?" Jasmine ran her fingers along the side of the half-empty flute. So, she'd already imbibed. With luck, it would make her chatty. The woman took a long sip, scrutinizing Toni over the rim. Her lips were freshly painted with a deep red gloss, liberally staining the rim of the flute.

Toni narrowed her eyes. "I've got things I should be doing. Either tell me what you've got, or I'm leaving."

The four-armed barkeep Jasmine named Jeri placed two flutes filled with a bubbly pink liquid in front of Toni and shot a warm smile at Jasmine. "Hey, girl, what are you still doing here?"

Jasmine pointed to Toni and then back at Jeri. "Hey, this is my friend, Jeri, Jer this is …"

Suspecting the woman was well on her way to very drunk, Toni sighed. *This is such a bad idea.* "Delle. Agent Delle."

"Have a drink, Agent Delle. Then we can have some fun." Jasmine smiled, exposing a lot of shiny white teeth. Her eyes remained sharp, though. Toni had the sudden impression of a carnivorous beast lying in wait. This was getting her nowhere. She needed to get back out searching for the pirates, not spend her night in a bar full of drunks. Toni stood.

"No wait, wait. Dan Colten. That's the name you want." One eyebrow cocked as if Toni should recognize the name. She didn't.

Toni sat back down, sipping from her flute when the other woman gestured to it pointedly. Toni ran her tongue around her mouth tasting the sweet berry liquor. She would have preferred water but they all knew how expensive that was. Especially the unfiltered kind. "Tell me about Colten."

"He's a smuggler. And a jackass," Jasmine said, slurring her words.

Oh great, a jilted lover. Toni didn't need this. Tonight was looking like a giant waste of time. "I take it you know him well?"

"He just shot you into an asteroid belt, didn't he? You must think he's a jackass too," Jasmine replied with a snort.

Toni coughed as she swallowed her drink. "How did you know about that?" She took another sip from her flute and leaned forward. A sneeze erupted from her nose. *Strong drink.*

"I know *everything*," Jasmine declared before swallowing the contents of her glass in a long gulp.

Toni watched, bemused. "He doesn't know you're here, does he?"

Jasmine grinned and raised her hand, gesturing for another round.

Resigned to a long night, Toni tapped the edge of her shades to signal the all-clear to Mate. "So, what happened?" She let her forehead crease and bit her bottom lip, an expression she'd learned from her sister. If there was anyone who could fake interest well, it was Serina.

Her mysterious contact waved a hand in the air. "I can't tell you."

"How did you know about the asteroid belt?" Toni asked. It was like interrogating a hostile witness. She was getting nothing. A tick twitched in Toni's right eye. *Mission. Remember the mission. Get the information and get out.*

Jasmine snorted. Toni couldn't help but focus on the way the woman's petite features scrunched, the tiny lines around her eyes deepened and a little crease appeared in her nose. *Kheghing hell, am I attracted to her?* Toni tore her gaze away and ran her hands over her arms, covering as much of her upper body as she could with the movement. Her cheeks burned and she grit her teeth. No, it wasn't attraction. It was envy. Toni felt so gangly in contrast to the woman's graceful movements. *What am I doing?* An agent didn't react emotionally to anything or anyone. This woman had no power to hurt her; she was an information source, that was all.

"Jasmine, why am I even here if you're not going to—"

"Okay, no. We need to clear this up straight away. It's just Jas, not Jasmine—never Jasmine. *They* call me Jasmine."

"*They?*"

"The smugglers," she hissed, her voice so soft Toni could barely make out the words above the chatter and laughter around them.

Jeri placed two more frothing flutes onto the table. "Jas," he warned.

"Oh, don't," the tipsy woman grumbled in reply, leaning back into her chair. She stared at Toni over the rim of her replenished drink. "They take me for granted."

"Is that why you're doing this?" Toni asked.

Jas's gaze drifted around the room.

I'm not going to get the truth, am I? She took another sip from her drink. Placing the glass down, Toni propped her arms on the table and searched the woman's face. There was no tension around her eyes, the lines and crinkles just gave her a tired air. Why had Jas contacted her? Toni knew she should storm out, but something about Jas made her linger. Her dark gaze locked onto Toni. Maybe it was the hint of loneliness Toni recognized. Mate and Zach were the best companions a woman could wish for, but they weren't alive. Mate had been designed as Toni's childhood companion and Zach—well, she hadn't worked him out yet. Not entirely. Her tweaks to his default programming seemed to be having a unique effect and as a result she wasn't sure what he was going to end up as. The cold hole in Toni's chest seemed to widen and for a heartbeat, Toni wanted. Wanted a warm touch, wanted a shoulder to lean on, wanted an ear to listen to her woes. Could this woman be all that?

What am I thinking? She's a contact, a smuggler. I can't trust her.

Did she need to?

For one night, Toni could pretend, couldn't she? That she was normal. That she was open and friendly. *Just keep your weapon close.*

Toni picked up her flute and swallowed the contents in one gulp. Fire erupted throughout her body. She swiped a finger below her nose to remove the sweat. *That kicks like a TAFF Generator.*

"Wooh, now we're talking! Here." Jas pushed over another drink. Jeri retrieved the empties with his lower hands and pointed one finger of his upper hand into Jas's face. "Be good, girl." With the fourth hand he pointed at Toni. "And you, too." His grin grew wide enough to take over his entire face.

Toni couldn't help but grin back. Jeri's lower hand rested for a split second on her shoulder before he turned away. Warmth flowed down her arm and spread to her chest. She blinked. *Work, remember, this is work.* She shook her head. *Screw it.*

"See, Jeri's terrific," Jas said loudly. Toni guessed Jeri heard her because one of his hands came around behind his back and held up a finger.

Toni giggled, covering her mouth with her hand. Her reaction made Jas shriek with laughter.

Eight drinks later, Toni told Jas all about her sister and mother. No names of course—she didn't think there was enough alcohol in the galaxy to strip her of the control that had kept her alive all these years. It felt great just to vent. Jas remained just as vague as she complained heatedly about her co-workers. A blank, spacy feeling crowded the usual sharp voice of reason out of Toni's head. Heat pulsed inside her skin. She flapped her hands in front of her face, suddenly uncomfortable with her emotions. Was she actually having fun? Urgh. Admittedly, she was growing to like Jas. Maybe not as a true friend, but the woman was listening when Toni spoke, making eye contact and groaning sympathetically. And khegh, it felt good to be heard.

Jas took Toni's wrist, comparing her dark skin to Toni's freakish non-color. "So clear. It's like I can see straight through you." Toni snatched her hand out of Jas's scalding grip. "No, no. I'm sorry. It's cool." Jas held her arms aloft. "I guess I shouldn't ask about the … you know." Jas touched her own neck. Toni shook her head, fighting not to cover her scars. "How about we do something else then?" She turned toward the bar. "You dance?"

"I … no."

"Another drink." Jas smiled. Her eyes glinted, brightening as her smile deepened the lines.

Toni glanced at the empty glasses gathered on the table. Jeri appeared. Two more pink monstrosities pushed close to her hand.

Another three drinks in and it was Toni who suggested they move to the top of the bar's counter. Jas grabbed hold of Toni's hand, declaring it was a great idea, and in moments the two women were dancing on the counter to the catcalls of the men and women lingering in the bar.

Slipping her jacket and badge off to hide her status, Toni worried briefly that the other agents in the bar would recognize her, but it wasn't as though she was nondescript. Shenghi, practically everyone in the room had to know who she was. No one approached her though. Of course they didn't. She'd been just as alone at the Academy as she was in her personal life. No one ever really spoke to her, got to know her. Why would they now? Her difference kept them all away. The usual cold feeling in her chest at the thought wasn't as cold. She blinked. *Huh!* They were fabulous drinks that Jas kept ordering. Toni had to remember to get the name of it.

Jas kicked out a squishy pouch she'd pulled from somewhere and berated the drunken agents until they started throwing their coins into it.

Toni thought it was all hilarious. She'd never experienced this kind of attention before. She fantasized the unfocused eyes stared at her with desire. Her jaw ached from all the smiling. She'd never felt so carefree, nothing bothered her.

"You're all right, Delle," Jas told her. Toni quickly interrupted to insist the woman call her Toni. After all, it was only for one night. She'd never see Jas again. What did it matter?

The fun came to an end when Jas tried to climb off the counter. She slipped, letting out a sharp cry. Toni reached for her, heart pounding, but her reaction time was impaired. She could only watch as Jas crashed to the ground.

Toni jumped off the counter and dropped at the woman's side. "Jas?"

Jas grabbed her hand. "Whoops! Oh damn." Her grip tightened on Toni's fingers.

"You're hurt." Toni braced Jas's back when the injured woman tried to roll over. Jas let out a little whimper. Toni cradled her shoulders. "Hang on, move slow."

A wobbly smile greeted that comment.

Jeri appeared out of nowhere. He waved off the red-headed barkeep who he'd called Peti or Peta or something like that and scooped Jas into his arms. "Grab the bag, kid," he ordered.

Toni snatched up the soft leathery pouch, overflowing with coin, and followed Jeri to the back stairs, apologizing profusely with every step.

"Forget it, Tones, it's all good. Can't feel it anyway," Jas mumbled into Jeri's shoulder as they climbed.

The roar of bar noise was still thick in Toni's head, muting her hearing in the silence of the upper floor. Feeling seasick, she swayed from side to side, but the corridor seemed to bend in the opposite direction. She scolded the walls and demanded they stay still. Jas … Jas was hurt. "I'm sorry." She never should have suggested dancing on the bar.

"Seriously, she's fine, kid. Here, go in and drag the blankets off the bed, would ya?"

With her head unbalanced from alcohol and the climb, Toni staggered around Jeri to open the door. A large enticing bed was the first thing she saw. Tearing her gaze away, she glanced around the minimalist room. Comfort but not personal was what sprang to mind. One window, slightly blurry, was large enough to climb through and the door behind Toni seemed the only way in or out. It was secure enough. Toni wavered her way to the bed and pulled the comforter off. "Is she okay?"

"Just the ankle. Does it every kheghing time and no doubt she'll do it next time, too. You shouldn't have listened to her." Jeri looked at Toni with his deep-set eyes. His face was barely flushed after his climb carrying Jasmine's practically dead weight.

Toni winced. "It was my idea to dance on the bar," she said, clutching at her aching head.

"Was it, kid?"

What? Her head hurt too badly to respond. *What does he mean?* She was sure the bar dancing had been her own idea. She swayed and stumbled into a wall. *Huh, where did that come from?*

"Kid, you're both plastered. Sit down on the bed, would ya? Before you fall down."

"I have to get back to my ship."

He peered down at her. *When did I sit down?* Jas snored softly beside her as Jeri removed Toni's shoes. "What are you doing?" she asked, her thoughts muddy. He shook his head at her, and that was the last thing she saw before she woke up on a giant bed next to a dark-skinned Belani woman and a man with four arms. Somehow, her shades had stayed on her face.

What the khegh happened last night? Toni rose part way off the bed only to collapse back down with a loud groan. Her head thumped. Her mouth felt like she'd swallowed her own shoes. *Where the kheghing hell am I?*

A moan escaped her lips. It was echoed by the women beside her. "Kheghing firepits, that's awful."

Toni didn't want to risk moving again but managed to turn her head; happily, her stomach stayed where it was. She squinted at the woman. "Hey."

Jas cracked open one eye and glared in Toni's direction. Her ears twitched and lay flat. "If I tell you I hate you right now, will it ruin the friendship?"

Friendship? "It might." Toni forced herself to her feet. Either she needed another drink or a massive cup of caff—like a mug the size of Mate. *Speaking of ...* She stumbled determinedly from the small room, knowing she had to contact her partner.

A male voice croaked from the bed. "If you hang about, breakfast will be downstairs in thirty."

At the thought of food, her stomach immediately rebelled. Toni raced from the room as laughter erupted from the bed. Dragging herself from the tiny washroom after revisiting her alcohol-filled evening, she slumped against the wall outside and activated her shades. Two pop up messages began blinking at her. She groaned. "*Shh,* not so fast."

Mate: Boss, do you require assistance?
Zach: Boss, where are you?

"Still at the bar. I'm good, immensely hungover, but I'm fine."

Zach: The contact?

"Still working on it." If she didn't move then the room didn't spin. Right now, that was the best option.

Mate: Do you require me to enter?

"No, it's fine. I'll be out in a few hours. My contacts are making me breakfast."

There were no further messages in response to that. The bar was empty when Toni made it downstairs. She sat—well, more like fell—and dropped her head into her hands. The pounding had become a steelcrete jackhammer. Who authorized construction works to start inside her skull?

The tumbler placed beneath her nose startled her upright. Toni's hand darted to her hip, but aborted the move—it was only Jeri. *I fell asleep again.* She leaned back and moaned. The sickly sweet smell of overripe fruit wafting up from the drink turned her stomach. She slapped a hand over her mouth.

"This will help," he said. Jas fell into the chair opposite, and the two women stared blankly into the blue liquid.

"It actually does help," Jas muttered. "It's just getting to the part where you can drink it that's the worst."

"Worst," Toni confirmed, squinting at the other woman. She figured she felt as bad as Jas looked—drawn and pale, rubbing wearily at red-rimmed eyes. Her hair even hung limply around her face as if it was too tired to look spectacular. "You look like crap."

"You too," Jas replied with a nod.

Both women grinned and groaned at the pain the movement caused before they downed their glasses. "Oh my gods," Toni choked out. "What the khegh is in that?" She instantly felt better. Her stomach settled and her head started to clear. Toni looked up at Jas with wide eyes.

"Jer won't tell me. Icy, isn't it? Like a pure shot of sunshine. Right, now down to business."

"What?" Toni blinked. *What is she talking …? Oh.* Toni sat up.

"Well, yeah, do you want the information I have or not?"

"Yes, of course," Toni replied.

"Dan didn't do it. I don't expect you to believe me, but he didn't do it. He's an ass, but he wouldn't steal shipments marked for Milten Seven. That water is desperately needed."

"Desert world? Yeah, I can see why Marn's water is necessary but he's a smuggler—so are you. Why do you care?"

"People will die without that water."

Understanding suddenly, Toni sat back. "You've got a base on Miltern Seven?"

Jas snorted. "The Cross doesn't have bases anywhere."

Toni doubted that was the truth and made a mental note to visit Miltern Seven soon. Just to make sure those shipments were only going to the human settlers. Jasmine's face was serious. Toni couldn't detect any of the facial tells that indicated it was a lie. Still, she didn't really know this woman. She couldn't take Jasmine's statement on face value, no matter how much Toni might like her.

"What makes you so sure? He flies a Stargazer called the *Renegade*, doesn't he?"

"Yes …"

"And the *Renegade* was spotted in the vicinity of every ship that's been hijacked in the past five weeks, hasn't it?"

"Yes, but—"

"And you're telling me there's no connection?" Toni raised an eyebrow and waited.

Jas pointed a finger, her face remaining a mask. "Technically, I'm not telling you that. Only that Dan didn't take the shipments."

"He's a smuggler, isn't that in the job description?" Toni accused.

"You agents always get this wrong. Listen, pirates steal for themselves. Smugglers ensure shipments get to where they're meant to be."

"For a fee."

"Of course. But we don't steal."

Toni rolled her eyes and leaned back. "You really expect me to buy that?"

"I just—"

"Tell me where he is and I'll ask him myself." Toni's stomach growled, waking her up to the fact that it was empty. *Shenghi, I could eat a spaceship!* She also had to get back to work. If Jas couldn't give her anything steelcrete then she had to get moving. Besides, she had a name. She could hunt the smuggler down herself now.

"I can't do that."

"Jas." Toni let her voice become a growl as she leaned forward. *Time's up.* "You came here because you had something for me. What is it?"

"I told you, I work for them. He didn't do it." Jas's clear gaze didn't leave Toni's face. She hadn't twitched during her impassioned speech. But she worked for them. Toni knew she had to take everything Jas said with a healthy dose of caution.

"Then who did?"

Both of Jasmine's eyebrows rose and her right ear flicked. "I don't know."

"Jas." Why would she bring Colten to Toni's attention? There had to be something else going on here. Perhaps it wasn't what Jas knew at all. "You think Dan Colten knows who is hijacking the ships?"

Teeth shining brightly, Jas pointed a finger again just as Jeri placed two steaming meals in front of them. "Feeling better?" he asked. They both nodded. "Good." Jeri patted Toni on the back. "Can't wait until next time, girls. You make a great show."

What did he mean by that? At Jas's laugh, the memories came flooding back. "Wait, I danced on a bar? Oh, shenghi pit demons!" Toni dropped her head into her hands. Heat flooded her body. *Oh no no no.* What had she been thinking? And in The Reef? She'd be a laughing stock. *Oh khegh, Zaambuka will hear about it!* She sighed, pretty sure this was the most embarrassed she'd ever felt. *What else?* Toni leaned back to glance under the table. "How's your ankle?"

"Eh, sore, but Jeri strapped it. I'll get it zapped tomorrow—happens all the time. Don't stress it. Speaking of ... here's your cut." Jas pushed a bulging hand-sized bag over the table. Curious, Toni took the leathery pouch and peered inside. It was full of glittery beveled discs.

"Not bad, huh? We are *so* doing this again."

Toni stared at the coin. *Why on Marn am I working as an agent when one night of drunken dancing nets this?* Catching Jas's eye, Toni grinned. "Khegh, yes." Her momentary sense of pleasure plummeted. What would Zaambuka say when he found out about her wild behavior? Rubbing at her chest, she pictured his disappointed face. An agent shouldn't behave that way. "Look, where can I find Dan Colten? I promise I'll only talk to him."

Jas narrowed her eyes.

"Agent's honor, I promise." *Mostly.* Toni held eye contact, burying her emotions deep down. Years of being her parents' disappointment made it pretty easy. Jas's eyes scanned Toni's face—the woman was obviously used to being deceived. But Toni was a pro. After a moment Jas leaned back and nodded, clearly satisfied.

"I'm heading to Bar Four on the island of Iikie on Nizlec Six. I think you should come with me. I really want you to try a Zeev. It's a drink I like. Bitter, but you grow to like it."

"Zeev, huh?" Toni filed that away. More mysterious messages. Who did Jas think was listening in to their conversation? There was nobody in the bar. Actually, Toni understood. If you were always watching over your shoulder, you assumed someone was lurking within earshot. "I guess I could try that. If there is anything else you can tell me, you'd tell me, wouldn't you?" Toni let a hint of uncertainty creep into her voice.

"Sure, of course," Jas answered, smiling brightly.

Toni recognized the lie. She held back a snort, knowing she was probably just as transparent. She wanted to smile when the woman said nothing to call her out. Yeah, she liked Jas. Toni would go to Nizlec Six, but it would not be to *talk* to Colten. "When?"

"Tomorrow night."

Toni nodded. Mate appeared at her side as she left The Reef. Of course he'd waited. She dropped her hand to his head and ruffled his fur.

"Well?"

"Yeah, I got something." She wondered if Jas would actually show up on Nizlec Six. Recalling the awful headache she'd suffered from this morning, she almost hoped Jas wouldn't show. Toni didn't think she'd survive another party like the one she'd just woken up from.

CHAPTER FOUR

Sweat dripped between Toni's shoulder blades. She shook her head frantically back and forth, bouncing and swiveling to the thumping music. The beat vibrated through her entire body. Her heart, in sync with the drums, pounded in her ears. Playing a woman who enjoyed dancing was one of her hardest performances to date. She genuinely hated dancing. Probably because her sisters enjoyed it so much.

Blue moonlight streaked across the sandy floor of the outdoor bar, strobing beneath the flashing lights, causing her eyes to water. Smoky air irritated her skin and she was freezing in this kheghing outfit. She felt too exposed and it made her scars itch. Jas waved to get her attention. Leaning close, Toni tried to make out what Jas was screaming. Over Jasmine's shoulder, she spied the man at the bar.

His white shirt looked blue under the bar's flashing lights. Sweaty black skin shone as he swallowed the contents of his stein in one long gulp and slammed the empty glass on the counter. Though she couldn't hear it over the deafening beat the three men surrounding him appeared to roar with laughter, clapping their hands against his back and shouting into his ear. He began coughing. His friends laughed again. When his breathing cleared, he looked up. His piercing gaze locked on Toni. Bushy eyebrows deepened the intensity of his stare. He ran a hand over his closely shorn scalp and his lips curled in a slow-moving smile. *Well, hello there.* So this was Dan Colten.

"Another dance?" Jas shouted into her ear.

"Thirsty," she said and headed toward the bar, pretending she couldn't hear Jas's snort over the pounding music. The woman hadn't mentioned Colten would be so yummy. *How do I play this?* A flash of her mother schmoozing at dinner parties appeared in her mind. *Oh yes, that.* It would take everything in her to behave that way. Mouth dry, she blamed the humid room and waved at the bartender for a drink to quench her thirst. The barman didn't appear to see her. She sighed, her thoughts returning to Colten and how to get his attention?

"Hey," he said, sliding up to the bar next to her. Apparently, she wouldn't have to do anything. Although his accent, strong and gruff, was unfamiliar, it curled around her body, caressing her. Likely he was human, particularly with a name like Dan. Her eyes travelled over his chest, thick muscles stretching his shirt, over his full lips and up to his nose. The slight bend indicated this guy was no stranger to a fight.

She turned her back to him and waved toward the bartender, finally catching his eye. "Another Zeev thanks."

She felt a tap on her shoulder. She glanced over. The smuggler raised a brow. "Really, a Zeev?" He gestured to the bartender holding two fingers high.

"What?" Toni asked, leaning down on the bar so her silk shirt gaped a little. She'd dressed to hide her agent status and, as her mother always said, the more skin on display, the less a man noticed the details. If Colten was focused on her body, he wouldn't notice her sobriety or alertness. Not that attention was something she ever lacked, though usually her appearance turned heads away. Still, she was a woman with assets and boy was she putting those assets out there tonight. The loose-fitting shirt—long enough to conceal the weapon tucked into her belt—dropped open further to display more cleavage. Paired with a mini skirt, she was guaranteed to get attention. She had it and she hated every minute of it.

As soon as she walked in the door, men and women watched her both covertly and obviously. She ignored them, already deep within the character she was portraying and hunted for Jas. The other woman stared when Toni stopped in front of her. Jas shook her head, shot Toni a long look, quirked a smile and tugged her onto the dance floor.

"It's an interesting flavor, right?" Dan asked, leaning into Toni's personal space, one hand resting casually against the bar close to her waist. Toni twisted her body not wanting him to feel the concealed pistol in her belt.

"You get used to it," she replied as the drinks arrived. He slammed back the drink like he had before. Toni did the same, coughing harshly as the liquid burned her throat.

"Get used to it, huh?"

"Well, the intention was there," she croaked. Colten placed his hand against her upper back and rubbed small circles. Toni paused for a brief moment and then turned away with a wave, intending to head back to the dance floor.

"Leaving so soon?"

Pointing, she said, "Friend, floor, dance," and tugged her hand from his warm grip, laughing when he refused to let her go.

"You haven't told me your name, though."

She smiled up at him, peering through her eyelashes. What a shame; he really was a handsome guy. "You never asked for it." Channeling her mother, she giggled, covering her mouth with her free hand. He still held the other. It was a heady feeling, having his attention like this. He maintained eye contact and prolonged touching her. *If only.* She forced the fantasy out of her mind.

"Daniel."

"What?" She tilted her head.

He pressed his lips to her ear. "My name is Daniel."

Toni shivered. The smuggler's breath was warm against the delicate skin around her scars. Sensitive to their unsightly appearance, she pulled back abruptly. To cover her move, she turned and brushed a light finger against the hair below his ear. "Trina."

Colten smiled and caressed her hand. He stared at her skin as if it were a delicacy he was desperate to taste. Her heart rate achieved orbit. *Good gods!* Toni playfully twitched her hand in a silent request for him to let her go. He held it up and kissed her palm. She felt it right down to her toes. "Amazing. I've never seen translucent skin. I can actually see your veins. Can I buy you a drink?"

She barely held back her eyeroll. "Friend, remember?"

"Your friend won't mind. Trust me, I know her."

"Do you?" She glanced up, feigning interest in his answer.

"Old friends, yes." He bent his head closer. "How long have you known Jasmine?"

Toni let herself giggle again and hated herself for it. "Not long."

"Jasmine definitely won't mind, then. Stay and chat to me for a little longer?"

Toni shook her head. "It's too loud in here. Besides, I came to dance." She pulled her hand away but allowed him to capture it back.

"Then let's find somewhere quieter."

This was too easy. She hesitated as a river of ice ran down her spine. *Who was playing who?* Was Jas setting her up? No matter. She was prepared. She nodded and followed Colten from the bar. *Keep your weapon close. He's up to something.* For a while they walked along the beach in the moonlight. Thankful for the excuse, Toni kicked off her strappy, impractical shoes and trailed her feet in the warm, wet sand. It would be easier to fight this way. In the moonlight, her feet seemed to glow. The briny smell of the sea tickled her nose.

"How long have you been on Nizlec Six?" he asked.

A cool breeze caressed her skin, bringing a real shiver to her body. Channeling her mother again, she began a story she'd heard the woman give several times in various forms. Lowering her eyes to stare at the sand beneath her feet she said, "I'm a scout for the Holoshot Media Conglomerate. I'm officially here looking for a set, but really, I've always wanted to visit. It's beautiful, isn't it?" She faked a look out to sea, sensing him move closer.

There was no one else at this end of the beach and the further they walked, the darker it became. She brought her gaze back to her feet. He was so close to her side his hands appeared in her field of vision. His thumb twitched. The footprints he was leaving in the sand grew deeper. Her hand dropped so she could draw her weapon should he move to attack her. She had to get him a little further from the lights of the bar before he made his move.

Letting out a whoop, she raced down to the shore line. The cool ocean water kissed her toes, sending more shivers over her body and goosepimples to her exposed skin. A lone avian cry sounded in the distance. When Colten caught up she continued, "The main scene in the movie involves a beach like this one but during the day. I had to come here and see it like this. If I can convince the assistant prod a night scene would work just as well …" She shot him a shy smile to see how he was taking her little story.

Colten watched her intently. By the light of the moon, his eyes were two orbs focused only on her. It sent a buzz through her body making her tense up. Her involuntary reactions were going to tell him she wasn't quite as tipsy as she had wanted him to believe. She didn't want him to sense how alert she was or how skittish she felt but she didn't know how to stop it.

She skipped away, turning toward the upper beach. The lapping waves hid the sound of her rapid breathing. That lonely birdcall sounded again. Circling the path, Toni slipped a little in the dry sand. Colten grasped her arm, his warm fingers curling around her elbow. "I've been here before." His voice was soft, disappearing into the darkness around them. "With several pals. The night was not this beautiful though, or perhaps that's the company." She forced herself not to pull away and allowed him to direct her into the shadows of the surrounding beach huts.

"I remember Rycee and I found this graying sandcat. It must have lived behind those huts." As he spoke, he pointed toward several wooden huts hidden by tall trees that edged the beach. Toni wasn't listening. She murmured soft sounds to keep him talking, and as they rounded the first building she spun, drawing her weapon, and came face to face with Colten's pistol. She stared up into the smuggler's cold, dark eyes. The gun in his hand did not waver.

"Interesting," he said, his voice sharp. "Who are you?"

Shenghi! Her heart now raced for another reason. She sucked in a breath and steadied her aim. "You pulled a gun on me. You first."

"You pulled a gun on *me*," he countered. "What do you want?"

"To ask you a few questions."

"And you need a gun to do that?" He waggled his own weapon back and forth. "Looks like you're at a disadvantage. I suggest we lower our weapons, leave in opposite directions and forget we ever met."

"Who says I'm the one disadvantaged?"

"I have the better position and I'm bigger than you are. Trust me, *you* are disadvantaged."

Toni smirked. "You don't say?"

Out of the darkness behind the smuggler came a low growl. The growl built as Mate prowled from the shadows of the second hut. His snarling snout dipped, and moonlight lit up the jagged edges of his teeth. Warmth filled Toni at his presence. Right on time.

"Unexpected," Colten said backing up, his gaze swinging from Toni to Mate and back again.

"I'm sorry, can you tell me again who is at a disadvantage?" Toni flashed him a sweet smile.

"I guess he belongs to you?" Colten holstered his pistol, his movements slow and steady. Toni kept her weapon on the smuggler as Mate crept forward to sandwich Colten between them.

"About those questions."

His shoulders slumped. "It's your show, sweetheart."

"The shipment of supplies bound for Milten Seven. Where is it?"

Colten's head snapped up. "Who are you?"

Toni raised her weapon higher. "My questions, your answers. My show, remember?" Power was a heady thing. Her body pulsed with it. Was this what it was like to win? No wonder her father loved all his manipulation games. *I could get used to this.*

"I don't know where they are."

"Oh, come on. You've been seen twice in the area of the hijacked ships, searching the same corridor off Waystation EEXDU. Where are the supplies?"

"How do you know about … *oh*, the Hegnforth lightship, she's yours?" He stepped forward. At Mate's sharp bark he froze. Slowly, he raised his hands. "I'm looking for the shipment, too. I don't know where it is."

Oh, come on! His expression was earnest. Perhaps a little too convincing. "You expect me to believe that?"

"It's the truth. I know a few of the people relying on that delivery making it to where it's meant to go. I'm just keeping a casual eye out for it. I was hoping to get lucky."

"Friendly interest, huh?"

"Absolutely."

"Who took it?" She lowered her weapon a fraction. If he was speaking the truth then she needed this information. But she had no way to know if he was being honest with her. He was a friend of Jasmine's and Toni figured Jas had been playing the same game Toni was, manipulating the conversation for her own interest. So what game was *he* playing? The same one as Jas, or something else?

His eyes flicked away. "I have my suspicions." His body was still tense, but his shoulders dropped and his fingers relaxed.

"Care to share?"

"As you're currently holding a weapon pointed at my chest, no, not really. What's it to you, anyway?" He shifted weight onto his front foot. Toni hitched her gun arm straighter.

"Interested third party," she told him. "Look, say I'm willing to believe you. Just give me a name and we can go our separate ways." Not that she would actually let him go. He was a smuggler after all, and it was her duty to arrest him. But if he believed she'd release him, he might give her the answers she needed. Colten seemed to consider that. He shrugged.

"Pirate by the name of Dalmith. He's a bad guy. You don't want to go after him alone."

Toni gestured to Mate. "I'm not alone."

Colten inched forward, his eyes glittering. "I'm serious. Dalmith is bad news. You'll need back up."

Toni tugged her badge from her bra with her free hand and flashed it at him. "I'm covered, thanks. Now turn around and put your hands behind your back."

The smuggler glared. "I thought you were letting me go."

"Right," she said with a laugh. Waving her weapon at him again, she ordered, "Turn around."

"You don't want to do this. You don't understand what is going on. It's not just the supplies," he told her, his voice dropping low. She shuffled forward to hear him. "It's not what you think."

"Turn around."

He shrugged and raised his hands higher. Moonlight glinted off something between the fingers of his left hand. Small, round and metallic. *What is that? A personal alarm?* He threw it into the air. Her stare locked on the device. Colten dropped to the ground as a blinding flare flashed across the black sky. Toni's sensitive eyes screamed, and she hit the sand hard, clawing at her face. Blinded, she struggled to her knees and froze at the cold touch of metal against her neck. Mate's growl rose. Colten spoke quietly. "Call your robot off, Agent."

"Mate, hold," she cried, her eyes streaming with tears. Her heart thundered, and sweat broke out over her body. *I'm dead. He's going to kill me.* She gasped but couldn't find air.

"The blindness will last a few hours. You're going to need your bot's help to get to safety. Call him off and I'll disappear."

He's not going to shoot? She gulped salty air, finally getting some of it into her lungs. *Khegh it!* She had no choice. Clenching her eyes shut, she realized her face was wet from her streaming tears. Swearing softly, she raised her hand. "Mate, stand down."

His growl grew louder.

"Here," she ordered. After a pause that went too long, she heard his feet pad toward her. His growl became a rumbling snarl as he approached. Colten jammed the gun harder into Toni's neck.

"No sudden moves now," the smuggler said loudly.

Toni held out her hands until she felt Mate's fur beneath her fingertips. He scooted close to her side. She clutched his body with shaking hands. *Mate's here. He'll help.* She heard the smuggler step away and the cold barrel left her neck.

"If I see a twitch, I shoot. Do you hear me, Agent?"

"Yes." She listened to the man walk away. When she could no longer hear him, she buried her head in Mate's metallic smelling fur. "Mate, I can't see." Toni could hear how terrified she sounded and swallowed back a scream.

"I am here, Toni." Mate's voice was a comfort in the endless darkness. *I can't do this.* She'd had the smuggler on the ropes and he'd got the drop on her. She could have died. *Why didn't he kill me?* Confusion spiraled her thoughts faster and faster.

"Help me," she whispered.

"Always." Mate nudged her with his nose. Toni gripped his neck fur tightly and struggled to her feet. Trusting her partner and friend to act as her eyes, she let him lead her back to the *Blackflame*, and to safety.

CHAPTER FIVE

Pain exploded around her knee. "Khegh it!" Freezing in place, Toni tried to work out where she was. Her breathing was too loud. The scent of ozone and copper didn't give her a clue "Mate?"

When he didn't immediately reply, her pounding blood thudded harder. "Mate?" *I can't even find my way around my own kheghing ship.* In two days, there had been no change in her vision. She was afraid that with her sensitive eyesight, the effects of the flash flare would be permanent. Mate and Zach attempted to keep her calm but it was a losing battle.

"I am here, Boss. You are three paces from the passageway entrance. Step back half a pace and over half a pace to your right."

Following his order, she found the wall and traced her way into the *Blackflame*'s central room. *I'm completely useless.* She'd never been so aware of how dangerous the *Blackflame* was and vowed to clean the entire ship if only her sight returned.

She refused to imagine what her life would become if it didn't. Fear lurked in the periphery of her mind. She could feel it waiting for her to drop her mental shields.

Her body ached. She was sure her blood pressure was too high and she wasn't getting enough air. Colten got so close. She was such a fool to think she could bring down an experienced smuggler. *What if my eyes don't get better?* She'd always lived with the fear that her delicate skin and eyes would be her downfall, and blindness had always been a threat, but to have it made real in this way truly hit home how vulnerable she was. If she was permanently blinded, she'd lose her job—she'd lose everything.

Thank Xendia for Mate, her calm center, her focal point. He'd been designed to be her companion as a child by parents embarrassed by her appearance and lack of friendships. She learned how to program because she'd wanted to make him a true friend. When Zaambuka had arrested her and offered her the choice to enter the Academy, he'd told her to leave Mate behind. She'd outright refused. She couldn't do it without Mate. He was her partner and now her lifeline.

To keep her mind occupied, she asked Zach to run a search for the name Dalmith. So far, nothing had popped.

By early evening, she began to distinguish shadows. Relief of a sort settled into her belly when she avoided bashing her knee against the bench a heartbeat before Mate warned her away from it. "I think, I think I . . . something's changed."

"What do you see?" Mate immediately asked.

"Not a lot, a slightly darker shadow in front of the never-ending darkness."

"That is a good sign."

"I'll kill him," she said for the umpteenth time.

"Are you positive the smuggler is not connected to the hijackings?" Mate asked.

Toni took a deep breath as he brushed against her leg. Her pulse settled. Just the sound of his voice, the feel of his fur at her side, was all she needed. Never had she been so thankful for such a special friend.

"I have a strange feeling he was telling the truth." Toni cringed. Admitting that hurt somewhat, but she couldn't shake the feeling. Nibbling at her bottom lip she stretched out with a hand. The chair was around here somewhere.

"You cannot trust him, Boss. He blinded you."

"Really, Zach? You thought I forgot?" Zach fell silent. "Urgh," Toni rubbed her eyes. "Zach, I'm frustrated …"

His reply, when it came, was a lot softer. "I'm sorry, too, Boss."

Toni's questing hand found the leather and turned the seat toward her. She sat gingerly. The smell of her ship was so clear to her now her eyesight was compromised—a mixture of electrified air and ozone with a hint of oil, grease, and burned hair. *Khegh it*. A rodent must have invaded while they were docked at the Waystation. Beneath the sound of Mate's servos was the rumble of the *Blackflame*'s powerful engines.

"Do you have anything to report, Zach?"

A grin twitched her lips. Trust Mate to get things back on track.

"I've searched the embarkation records for the Waystations along the shipment routes and uncovered a ship registration for a man named Dalmith. He appears to be a frequent visitor to Waystation Tildex."

"The second Waystation," Toni mused. The dots of the case were starting to connect. "Wait, the registration was under his own name?"

"He also has a business registered in his name. A bar and several warehouses."

"If this man is who Colten accused, would he not attempt to disguise his identity?" Mate commented.

"You would think," Toni muttered. Did it really surprise her that Colten had lied? She could talk to Dalmith and rule him out as a suspect. By that time, her eyesight should be returned and she could go after Colten with a vengeance.

"So, we are going after Dalmith?"

"For now, Mate," she confirmed. "But Zach, keep a search window open for Colten."

"Absolutely, Boss."

*

Colors and shapes were still blurry, but she was able to distinguish between people and inanimate objects by the time they landed on Waystation Tildex. It helped that people moved. She set her shades display to heat vision to give her more clarity, and Mate stayed close to her side in the event she needed his assistance. Since her balance was uncertain, she had Mate in a harness and was using him to guide her around the station. It was a comfort to know that if she missed anything, the C-bot would not.

The station smelled old, like moldy grease and dry oil. Mate spoke to her softly. "Are you sure you cannot wait until more of your vision has returned?"

Toni was not helpless. She refused to be helpless. "No time. The next shipment leaves Marn tomorrow. If we don't stop the hijackers, it will be weeks before Milten Seven can receive any water. People will start dying. We have to stop Dalmith now if he's the one behind it."

"You suspect he is not?" Mate asked.

Toni tightened her grip on his harness. "I don't know."

She kept her pace steady, taking careful steps and feeling Mate's fur brush against her leg. He was leading her toward dock seventy-nine, where Zach reported Dalmith's ship was berthed. Voices echoed the halls but did not come close, squeaks and hissing followed their path. Thumping vibrations rose over her feet and up her ankles, something heavy, machinery of some kind, operating below decks. As the ship came into view, Toni scanned it with the various settings of her shades. "Khegh it!" It was a monster. Her glasses outlined seven external gun mounts on this side alone, and there were ports for torpedoes as well. She picked up a shimmer that indicated some kind of stealth technology had been paired with the ship's shielding. A man stood guard outside the lowered ramp. Her blood ran cold.

Shenghi. There went her idea to sneak on board. She strengthened her grip on Mate's harness and let him lead her forward, making a show of tilting her head from side to side at any sound. If she was going to appear blind she might as well use it as a disguise. Holding aloft a small container, she called, "Hello? Is there someone here?"

"Hey, you, this is a private dock. You need to leave."

"Please, Sir." She moved in the direction of the voice. A red body blob moved into the center of her vision. She rattled her container—the coin she'd collected with Jas lent reality to her ruse. "Please, Sir." She let her voice wobble, and listened to it echo around the quiet bay. "I am poor and unfortunate. My condition has caused me to become blind at an early age. Would you have any coin to spare for food, Sir?"

The man-shaped blur grew even larger as he approached. She flinched when something heavy dropped into the container. Then some of the weight disappeared.

"You sure are, Freak." He pressed hard against her shoulder. "Get out of here. I said this is a private bay."

Toni stumbled back from the unexpected push, remaining upright more through luck than skill. Her heart pounded, the lack of sight bringing her imagination to the fore. She was so vulnerable in her current condition. The shadow of the guard was big—she shouldn't be taking this risk. At her knee, Mate growled.

With a tremble in her voice that was not entirely forced, she asked, "Perhaps there are others on board your vessel, Sir? Your master, maybe?"

"He ain't here. I said go, little girl."

Tugging on the harness, Toni indicated Mate should turn around. Behaving like a proper Seeing Specialist, he led her slowly from the bay. Over her shoulder, she called, "Humble apologies, Sir, for taking up your time."

"Anything?" she asked when she was sure they were out of sight. Her chest heaved, her breathing unsteady.

"No. Maybe Zach will have found a better way in?"

She wasn't hopeful. Dalmith's ship was giving off all sorts of signals. Bad ones. A ship that well-armed and guarded was definitely hiding something.

"Where to now?" Mate didn't comment on her trembling hand, but he had to feel it.

Back home. Clearing her throat, she suggested, "Let's check in with the local bars."

Minutes later they stepped into The Wayfarer, a dark, dingy room—as Mate described it—on one of the lower levels. Toni registered only three heat signatures and two of those were behind the counter. Waystation bars, as a rule, were overcrowded with stopover pilots looking for a drink and a hot meal between hops. Her hearing and sense of smell confirmed what her shades told her.

Mate led Toni to the counter, and she went through her begging routine again. One of the barmen offered her a few coin. She felt bad about it—it sounded like he could do with the money. "It's quiet, are you closed?"

"It's that place! Stealing all of my regulars."

Strange. One full bar usually cascaded customers down to the rest. There was no logical reason for a Waystation bar to be empty. "What do you mean? What place? I'm afraid I haven't been here very long. I'm hoping to get enough for food and passage to Sovi Coph A. They have surgeons there, and—"

"Oh, kid, you know surgeons are expensive."

"I know." She put on her most dejected face and felt around for a stool. The only customer in the room quickly hobbled forward and pulled one over for her. "Oh gosh, thank you! Wow, I didn't even know you were there."

The man grunted and returned to his seat. She watched him go. The heat map disappeared where his right leg should be—mechanical limb. It explained the limp.

The barman who'd offered her the coin took her hand and wrapped it around a cold glass. She flinched at his touch. "On the house, love."

Now she felt *really* bad. "You said the other place? What happened?"

"It's bad. Don't go there. The owner moved in weeks ago. Bought out two bars and ran the third into the ground. I'm the only independent still standing. Well, mostly."

The man seated behind Toni grunted again.

"That sounds awful." *And highly suspicious*. The bar was worthy of a look, so to speak.

"The owner is dangerous. You don't dare cross him."

"And yet you're still here. I think that's very brave of you."

The red blur grew closer as he leaned down. "Well, look around ... oh ... uh, I mean, you can hear this place is completely empty, other than for Stan over there. I'm not exactly competition. I think Dalmith lets me stay here as a warning to everyone else."

So the empty bar *was* Dalmith's doing. "Oh, dear."

Toni was about to ask where the bar was located—insisting of course she only wanted to know where to avoid—when he added, "I'm sure there's something shady going on. All those guards standing around an empty storeroom, ships that come and go but barely stay for more than a night. The crews all head straight to the Safe Harbor."

Empty storeroom? It was sounding more and more like she'd found her pirates. Colten had been telling her the truth. "Safe Harbor?"

"The bar."

"But this is a Waystation. Ships don't usually stay, do they? What's weird about ships coming and going all the time?"

"It's the type of people."

"What do you mean?"

The barman backed away. "Ah, nothing, nothing. I shouldn't have said anything."

Toni hadn't heard anyone come in through the door, but the room grew suddenly colder. She glanced over her shoulder. There was a heat signature in the doorway. She dropped her hand to the top of Mate's head and tapped wanting an image of the person. "Is someone there?" she asked projecting a little fear into her voice. The scent of tobacco hit her like a fist. Along with the body odor of someone who hadn't bathed—ever. The red blob wavered for a moment and then disappeared. Toni turned back to the two barmen but they had also disappeared. "Sir?"

Toni called. The old guy at the table grunted. Her head snapped toward the sound.

"Knows better than to start flapping his mouth. Go home, kid. Don't stay here. This is a bad place."

"Yeah, I'm getting that." Toni stood and gestured toward the door. Mate led her out. They wandered, apparently aimlessly, while they waited for Zach to check in. Ending up near the suspiciously mysterious storeroom was a pure coincidence. At least, that's what she'd tell anyone who asked. She knew they were close when the lighting grew bright enough to irritate her eyes beneath her shades, making them water. Eight, nine, ten blurry shapes, and over her left shoulder three more. She could feel the rumble beneath the deck. Slightly more violent here than upstairs. Raised voices stilled her feet. "Careful." They crept to the corner. Toni whistled at the number of guards stationed around the giant plasteel revolving doors. They looked like they were expecting an invading army.

"Do you want to go closer?" Mate asked, not sounding as though he approved of that option.

"Want to, but I don't think the blindness excuse is going to fly with these guys. Maybe you can—"

"No, Boss. I will not leave you here alone while you are unable to see."

"Mate …" Warmth filled her at his concern. She ran her hand over his head in a thank you, but she needed to know what was being kept in that store room. The two agents backed down the corridor. They were stopped by the sudden appearance of another guard. It smelt like the same man who had stood in the Wayfarer's entrance. Mate growled, low and terrifying. Toni immediately tensed. Should she make a move for her gun or wait it out? Her breathing sped up as she heard a click and a slide of metal through leather. She recognized that sound.

The red blur in Toni's vision flared brightly as the guard's weapon primed.

CHAPTER SIX

It took everything she had to stare ahead unwaveringly. Forcing her breathing to slow, she gestured for Mate to continue walking.

The guard cleared his throat.

"Is someone there?" she asked, swinging her head from side to side as if trying to pinpoint the direction of the sound. Her heart raced.

"Move and I will shoot you."

"Oh, but—"

"Remove the shades."

Shenghi. Toni slipped the shades from her face, thumbing the display off as she did so. Her vision had improved—sort of—and she was able to make out his flinch as he took in her visage. She stared as blankly as she could. "Excuse me, Sir, but why—"

"Quiet," he ordered and snatched the shades right out of her hand. She didn't react. If any part of her cover still existed, she'd have to play this carefully. She stood still while the guard examined her glasses before he dropped them to the floor and stood on them with a heavy boot. The crack of the frames was loud in the otherwise silent corridor. It was only then that Toni reacted.

"Was that my glasses? Did you drop them, Sir? What happened?" *Khegh it!* They were her favorite pair. Thankfully she had another back on the *Blackflame,* but still …

"Shut up," the guard growled. Shoving his weapon into her chest, he prodded Toni back along the corridor toward the storeroom. The C-bot remained silent. His body vibrated against her knee, clearly struggling to contain his desire to attack. She was trembling too, only from fear. Why had she thought she could do this with impaired vision? What kind of agent was she? She could do nothing right. *I'm not ready. I can't do this.* Sweat soaked through her shirt. She scrubbed damp palms against her trousers.

The guard was not the only one now. They were marched past several men holding big guns and into the storeroom. "What's happening?" No one answered.

With another jab, Toni was encouraged to head down a long corridor created by columns of crates. Unable to make out the logo stamped on the side, she would pay good coin that these crates were from the hijacked ships. So that's what was going on. The shipments never left the second Waystation. Presumably, the original crews were killed here, or even prior to arrival, and the transponders that sent the ship's registry details through forcedspace switched off, giving the appearance that the ships disappeared.

"Did you think I wouldn't know who you are, Agent? I know everything that happens on this Waystation, including who does what and when. And let's face it, you aren't exactly forgettable."

The man who spoke stepped from between the stacked crates. Toni could make out his basic features: black hair possibly receding—it was a little blurry—on a large head with a square nose. Darkness around his mouth and chin was probably a neat beard. She'd know for certain if he came closer. Wide shoulders and an even wider waist.

Mate was tense, watching the guards with a careful eye. Toni gripped his harness and shook it in warning. Now was not the time to attack. She hoped Zach got out a signal for Agent assistance when her shades were destroyed. At this point, she was pretty much banking on it.

"You're actually the man I'm here to see, Dalmith," she said. He twitched, exposing the fact he'd counted on his anonymity. "Do you really need all of these men here just to chat with me? Let's go somewhere a little quieter, huh?"

Dalmith laughed, stroking his chin. "Bold suggestion, Agent, I'll give you that. How did you find out about me?"

She didn't reply. Her mind frantically searched for a way to distract them. *I don't want to die here.* She'd been so close. She had the pirates who stole the supplies. Shenghi she had *the supplies*, and Zaambuka would never know she'd solved the case. Would he even know she was dead? Or would she become a mystery, just like the hijacked ships? It was the smuggler's fault. Dan Colten. If he hadn't blinded her … Oh yes, she had been blinded, but not from the flare. She only wished she could have witnessed his eventual comeuppance.

Dalmith laughed again and gestured to the men around him. "So this is all they sent to stop me? A girl with a dog?"

Toni almost rolled her eyes. It looked like she wouldn't need a distraction after all. Dalmith liked to gloat.

"Look around you, Agent. This Waystation belongs to me. You were only allowed to land because I permitted it."

Mate growled and Toni shushed him. What information could she taunt Dalmith into revealing? The longer he talked, the better. Still, she needed a way out when the time came. Dalmith was only speaking to her now because he intended to kill her, that was obvious. Her heart pounded, this time in anticipation. She would get out of this. She had Mate and Zach was still out there. This time, Toni wouldn't underestimate her enemy.

She took stock of their strengths. The storeroom had one entrance. Four heavily armed men stood just inside, listening to their boss pontificate. And their weaknesses. They shuffled their feet, looked away or picked at their nails. One guard stood behind Toni and from the corner of her eye she could see his weapon pointed to the ground. *Big mistake.* The two men hovering behind Dalmith were the only ones who looked focused. Including Dalmith, that was eight. She'd have seconds at best. All she needed was a weapon. And, of course, Mate.

Dalmith continued loudly. "Do you think anyone can stop me? Five ships taken, a sixth tomorrow, and any other ship they send our way. The supplies are *mine*. If the folks on Milten Seven are in such desperate need for water, they will pay to get it back. My ships restock here. *My* crews, MY people, MY WAYSTATION!"

His gestures grew more and more outlandish. The guy was egomaniacal, and quite possibly crazy.

The distraction she was waiting for came only a moment later, when a massive blast shook the entire station. The floor continued to vibrate under her feet long after the explosion died away, shaking the crates so violently they started to shift. The two guards flanking Dalmith spun, searching for the cause of the blast, the others shuffled backward out of the path of the potential avalanche of crates and while they were distracted, Toni tapped Mate on the head. They wouldn't get a better opportunity. *Time to go.*

Mate leapt at Dalmith. Toni tackled the guard behind her, wrestling for his weapon. When he didn't release it, she elbowed him sharply in the head. He fell, dazed, and she snatched the weapon out of his lax fingers to slam him over the head with it. He collapsed.

Mate knocked Dalmith onto his back and kept going, leaping over his body to plow into the guard behind, barking and snarling loudly. With all eyes on Mate, Toni turned the dial on the weapon and shot wildly in the direction of the remaining guards. Through more luck than skill, all three went down, stunned. Mate ran at the men outside the door. Toni fell to her knees as one shot back. A spray from her weapon dropped him and Mate finished the last guard with frightening efficiency.

Breathing hard, she climbed unsteadily to her feet and checked on Dalmith. He was out cold. She rolled him over and cuffed his hands behind his back. She swiped a hand over the sweat on her face and pulled the errant strands of white hair out her eyes. Straightening her body, she glanced around the now silent room. Her lips twitched. The ball of cold in her chest melted as warmth heated her blood. Looking down at Dalmith, she said, "Yup, all they sent was a girl with a dog."

*

"The explosions were you, Zach?" Toni snorted as she cuffed the last guard. Of course they were. Her CII was apparently the technological equivalent of a pyromaniac.

"I called the Specialist Terrain Combat Troops. They reported the closest squad is six hours away. I wasn't going to wait that long and I didn't think you could either, so I hacked into the Waystation's engineering systems." Zach's voice rose from Mate's speakers.

"What did you do?"

"I checked the maintenance logs. Since Dalmith took over, the Waystation's disabled NSD has fallen into serious disrepair. They hadn't checked the containment shields in over six weeks. I might have tweaked them in a downward direction. Honestly, Boss, it did not take as long as you would think for the core to go into overload."

"Good work." Toni was impressed with the *Blackflame*'s CII. His ingenuity was unexpected to say the least. Given this was their first mission together and she didn't yet know all of his capabilities, she was pretty pleased with his initiative. Pleased and thankful. "I assume you've reset them now?"

"Yes, Boss," he confirmed.

Toni shook her head. "Any damage?"

"Not if maintenance examines everything reasonably quickly," he answered.

She left the seven men trussed up on the floor and flicked her gaze over the wall of stacked supplies. "Zach, how many crates should we have here?"

"One hundred and eight-seven."

"Mate, start scanning. Let's make sure everything is here."

The count didn't take long. "What do you mean we're four crates short?" Toni stomped to Dalmith, who she'd been forced to gag, and tore the tape away. "Four crates short? Who did you sell them to?"

"What? The count is not short, all the guns are here."

"Wait, what? What guns?" Without waiting for an answer, she raced to the nearest crate. The lid was partially sealed.

Straining muscles not built for brute strength, she managed to get the lid up enough to look inside. She swore loudly.

"Boss?"

Reaching out with a finger she caressed the shiny black surface of the topmost weapon. "Guns. A lot of 'em." She turned on Dalmith. "Who are they for?"

He didn't answer.

"Mate?"

"Confirmed. Four crates missing, Boss," Mate reported.

"That's not right," Dalmith complained. His face turned red and he struggled within his bonds. "That kheghing thief! I knew he was up to something. Rycee is going to kill me."

"Who is Rycee? What thief?" Toni shook Dalmith several times before he responded.

"A smuggler named Colten. I let him stop here to avoid an agent. Let me guess, that was you?"

Toni slapped the tape back over his mouth. *Shenghi*. Her stomach tightened as heat rose into her face. The smuggler, the same smuggler who had escaped her custody and blinded her, stole four crates of weapons from Dalmith. And she'd let him get away. *I'm a fool.*

"Ping received from a neighboring system, Boss. A ship has dropped out of forcedspace. It's the *Renegade*," Zach reported suddenly.

Toni bounced on her toes. The gift she'd asked Zach to leave back on the Waystation—a virus that would load when he docked and linked to the station's server, had worked. *I can fix this.*

"Call the STCT. Tell them to jam their TAFFs into overdrive. We need to get after that smuggler."

*

While Zach insisted the smuggler's signal was still active, Toni didn't trust that Colten hadn't discovered Zach's hack, spoofed the signal, and disappeared already. She thought the smuggler would be very happy to leave her floundering in space, searching for a ship that was no longer there.

In order to prevent the *Blackflame*'s entry into the system being discovered, Toni dropped out of forcedspace a few light years outside the Shetii system and used her NSD to bring them closer. They were relying on passive sensors and a visual inspection to prevent the *Renegade*'s captain registering their presence and jumping too soon.

"Any sign?" she demanded, sitting tensely. Her eyes darted from her scanner display to the overhead screens, watching for any sign of the smuggler. Her teeth ground together so tightly her jaw ached. Colten picked a good system to hide in. Shetii was an aging solar giant with nine circling planets. Each planet was uninhabited but several of the moons around Jatele, the third planet, were in a stable orbit.

Toni was tired, frustrated, and growing angrier by the second. She would *not* let Colten get the drop on her again. This time, she'd either take him in or shoot him down.

As they crept further into the system, Toni and Mate fell silent, waiting patiently for any sign of their elusive prey.

Light pulsed at the top right of the *Blackflame*'s view screen and a force bubble tore open. "Two point eight KL!"

At Zach's shout, Toni slammed everything to full and took off after the *Renegade*. A pop-up counter appeared in her view, descending as they raced through space.

The enemy ship's engine flared as it raced away, but Toni had seen him first and closed the gap quickly. Colten must have augmented his ship with something to boost his speed, because Toni had barely inched into range before he darted away again. Inverting the *Blackflame,* she looped up and slipped closer to the fleeing ship. Her body perched on the edge of her seat as her fingers tightened around the control stick. When the *Renegade* fell into her targeting box, she ordered Mate to start firing.

"Boss, are we shooting to destroy or disable? Remember our directive. We are supposed to return those crates in one piece," Zach recited from the mission file.

Toni's blood was coursing hot and fast through trembling limbs. "Disable, of course. We just want to scare him, Zach, make him sweat a little."

Her desire to destroy the smuggler was strong. She wanted him down and would happily do it with lethal force if necessary. Her eyes ached. She was still struggling to focus when reading anything positioned more than a few feet from her face, but any embarrassment over her injuries was nothing compared to the knowledge Colten almost shot her down the last time they'd gone ship to ship. She had no intention of showing him any mercy now.

"The *Renegade* is attempting a communication lock."

"Deny it," she ordered. "Keep firing, Mate."

"Yes, Boss."

Toni pushed her TAFF drive harder. "Give me more power, Zach."

She imagined she felt the burst Zach gained from some-where and checked her screens. The distance between her and the *Renegade* was growing smaller. The fleeing ship banked sharply. It looked like Colten was going to try and lose her in the atmospheric storms around Jatele's second moon. Toni raced after him.

"The *Renegade* is still attempting communication," Zach announced.

"Reject it and flash a message. Tell him to shut down his TAFF. I'll give him the chance to talk in person after I arrest him." Her fingers were sweaty around the stick. One button. She could reach it, press it. It wouldn't take much. The stock of missiles within the *Blackflame*'s hold flashed into her mind. *Overkill?* Then she remembered the asteroids, and the flare. *Do it.* Without his ship partner, the tables had turned and she was in the stronger position. She could shoot him down. A swooping feeling hit her chest.

A moment later Zach reported, "No response to the message." Toni snorted.

Mate's shots were starting to land against the *Renegade*'s shields. Toni ordered him to target Colten's NSD or TAFF generator.

"Why isn't he shooting back?" Zach asked.

It was odd. A chill crept down her back. Toni frowned. "Mate, Zach, what's causing those atmospheric storms?" The *Blackflame* broke through the moon's exosphere and dove down. A glance at the readouts confirmed nine hundred mile an hour winds buffeted the ship, and its inhabitants, in a dozen different directions. Toni grabbed for anything she could reach as she was rattled hard. Her seat straps bit deep into her shoulders and stomach as they bound her in place against the violence outside.

Mate's fire pounded one small area of the *Renegade*'s shields, which started to spark.

"What is that?" Toni cried out. Lightning out here? It wasn't possible.

"Feedback from the surrounding thermosphere. There must be a particle response affecting the lasers," Mate answered.

"Result?"

"Unknown." That cold feeling swept into Toni's chest.

The *Blackflame* bounced and broke through the mesosphere. Something smashed into them, hurling them sideways. Toni held on tightly, forgetting all about the other ship. "I have disabled the *Renegade*'s TAFF drive," Mate announced, but it didn't matter. A loud crack thundered and the *Blackflame* slammed violently to one side. Power fluctuated, sending sparks through every console and shooting up Toni's arms.

She screamed as something hit the ship again.

Then the power flicked out. The *Blackflame* plummeted.

CHAPTER SEVEN

Toni gasped for air. Pain, an immense pressure, spread across her chest. She groaned. What happened? Not ready to open her eyes, she focused on her body—fingers, toes, arms, legs. They tingled, aching like she'd depressurized from Zero G too fast. It hurt to breathe. *What happened?* After several attempts, she pried her eyes open. Blinding light speared into her brain. She let out a scream and slammed her eyelids shut. *By Xendia! I can't remember.* Moaning loudly, she could hear herself, so there was that. The scents of ozone and oil saturated the air. *Too much.* Had there been an accident?

She cracked open one eye and stared at the giant tear in the wall. With a groan that became a gasp, she twitched her arm and raised her head.

Something heavy shifted against her legs. She froze.

"Mate?" Her voice came out as nothing more than a croak. There was no answer. "Mate?" she tried again, fear infecting her voice. Shenghi, what happened? Memory returned with a flash. There had been a bright light and sparks, a feeling of fire and pain and ... *Oh gods, my ship!*

They'd been hit by something. Zach, Mate! She dragged herself upright to look around.

Ow. Something heavy pressed hard on her shins as she twisted. Air fled her lungs. Part of the console, cracked in the crash, trapped her legs. In the distance, Mate lay on his side.

"Mate?"

He didn't stir.

"Mate? Mate, please Mate." Toni sobbed, reaching out a hand to him. Oh no. *Please no.* She stretched her arm and again pain pushed the breath from her lungs. Oh, gods! Kheghing hell. Her mind held only one thought. Get out! She rocked and wriggled back and forth in the tight space. I can't! With every jerk, fire radiated further along her side.

Stabbing shocks of nerve fire attacked her body. Flashes of light exploded behind her eyelids. She lost focus. Everything felt weightless; her head was thick with wooly thoughts. Blackness fell in a sudden curtain fall.

*

Blinking her eyes open she stared at the crack in the *Blackflame*'s side panel. *What happened?* Her head twisted from side to side as she took in the state of the ship around her. *Accident? Crash.* Her ship had crashed. She lifted her wrist, the stretch of her muscles brought a gasp to her lips. Her other arm was numb. She looked down but couldn't see her feet. *How long was I unconscious?* Wriggling her toes, she called, "Mate? Zach?" The ship was silent. The smell of oil and chemicals, probably toxic, was growing stronger.

It would take something jammed under the console to shift its weight. Over her shoulder, she spied the emergency beacon and reached for it. Pain tore at her side, ripping a gasp from her throat. She flopped back into her chair. *Oh, Xendia!* Fear settled heavily in her stomach. *What am I going to do?* The moons around Jatele were uninhabited. She wasn't even sure where on the moon she'd crashed. She could be anywhere and she couldn't reach the emergency beacon, if it still worked. Jagged knives ripped through her limbs as she thrashed frantically back and forth. *Free! I have to get free!* She blacked out.

*

"Rise and shine, sleepy girl." A man's voice whispered into her ear and something warm brushed her cheek. *Dad?* Toni forced open her eyes and looked up into unfamiliar dark eyes. They blinked. *Such long eyelashes.* Full lips smiled, exposing white teeth. One tooth was crooked, and his nose looked like it had been broken once, a small bump marred the otherwise straight line. Still, he was pretty handsome. Awareness returned with a snap. Daniel Colten stared at her, grinning broadly, waiting for recognition to dawn.

"Hello there," he said.

Her mind went blank and all she could do was blink. "You!"

"Welcome back. I was wondering how long that was going to take."

Toni struggled to sit up but the smuggler pushed her back. "Lie still. You were pinned for a long time. I'm sure everything hurts like hell right now."

It certainly did, but she'd never admit that to him. She shoved his hand away and sat up, stifling a wretched moan. *Oh gods!* He muttered under his breath but backed away. Glancing at her feet, Toni experimented with twitching her toes. They moved easily under the scratchy blanket. *Blanket?* The scent of cooking meat floated to her through the air. Her stomach heaved. She clasped a hand over her mouth and swallowed until the waves of nausea settled. "What happened?"

"I found you. You were stuck under the console of your ship's control center. I got you out and here we are."

Positive it had not been that simple, she glared at him and her hand formed a fist around stiff grass. She lay in a circle of shade cast by a shimmering golden tree. Leaves glinting brightly beneath the burning sun. A thin vein of silver ran through each rounded leaf. Twisting her head, Toni saw they were at the entrance of what looked to be a forest. Toni inhaled then coughed; the air was so dry, hot, like another thick blanket draped over her. She tried to moisten her mouth but nothing happened. The overladen branches above created a large canopy to shade her. A few feet from her side the finest white sand she'd ever seen. It looked like glass. A body of water, maybe a sea or a lake, stretched to the horizon, glistening diamonds under the intense heat. She couldn't see the *Blackflame* anywhere. *Mate?*

"Where's my ship?"

"You crashed further inland, about a mile from here. I came down over there, just out of sight, near the shore."

"Crashed?"

"Yup, same electrical eddy that hit you. I saw you go down and tried to land nearby."

"Why?"

He stirred a bent stick around a steeltale bucket staked over an open fire. He knocked his boots against the stones placed in a circle to contain the flames. So that was the source of the smell that sickened her earlier. "How long was I out?"

"Six and a half hours. My aid kit is limited, and I couldn't find yours, but I'm pretty sure you've got a couple of cracked ribs and a concussion. Severe bruising to your shins and left knee, nothing worse. Didn't even penetrate your skin. You're a lot hardier than you look. If you've got a bone regenerator in your ship, I can zap your ribs. You were lucky."

Yeah, I sure feel lucky. She met his eyes. "Why did you get me out?"

He aborted a shrug, air hissing through his teeth. When he moved the pot, he didn't bend. The muscles in his arm twitched and the side of his mouth tightened. "What, Colten? What aren't you telling me?"

He glanced at her out of the corner of his eye. "This moon is uninhabited and both of our ships are damaged. We're stuck here, together."

She blinked at him. *What? Alone?* If both ships were damaged how were they going to escape the … oh she was stuck here. With *him.*

He continued, "Your ship is badly damaged, but I think we can pull enough parts from yours to fix mine."

He wanted to junk *her* ship? A dagger of pain stabbed into her brain behind her right eye. She pressed into her temple, freezing at the feel of a bandage wrapped around her forehead. "What is this *we* you're talking about?"

He grinned. "My ship is the better option."

"Oh, come on." She flopped back on the ground, landing on something squishy. Twisting, she examined what it was and found Colten had put her jacket there. *Huh, that was nice.*

He nudged her a while later. She stirred, opened her eyes and blinked up at the darkness above her head. *What happened? Where am I?* Sparks of electricity dug into her side when she tried to roll over. Sniffing, she wondered what was on fire. She found a pair of red-stained boots and looked up into Dan's face. *Oh right, the crash.*

"What?"

"You fell asleep again. Eat this." He held out a steaming bowl. Her stomach lurched at the thought of food and she quickly turned away.

"You have to eat," he told her.

She clenched her teeth together and shook her head mumbling, "Not a good idea." After a moment of silence there was a loud slurp. Fighting the pain Toni rolled over. Colten sat a few feet away on a fallen tree trunk and slurped at the bowl in his hands, smacking his lips together after each mouthful. Her skin crawled and she twitched with every sound. Rocking from side to side, more sparks shot down her spine. The burnt-milk smell of the soup drifted to her nose.

"Do you mind?"

"What?" Liquid dripped down his chin, and he wiped it away with his sleeve.

"That's disgusting," she groaned. "You're doing that on purpose, aren't you, Colten?"

His grin infected his eyes. "You know, you should call me Dan. We're going to be stuck here a while, together. I can't keep calling you *Agent*."

"You could." Sliding her butt back, her head whirled. A sharp pain sliced into her hip. She mashed her lips together and forced through it. Arrest him, or at least chain him to something nearby until she could move properly. Laying back down, she moaned. Maybe she'd arrest him in the morning.

A laugh from the other side of the fire made her suspect he knew exactly what she was thinking. She scowled up at the sky. *Where are my shades?*

"Broken. I found them in the wreckage when I pulled you clear."

Khegh it all, I said that aloud. She'd have to be careful with what she thought about. Clearly she wasn't focusing well enough to stop from saying whatever popped into her mind. She did voice her other fear. "Mate? My C-bot?"

"Disabled or injured. I don't know. Non-functional, at any rate. I couldn't get a signal off him."

Mate? Oh no! If he was down, then so was Zach. *I'm alone.* Toni closed her eyes massaging the skin between them. *You have him.* Her eyes sprang open at the betrayal of her thoughts. "Speaking of signals ..." she prompted hopefully.

"No electronics at all."

There went her plan to trigger the emergency alert manually. Then again, if she could get a look at her ship, maybe she could cobble something together to send out a limited signal. "You said we might be able to get your ship to function?"

"I'm thinking if we dismantle your NSD we might be able to boost a—"

She shook her head. With no charge to the Normal Space Drive, it wouldn't matter. "We have to change the switches first." *I never checked my spare supplies.* Did she even have replacement switches?

He eyed her with interest. "You sound like you know what you're talking about."

She grunted. Electronics and programming were her thing, not mechanical repairs, and she said so. His early words replayed in her head. "We're stuck here, together." *Shenghi.*

"Like I said, between the two of us we might be able to get something up and running. Look, if you can't eat, then at least try to get some rest. Neither ship is going anywhere for the time being."

He was right about that. And she wasn't going anywhere until she could stand up without falling over. *How can I sleep?* Colten—Dan, his name is Dan—was wide awake, and who knew what he could get up to while she was out. Then again, all he'd done so far was rescue her from her damaged vessel, patch her injuries and try to feed her. Not what she'd have expected.

She was safe and warm and he'd even cooked for her, though she couldn't stomach the thought of it. She allowed her eyes to drift closed. She'd have to rely on him—at least for now—but she wouldn't trust him.

*

"Get up. We have to move, get up!"

She was prodded and pushed hard, then felt herself moving along the ground, a tight band tugging hard on her ankle. "Wha ..." she mumbled, gasping at the spike of pain that stabbed through her leg.

"Get up," Dan demanded.

Toni pried open her eyes to find him towing her across the sand toward the tree line by the ankle. "What, what's wrong?"

Dan dropped her ankle and hoisted her upright.

"What? What is it?"

"We have to move. Trouble's coming."

"What?"

"Just move!"

With his help, she limped under the cover of the trees. Twigs and branches scratched at her legs as she stumbled trying to keep up with the powerhouse pulling her forward. He kept his arm around her back; his body heat soaked into her skin. *Why isn't he wearing a shirt?* A rumble rattled the trees around them. She slowed and glanced over her shoulder. *What on Marn?*

"Keep moving!"

The rumbling increased, making the dirt beneath their feet tremble. Toni tripped. Her sides ached and her left knee was throbbing like a bitch. She pulled back on Dan's arm. *I need to stop.* He grabbed her around the waist and swung her over his shoulder breaking into a run.

"Woah, hey!" From her new vantage point, Toni could see ... *Oh, my gods!* Thin tree trunks snapped or fell, tumbling around the stampeding grey-skinned, four-legged animals. Eyes wide, they snorted and bellowed as they crushed everything in their path. At first, she thought that was what Dan was running from. Then she saw the monstrous creature bearing down behind the three animals. At least, she saw its big, clawed feet. "Shenghi!" Dan ran faster. Toni's heart sprang into her throat—she couldn't breathe. Her ribcage was pressed against his shoulder. His body odor filled her nose. Every step he took forced the breath from her lungs. She could only gasp, and watch in horror at the approaching stampede.

The grey animals—at least four times Mate's size—drew closer. The whites of their eyes shone almost as brightly as her skin. Nostrils flared wide as they snorted terrible, terrified sounds.

The monster put on a burst of speed and snatched up the trailing beast. It consumed the animal in a crunch of bone. Toni screamed again, digging her nails into Dan's damp skin. A sudden iron-rich smell of blood overpowered Dan's scent. Her stomach quivered and she swallowed back bile. Everything went dark as rock surrounded them.

"For Xendia's sake, will you shut *up!*" Dan gasped.

He slowed as he stumbled toward the back of a cave. With every step, the walls closed in. Releasing a loud groan, he lowered her to the ground and then flopped beside her, panting loudly. They stared at the entrance, waiting for the animals to fight their way in. She ran her hands over her clothes. Her knife was missing, her holster gone. How had she missed that earlier? *I don't have a weapon.* Those things could have killed them. She was completely helpless. *What if he'd left me behind? Why didn't he?*

A roar and a shriek froze her mind. Stomping and stamping, the scrabbling of claws on stone, and then a sudden silence, sent shivers down Toni's spine.

"I don't think it can get in here," she whispered at last.

"I kheghing *hope* it can't."

She reached out a trembling hand and touched his arm. "Thank you." *Why did you save me?* Confusion filled her. No one had put her before their own safety before—well, no human.

"Did I hurt you?" he asked, sucking in great gulps of air. Beneath her fingers, his body trembled from the run. She inched away from his sweat-soaked skin.

"No, I don't think so. I'm a bit sore, but then again, I was sore already."

"Not going to yell at me for making it worse?"

Even in the murkiness of the cave his grin sent flames to her brain. "Give it a rest."

Now that her heart was settling back into its normal rhythm, the throbbing in her head took over. She needed to lie down. "Now what?"

Dan started to laugh. "Shenghi! Oh, I ache. You're not exactly light, are you?"

"Hey!" she snapped, poking him hard in the side. When he flinched, her eyes brightened.

"Oh, don't even think …"

She blamed relief at being alive for what she did next, reaching out to tickle his side as a giggle exploded out of her. In the back of her head, all she could see was Mate's unlit eyes and dead stare as he was swallowed by a thundering monster with clawed feet. Tears prickled. She laughed to hide her sob. She was alone here but for the smuggler twitching beneath her hand. The smuggler who'd just saved her life, again. He grabbed her wrist, stilling her move. His fingers pressed into her skin, and tingles raced up her arm. She pulled away. *What am I doing?* Her strange behavior had to be the result of concussion.

They sat in an awkward silence she didn't want to break. The damp dirt smell of the cave was seeping into her pores. There was something else in it, animal urine maybe? *Ew!* No matter which way she lay, the smell wafted into her nostrils. Finally, she leaned up on her elbows, "Why aren't you wearing a shirt?"

He rose quickly. "Uh, yes. Well, I was pulling the console from your ship and it was ho—"

"Wait, what? Why were you in my ship?" She tried to jump to her feet but everything hurt too much. She slumped back, and glared at his shadowy form. Between clenched teeth she sucked in a sharp breath. *Mate!*

"Hey, relax. I was only pulling the parts we need for the repairs. Was looking for a charge."

Her anger tightened like a fist within her chest. Breathing hard, she growled. "Do *not* go into my ship without me."

There was no movement beside her. Even the sounds of his breathing stopped. "You don't trust me?"

Not in the slightest. "No."

"I just saved your life."

She rolled her eyes, knowing he couldn't see it. "And that stops you from being a smuggler, does it?"

"No. Look, don't make a big deal—"

"It is a big deal! It's *my* ship." She slapped her hand against the damp dirt, scratching her palm against something sharp. *Khegh it!*

"Look, sweetheart—"

Sweetheart? Fury exploded as a ball of flame behind her eyes. She was surprised she couldn't smell smoke. "Khegh off! No ship, not without me." She didn't want him near Mate and Zach without her there to watch his every move. She scrubbed at her hand removing the dirt clinging to her skin.

His clothing rustled. The sound of his boots scuffed the rocky ground as he paced. The clomping moved toward the cave's entrance.

Her gut tightened. "Where are you going?"

"To look for our supplies. I'm hoping they didn't get trampled."

"No, you can't. Not yet. You can't go out there." She told herself she wasn't worried about the smuggler, she just didn't want to be left alone in here, unable to protect herself. *I need a weapon.*

"Well, it's a little small in here what with you and your ego."

"My ego? Listen here—"

"You listen. You're still hurt."

Through clenched teeth she bit out, "I'm fine."

"You're not. Stay here. I'll—"

"Those animals are still out there," she reminded him.

"They'll be gone and—"

"You can't go out there yet."

"Stop interrupting me!" he shouted, throwing his hands up. She could just make out his outline, a moving shadow.

She snapped her mouth shut. *Stubborn kheghing ass!* Huffing out a breath, she rubbed at her tight chest and focused her gaze on the blackness in front of her.

"Really? That worked?"

"Shut up," she said without looking in his direction.

It sounded as though he slapped a hand against his leg. "We need water, and I have to check the site."

"You don't even have a weapon," she pointed out. "Wait, why don't you have a weapon? What happened to your gun?" *And where is mine?*

There was silence. His voice softer when he admitted. "I took it off when I was pulling the backing from—"

"Oh my gods, you put your weapon down on a moon you know nothing about?"

"I thought it was deserted."

"Clearly the scary, hungry wildlife didn't get the message."

Dan grumbled quietly. She heard his body shift and the creak of cartilage as he knelt beside her. He reeked of sweat. "I won't be gone long. We need our supplies, and you're right, I need my weapon in case those things come back."

Trying to make me feel better? The adrenaline from their run had well and truly disappeared and her aches were growing stronger by the second. She'd probably pass out soon. And then she'd be all alone, in a cave, in the dark. Her throat tightened. "Yeah, good idea. You should go so you'll be back before nightfall."

His voice lightened. "Are you worried about me?"

"No."

Ugh, he was grinning. Of course he'd jump to that conclusion.

"You are. You don't want me to get eaten."

"Oh, go already. I need a drink and you're the only one capable of getting it, that's all," she mumbled.

The ruffle of his clothing grew closer. She pulled back, uncomfortable with his proximity. "I will come back," he said softly. He climbed to his feet and walked out.

She stared out of the cave long after he'd gone. That's what she was afraid of.

CHAPTER EIGHT

Toni roused.

Blinking slowly, she found the cave had grown darker in the time she'd been asleep. Heavy silence hovered around her and she became aware of her heartbeat thudding in her ears. *Why isn't he back yet?*

She scratched at the dried sweat on her neck, feeling it flake under her nails. Dan was a resourceful smuggler, so no need to worry, right? He wouldn't get into any trouble alone, and he certainly wouldn't need her help to stay alive. That thought gave her pause. He didn't need her help. He could repair his ship on his own, so why hadn't he left her to die? He could have then stripped her ship of the parts needed and left. They were enemies. It was her fault they were even here. Why did he save her?

No matter what game he was playing, she had to remain cautious. Whether Dan was helping her out of the goodness of his heart or because he needed something didn't matter. They were stuck together on this moon, and the longer she needed his help, the longer it would take to complete repairs and get out of here.

And when we leave, what then? She shook away the question. That could wait until they actually reached space. There was a lot to do between now and then, and she'd spent enough time thinking like an injured woman. It was high time she started thinking like an agent and fended for herself.

First things first, she needed a bathroom.

With sluggish movements, she dragged herself to the wall and used its uneven surface to pull her body upright. Dizziness hit her immediately. Leaning back, she closed her eyes and focused on breathing until her equilibrium settled.

Hesitantly, she took a single step and was pleased when she didn't fall or stumble, shuffled forward. What felt like hours later, she reached the mouth of the cave and glanced up. The sky was alight with wavy green lights. *Icy.* Finding a spot, she went quickly and yanked her trousers up, hating the feeling of being exposed. The longer she was on her feet, the weaker she felt. Her head was swimming again by the time she staggered back into the cave.

Damn it, she'd meant to look for some sticks or moss so she could start a fire. Her stomach lurched. Spinning on a heel, she limped back out of the cave and dove into the closest clump of bushes, dry heaving painfully.

Nothing made a reappearance. Thank goodness she hadn't eaten earlier. As the spasms tapered off, she broke out in a sweat, sending shivers through her body setting her limbs trembling like a newborn mooncalf.

"There you are."

She didn't react to his voice. His approaching footsteps could barely be heard above the buzzing in her head. Right now, she wouldn't have cared if he was the monster come back to eat her; in fact, she would have welcomed it. She moaned pitifully and clutched her head, too weak to move.

"Here," he said, holding a small container to her mouth. His other hand came across her waist to steady her body. She relaxed into his embrace, sipping at the warm salty liquid to rinse out her mouth. She spat on the ground and took another sip.

"Ugh."

"Let me help you inside, Trina," he said not moving away until she settled on the ground. Toni rested her head against the jagged cave wall and focused on Dan. He returned carrying armfuls of leaf matter and broken sticks, piling it high before setting it alight. He glanced up at her. "What were you doing outside?

"Bathroom."

"Should have waited."

Toni glared. "For how long? I had no idea if you were even coming back."

In the light of the newly built fire, his eyes widened. "I told you I was coming back. Didn't you believe me?"

No. Peering around, she was curious to learn more about their hiding place. Now that she could see she found the cave smaller than she'd thought. Shadows danced over uneven walls, naked roots poked through rock.

"You will have to trust me sooner or later," he told her, rifling through a bag at his feet.

She didn't answer that either.

Toni must have dozed, the scent of burnt moss and some sort of flower filling the air, lulling her into a relaxed state. She came fully awake when she recognized warmth and pressure from his body behind her. Instantly, she rolled away from him, her body twitching and her heart thumping. "What are you doing?"

"It's going to get cold in here. There's a frost outside. You need to stay warm until your head clears. Just close your eyes." He waited, staring at her, making it her decision.

It's not that cold. The next breath she huffed out appeared like a fog in front of her mouth. Reluctantly, she slid back to him. He threw a blanket over them both and tucked it in around his body. The banked fire threw a golden glow against the surrounding rock. She could hear the crackle and pop of wood and sap.

"I don't—"

"Not now," he grumbled against her neck. She flinched at the brush of his warm breath. "Just go to sleep."

Yeah sure, like she'd be able to sleep with him pressed against her like that. Slowly, the heat soaked into her and she drifted. His hand crept up to rest against her hip. She didn't move, telling herself it was because she didn't have enough strength to knock him away.

*

As much as it pained her to admit, he'd been right about the two ships. The *Blackflame*'s nose was gone. She couldn't bear to look at the gaping maw of twisted metal as they approached. Her examination of the TAFF drive was more promising. Running her fingers along the cables, she was pleased to find most of them intact. She could pull them, along with the initializer and the stabilizer. Without her shades, her vision blurred at a distance but in here she could use her sensitive eyesight to her advantage. Third chip down was cracked. She could see the faint green sheen of chelix gas leaking from the tube line behind it. She skipped the next chip too. The stack below seemed to be fine. Bending her head, she crawled deeper into the duct. Thankfully she was able to move her neck without stabbing pain this morning.

Yeah, that was plenty of switches. She could yank most of them though it mentally pained her to do so. Her empty stomach groaned. "Hey, grab the dehydrated packs if you can find them."

"You're already over my stellar cooking skills?" his voice drifted back to her. He insisted he could patch his ship's hull so she'd sent him to the lower hold to hunt for her soldering equipment—if it had survived the crash.

"No, just afraid you're gonna try and get me to cook."

"That bad?"

"Wanna try me?"

"Ah, that's a no."

Ass! She wriggled further, hissing with the pull of skin around her hip. She shifted her weapon to the small of her back. She wasn't planning to advertise that she'd found it and wouldn't put it down, no matter how many bruises she got winding through the innards of her ship.

"Anything useful in there?"

His voice sounded louder. He was coming back. "Yeah, enough that I should be able to repair your comms, get out a signal maybe. Try the engineering hatch."

"Below the generator?"

"Yup."

One more should do. Clasping her hand around the scrounged chips she scooted back. *Oh, yang cord.* Tugging the cable free from its connection, she climbed from the duct and headed for the hatch.

"That's not going to work," she said, staring at his hands.

"Well, we won't know until we try it, will we?" he snapped dangling from the power exchange tube. The hand holding the decoupling wrench was bent under the casing.

"It's not compatible with a Stargazer. I'll have to recode it and splice the connection cable."

He shot her a narrowed glare. She ignored it. "You've already blown two switches simply from using the wrong cable size."

"I blew it?"

"Yes, you wouldn't let me do it." Toni sat down at the open hatch and started stripping wires. Dan returned to dismantling the transformer box. Trying to, anyway. She suppressed a smirk watching him twist. There was no way his big man hand was getting behind there.

"Don't forget the—"

"If you say the tri-splice lines again, I am going to come up there and—"

"Threatening the injured woman? Nice, Dan, real nice." She shuffled sideways, her body still aching, and picked up her tablet. Writing a new line of code to convince the incompatible parts to work together should be pretty simple. She just had to tell them they really did use the same power structure. While she waited for him to prove his intelligence was greater than hers, she figured she'd get started. "You going to admit it yet?"

"Nope." She couldn't help the grin that crossed her face at his growled response. At least he couldn't see her reaction. She didn't need him thinking he was entertaining her or anything.

The code simulation flashed a red failed message. She ran it again. Red red red. She lifted the device to throw it, but instead slammed it on the floor and let out a howl of frustration.

"Hey? What?" Dan poked his head out of the hatch, his brows scrunched together. "Don't kill the tablet," he warned.

"It won't work." She stabbed at the command keys angrily. "The codes won't work. Why won't the codes work?"

"If that's the way you're treating it, I'm not surprised."

"For khegh's sake, if these codes don't work then nothing we're doing is going to work. Nothing! All this time wasted for nothing."

He pulled himself out of the hatch. "Well, I suggest you start by treating it better."

She contemplated throwing the tablet at his head. "It's your ship—*you* make it work!" She knew it was a stupid thing to say as soon as the words left her mouth. The look he shot her said it was, too.

"Time for a break, I think," he said, approaching to help her stand. She took one look at him and recoiled.

"You're not touching me with those."

He examined his grease-stained hands then rubbed them against his thighs. "Better?"

"Gods, you're disgusting," she groaned, wriggling back across the floor to get away from him.

"Let me—"

"No, no, you're gross right now. Go away." She slapped at his hands when he reached for her. He pounced. Moments later, she was lying in his arms grumbling quietly beneath her breath. When he put her down at the campsite outside, he left large stains all over her shoulders and waist. "Look at this—it's completely ruined!" she complained, gesturing to her silk shirt.

"I dunno, it looks fine to me."

"With your handprints all over it?"

"Yup." Grinning, he tore open a bag of dehydrated protein.

A white-hot heat flared in the center of her chest. She was not a plaything for his amusement. His disrespect made her blood boil. She was sure he wouldn't treat a male agent this way. Her silk shirts were necessary to protect her skin. *Like he cares about your sensitivities.* Tears prickled and she turned her head, blinking rapidly to hide them. Calling a halt to their repairs only added to her frustration. "I wanted to get it done today." The longer it took, the longer they'd be stuck on this rock. All he seemed to want to do was eat and sleep. And yes, her head hurt, yes a break to rest her eyes would be great, terrific even, but she hated appearing weak in front of him, and hated him for coddling her.

If he questioned her abilities again, she was going to explode. She clambered to her feet and limped into the jungle. *Yeah, I need a break. From him.*

"Hey?"

She didn't look back. Living alone with only Mate and Zach for company for so long showed in her irritation. His constant presence was giving her hives. Everything he said either made her furious or unreasonably upset, and she couldn't explain why her emotions were swinging so wildly. *Well, you could.* She told her brain to shut up as it wasn't being helpful. Parting the bushes, she stared at the damaged *Blackflame* and realized her feet had brought her to the only place she'd ever felt safe.

He thinks I'm useless. Hopeless. She sank to her knees. *Why do I even care what he thinks?* She stared at her grubby hands and ran a fingertip over her chipped thumbnail. *I miss Mate and Zach.* Sniffing hard, she let the loamy smell settle into her chest. An animal cried out in the distance. She hadn't seen what made the cry so she had no idea what to imagine but pictured something small and feathered. While she was here, she might as well pull the M-cable.

Climbing to her feet, she let her steps take her closer to the *Blackflame*'s hull. Touching the cold plasteel, she imagined Mate telling her they would find a way to repair the ship and not to worry. Her gut clenched. *Oh Mate.* She headed inside and slumped down beside her inanimate partner. He lay on a cushion near the wall closest to one of Zach's dead monitors. The first time they'd come in here to strip the ship, Toni had been unable to focus until Dan moved her partner from where he'd fallen in the center of the room to the wall and made him comfortable.

She remembered the quirk of his lips as he'd struggled with the heavy C-bot's weight, the way he hadn't looked at Toni, his hand brushing gently against Mate's fur to smooth it down where he'd messed it. "I think I like him, Mate," she whispered. It was impossible. He was the enemy. No matter how often he gave her the last sweet out of his dinner bag or made her laugh with some stupid story, as soon as they got off this moon, she would arrest him. She couldn't allow her feelings to get in the way of that. "I wish you could tell me I'm a fool." She ran her fingers over his fur and contemplated, as she did every morning, trying to repair his systems.

Initially, she'd hoped it was only a loose connection that stopped him coming back online and that a reboot would be all it took to get him running again. The basic repairs she tried did nothing. His systems would require an investigation, and her priority had to be the emergency beacon on Dan's ship. Her desperate need to fix Mate itched at her in a way that was almost impossible to ignore. She needed his calm, logical mind and comforting presence to help her focus. She'd never been without him before. No wonder she wasn't coping. The tremble in the pit of her stomach reminded her that without Mate to watch her back, she couldn't afford to lower her guard around the smuggler. A whisper in the back of her mind admitted it was already too late.

Stay here and fix him. She stood and hunted for her tablet. Her shoulders slumped when she realized it was back on the

Renegade, with Dan. *Why am I relying on him to get me out of here?* She turned back to Mate. "Because I'm not an engineer. I can fix Zach probably. You too, in time. But I can't repair the hole in the hull." She stared around at the damaged cockpit. Lifeless. With no power it was as silent as deep space. She could smell coolant leaking; the acrid taste tickled the back of her throat. "Of course, you could tell me how to fix it if you were working."

Nodding decisively, she decided to return to his ship to fetch her tablet. "Time to stand on my own two feet. I don't need him." She didn't need anyone. Her eyes flew to Mate. "Except you. I need you, Mate. I can't do this on my own."

Mate didn't reply.

The stillness of her ship was eerie. A tree branch cracked outside and her gaze darted to the open hatch. Her heart gave an uneven thump thump as it skipped a beat. That was why she stayed with Dan. *I'm afraid to be alone.*

Staring at Mate's body, she made a promise. "I will come back for you. After I fix the *Renegade*'s comms and send out a signal, you're my next priority." Her stomach let out a grumble. A laugh burst from her lips. "Well, one of them."

Reluctantly obeying the hunger call, she returned to the campsite. Dan didn't say a word as he flipped whatever was cooking on the broken plasteel panel he had hung over the fire, only pointed to her spot. She ignored him and made her way to his ship then plodded back to the campsite. Sitting down she wrapped her blanket around her shoulders and poked at the tablet to run the simulation again. Red flashed up at her. *Shenghi!* What was she doing wrong?

After insisting she found programming simple, her face burned with her failure. Her tapping grew louder.

"Did you check the line count?" he asked.

"Yes, I checked the line count." *He thinks I'm a kheghing idiot.* "And the relationship lines, and the memory conventions. I've checked everything."

"Well, you missed something."

She threw off the scratchy blanket and climbed to her feet. "Maybe it just won't work," she complained, stomping from the campsite toward the ocean.

"Where are you going now?" he called after her.

"To throw myself into the sea! Where do you think I'm going? For a walk. What are you, my mother?"

"You have one?"

"Cute, real cute," she said and slipped in the fine sand as her anger took hold.

"Don't go far."

She climbed back to her feet, furiously spitting, "Yes, Mother." He didn't look at her as she continued. "I need to think and I can't do that with you annoying me."

"What did I say?"

"You didn't have to say anything, just standing there is distracting."

His laughter followed her all the way to the shore. She scuffed her feet through sand, kicking great swathes up into the air. She never should have opened her mouth. Staring out into the water, she focused on the movement of the waves, listening to the crest and tumble of it onto the shore. Her breathing slowed. Warm water brushed her toes. *Why am I so angry?* Who was she kidding, the answer was obvious. She wanted Mate back at her side and Zach snarking on every screen. She wanted normal food and a real bed. She didn't want to be here ... with him.

Scoring her feet along the shore, she twirled and swirled the sand beneath her toes. *Why isn't the code working?*

It should accept the combined segments she'd written. It made no sense. She stopped and glanced back down the beach at the random and beautiful patterns she'd created shining in the moonlight. The long lines were broken only by her footsteps and ... *I need to break the code into smaller sections!* "Kheghing firepits!" She hobbled back to the campsite.

Minutes later, she ran the simulation again, and grinned at Dan when the tablet flashed a happy green. He matched her smile with one of his own.

*

Toni scratched at her neck scars and silenced a moan. Her skin was red in patches where she'd dug her nails in. Dan noticed when she was tired, though she was sure she hadn't complained. He noticed when she was hungry and always had a plate waiting or a container nearby to quench her thirst. Yesterday, she'd found him gently handwashing her shirts with the non-allergenic soap spray she had stashed on her ship. He even found an old pair of sunshades when he realized how painful the clear sunlight reflecting off the surrounding sand was to her eyes. He was everywhere she looked. He wouldn't leave her alone. Her only option was to avoid him. But how could she do that without him chasing after her?

Now that she'd solved the problematic coding issue, she was at a loss. She could try to fix Mate, but for some reason she didn't want him to know that's what she was doing every time she snuck off on her own. His attentiveness had her hackles up. *He knows.* And she'd pulled too many switches to repair Zach. She needed a distraction. One that removed her from Dan's sight. "I can try to fix your CII."

He shot her a long look. "Can you actually rebuild a CII?"

"You think I can't?"

"Well—"

"Seriously? Do you think a woman like me doesn't have the brains for such work? Too delicate, maybe?" She rose and stalked toward him, the wrench in her hand wavered threateningly.

"No, I just—"

"Come on, you thought I would be completely useless out here, didn't you?"

"You can't cook."

Her eyes widened. "So? I'm supposed to be able to cook instead of reprograming a fritzed CII?"

"No, I meant … damn it, you're doing it again."

"Doing what?"

"Interrupting me. Putting words in my mouth and thoughts in my head. I wasn't thinking that at all. Kheghing hell, you are so quick to jump on everything I say and twist it—"

"Well, what you say is so kheghing stupid!" she accused, turning away. The argument was over as far as she was concerned. *Wait for it.* Yup, the sound of his footsteps approaching. The itch beneath her skin grew as he came close enough to smell his musky body odor.

"You have no idea what I'm saying because you never let me kheghing finish!"

She raised her brow at that and, after a moment of silence, gestured with a broad hand for him to continue. He glared. But she was unaffected.

"No, I just figured, stupidly as it turns out, that a woman like you wouldn't need to learn how to program."

Toni's body straightened. *Always the same thing.* Her voice was cold when she quietly asked, "A woman like me?" *A freak, you mean?*

"A beautiful woman," he clarified. 'You could get anyone to do it for you."

Snorting loudly, she said, "Nice try." *What a joke. Does he think I can't see through that?*

He tilted his head at her reaction, his lips parting. "What does that mean?"

"You're delusional, that's what I meant. Are you trying to con me so you can order me to fetch you water or something? Maybe bake you a pie?"

"You can bake?" He shook his head and lowered the mallet. "You really don't see it, do you?"

"See what? See that you're trying to convince me to do something for you? No, I saw that pretty clearly."

He prowled closer. When he took her hand, a huff of surprise burst out of her mouth. He raised it to his eyes, turned her arm inward and pushed her sleeve back. She watched, frozen, as he traced the red and blue veins that ran under her skin. His touch was gentle, and the calluses on his fingers tickled. "Beautiful. There is no one in the galaxy like you, Trina. One bat of those eyes and you could have any man begging to do whatever you want."

Her mouth fell open. "Oh." Warmth flooded through her body as tingles from his words raced over her skin. Her stomach flip-flopped. His sweat-soaked scent wrapped around her, making her dizzy. Stepping back, she snapped, "Don't be ridiculous." She cradled her wrist where she could still feel his fingers ghosting over her skin.

"I'm not being ridiculous," he said. She could barely hear him when he added, "What do you want, Trina?"

"Nothing. I want nothing." She fled back to the *Renegade*, still trembling. The lie she'd told followed her every step of the way.

CHAPTER NINE

Toni wasn't hiding. She was working. Fortunately, her part of the repairs required her to be inside. Not only did it allow her to shelter from the painful midday sun, it also kept her away from him. It was a struggle to focus on repairing the glitches in D'ena's software and patching the communication logs, but she was finally making progress. Thoughts of Dan and the touch of his fingers were pushed to the back of her mind as she concentrated on each fragmented line.

Lost in a long string of code, her body thrumming with beautiful numbers, a loud explosion shook the ground. It sent her racing from the *Renegade* with her pistol in her hand. "Dan?" she called when she didn't see him. There was a smell of detonite in the air. "Dan?" Her heart pounded. Turning a circle, she searched for smoke, his dark form, footprints—anything. When she couldn't find him, her breathing grew faster. "*Dan!*"

"What? Settle down. What is it?" He appeared out of the jungle like a wraith, holding a large dripping bag.

"What happened?" she asked, looking over him quickly, searching for injury. He seemed fine. In fact, better than fine.

She tore her eyes from his bare chest. "What happened?" She tried to calm the fear in her voice and realized she hadn't succeeded when he grinned at her.

"Worried about me?"

"Yes actually. You haven't finished the patch yet."

"Oh, so it's my work you're worried about?"

She glared at him. "Yes, but only because I don't want to do it. I hate that burner."

He dropped the bag he was carrying and held out his arms. "I'm just fine, see? You've been holed up inside so long I figured I'd have to come in there and resuscitate you."

Toni rolled her eyes. "What were you doing? What was that explosion?"

Scratching at his neck, his face flushed. "Ah, I was hunting."

"Hunting? Hunting what?"

He picked up the bag and stumbled under the weight of whatever was inside. "Dinner. And if my memory serves, it's your turn to clean—"

"Oh, you know what? I've just had a crazy idea about a new line of code. I've got to go before I forget it." She threw him a grin and took off for the ship. "By the way, your hunting technique sucks. You stink, buddy."

Dan raced after her, chasing her all the way back to the *Renegade*. He stopped just outside the door. "Will you come out when dinner's ready?"

It took her a moment to reply. Panting, she finally got out, "Yes."

She stayed buried in the *Renegade*'s control center until tempted out by an incredible, mouth-watering smell. She started salivating. Dan had braced a network of branches over the open fire. Each stick held chunks of blackened meat close to the flames.

"Hey."

"Smells good. What is that?" she asked, coming closer.

"Do you actually want to know?"

She spied a bloody pile of animal skins nearby and shook her head. "No, no it's good." The tattoo on his chest just above his left nipple caught her eye as it always did. White against dark skin. A pistol outline crossed with a knife.

He pulled on a shirt, much to her disappointment, and started to strip cooked meat off a large shank. In the back of her mind, she was thankful she'd crashed with him nearby. If he'd landed on another island or on the other side of the moon, she'd have been forced to feed herself. She'd probably have starved to death by now.

They sat in a comfortable silence while they ate. In deference to the fact that he'd cooked, she cleaned up their basic dishes and returned to sit next to him in front of the fire. For a while, they sat staring up at the slowly waking stars, breathing quietly. "What are you staring at?" he asked.

She didn't move. Each night about this time, the silver lines in the leaves above them flared and then pulsed. "I'm waiting for the strobes."

"The what?"

"The silver lights. It's breathtaking."

"What lights?"

She turned her head enough to catch his eye. "You've never seen them? Oh! My eyes."

"What does *that* mean?"

"I can see colors ordinary people can't." She fell silent. The briefest flicker above her nose signaled the start. "There it goes." She watched in awe. The lights pulsed so fast it was like traveling in space. "I wish you could see it," she whispered.

"So do I." He rolled toward her. "So, you mentioned a mother. Any other family?"

She glanced at him curiously. "Why do you want to know?"

"Just making conversation. Xendia, it's not an interrogation. You don't have to tell me if you don't want to."

Groaning, she sat up and leaned back against one of the logs, stretching her legs out across the sand. "Yes, both parents, an older sister, two younger sisters, and a younger brother. What about you?"

"Only child. My mother passed, but Dad's still kicking around somewhere. D'ena is named after her."

Toni turned to him and asked the question she'd been itching to ask for a while. "Why'd you become a smuggler?"

His usually expressive face blanked. He climbed to his feet and paced in front of the fire. "It's funny how things happen, you know? I hadn't intended on it. It wasn't part of the plan. Big house, pets, wife and kids, but life's funny. As soon as you start making plans, reality tears them into little pieces, and then you're stuck trying to put them back together again."

"What happened?" She was afraid he *would* answer her this time. Instead, he slumped down onto the sand next to her and leaned against the same log.

His voice was soft when he replied. "Ry ... Made a few mistakes, ended up in the wrong place with the wrong people. It is what it is."

So he wasn't going to tell her. She stared into the flames. Her fingers curled into the cool sand forming strange abstract pictures. The scent of their dinner still lingered in the air, but it was fading. She could smell his soap. Scooting lower she kept her arms close to her body. *I must reek!*

Curiosity finally forced her to break the uneasy silence fallen over them. "Have you always worked alone?"

He barely hesitated. "Yup. Don't need anyone else to do what I do. Heck, the pay is great. You need a job? The hazards are insane but the people you meet are mostly good. There are some nut jobs, but you get them everywhere, right? People to avoid, that sort of thing. You'd be good at it."

She laughed at his obvious attempt to change the subject. Silence stretched between them, but it wasn't hostile—more comforting than anything. Warmth kissed her face on the side that faced the fire. The smell of burning wood familiar—her grandparents kept a working fireplace in their small house. The memories of their crinkly faces and the hot cocoa they always had on hand filled her with melancholy. Popping wood sap sent sparks into the air. Toni pulled her knees up to move her toes away. After a little while she sighed. "My name is Toni."

"I know."

"What?"

"Jasmine."

Of course. "Why didn't you say anything."

"I was waiting for you."

She thought about that for a while. "This is kinda nice."

He nodded. "It is. When I look up at the sky dancing around like a great celestial show just for us … I think I could stay here, live here." He turned to her then. "We could stay here."

She laughed, thinking he was making a joke, but his face was serious. He stared into her eyes. "We could. Just the two of us. No need to go back."

Toni shook her head. "Be serious, Dan. It would never work."

"You could make it work, if you really want to."

He looked so earnest. She tried to imagine it, but every time she pictured the two of them together, the image dissolved like a water-based image in the rain. Ephemeral, intangible—it was a dream, nothing more than that.

"Can I ask you a question without you exploding at me?" he asked.

"Depends on what you ask." She was sated, warm, and exhausted from staring at strings of code. In a few days she might be ready to reactivate the CII, maybe even as early as tomorrow. It was time to start thinking of the future, the realistic future. What was she going to do when they got off this moon? Could she really arrest him? What if she turned him instead? Make him into an informant. Would he go for that? It was certainly more palatable than just letting him go. And then she'd get to see him again.

"Do you really think you're a freak?" In the light of the fire, orange flames danced in his eyes. He stared at her unblinkingly. Firelight cast half of his face into shadow, while the side she could see glowed.

"I am."

"Why do you think that?" he asked, exhaling a long breath almost like a sigh.

How could he ask? *Look at me.* She turned her face up to the sky. "I'm not normal. I'm too pale and sickly looking. I make people uncomfortable. I burn too easily, my eyes hurt in just about any light. My DNA is damaged. I shouldn't exist. I'm an anomaly."

"I think—"

She didn't want to know what he thought. "My scars. I was born with them, you know. They don't just stop at my collar. I have them on my ribs too. I *am* a freak."

"Did someone tell you that?" His voice sounded flat in the darkness. No expression crossed his face when she peered at him. He was holding his body so still, no part of him twitched. She couldn't tell what he was thinking.

"Who hasn't?"

"I haven't."

Toni snorted. "Yet."

He knelt forward to nudge a block of wood further onto the fire and when he sat back he was a lot closer, close enough that Toni could reach out and touch him—if she wanted to. She clasped her fingers tightly together over her belly, feeling his gaze on her face. After a few minutes, she turned to look him in the eyes. "I don't know what you're trying to do here, Dan, but this thing, whatever it is, can't happen. We're enemies. Maybe not right now, but when we get off this rock we'll go back to being who we are. You, a smuggler on the run, and me, hunting you down. Just let it go."

"Thing? You think this is a thing?" His voice was low when he added, "Are we really enemies, Toni?"

"Don't," she begged, hoping he would let it drop. She licked her lips to moisten them and for just a moment, she didn't think she could say no if he pushed things further. She didn't think she'd want to.

"It's not true," he told her, looking away.

"What?"

"You're not damaged, or broken, or a freak. Whoever told you that was very, very wrong."

"Everyone can't be wrong, Dan," she said, rolling away from him at last. She lay down on the blanket they'd been using as a bed. Moments later, she felt him take his place at her back. He flicked the blanket over them and breathed into her neck.

Toni was mostly asleep when she thought she heard him say, "Not everyone."

CHAPTER TEN

"I think we can try turning her on," she called to his feet late the next afternoon. The sun's bite was sharp on her face. Toni shaded herself with her hand, peering down from the top of the *Renegade*'s ramp. Dan lay beneath the wing, but toed the trolley out from underneath at her announcement.

"Wait for me," he called up. Oil painted his face. She turned away from the sight, hiding her grin.

Two and a half weeks since the crash and *Renegade* was finally patched and rebuilt. It wasn't pretty by any means, but hopefully the Stargazer would be functional. Toni led him into the cockpit.

"Shenghi! What did you do in here? Throw an end-of-solar-year booze up?"

"Funny. I've been working on your CII, not as your house-maid," she replied. Lifting the rewired board she'd created to act as a new interface, she waved it around. "I've got one speaker attached, but no screen, so you won't get the CII's face. Ready?"

"As long as you've got her working, that should be fine. We'll need her to manage the fuel changes on the burn up."

She looked at him drily. "Yes, I know."

"How did you learn to do this anyway?"

"What? Reprogram a CII? I get bored."

He snorted. "Bored?"

Toni climbed under the console and connected the last of the lines to allow the meager charge he'd generated outside to trickle into the system. They waited for the NSD to reboot. *Come on, come on.* She'd practically rewritten the entire program. Was there a chance she'd missed something? Highly likely, given the situation. Still, she had her fingers crossed. All she needed was a little "hello." *Come on.* She thumped on the console with her fist. "Anything?"

Above her head, Dan cleared his throat and called, "D'ena? Are you with me?"

There was a burst of static in reply. *Yesssss.* "Hang on," she said, and stretched further within the confined space under the console to manipulate a few more connections. *Maybe something's loose?* She climbed out and stared at the cockpit lights. Connecting them to the CII was a good way to test signal strength. "Try again."

"D'ena?"

The *Renegade*'s lights flickered. A computerized voice said, "Boss?"

"Hey, you did it!" Dan grabbed Toni around the waist, hugging her tightly and laughing into her ear.

Toni grinned, watching the lights flash.

Dan's fingers touched her face, turning her to look at him. He kissed her. She froze at the touch of his lips. *Oh.* He tightened his hold and pulled her closer. Her eyes drifted closed. She sighed into his mouth, raising her hands to loop around his neck. His lips were warm and wet. His hands pressed fire into her skin everywhere he touched. Even the usually numb area around her ribcage scars tingled. He ended the kiss, lifting his head slowly only to kiss her again when she dragged him back.

"D-d-d-a-an?"

He raised his head at the static filled sound of the CII's voice. "Welcome back, D'ena."

The relief in his voice was so great Toni turned away to give him privacy. Her hand rose to her lips. Her first kiss. She wanted more. Dan sat down at the control center and didn't look back. The kiss probably meant nothing to him, but for her, it meant everything. Her head swam. She needed air. "I'll leave you two alone," she said, and escaped through the open doorway.

Grabbing the blanket to protect her skin from the sun, she sat down on the shoreline, facing the ocean. Every time a wave crashed against the sand water licked her toes.

What was that? She knew Dan was happy to have D'ena back, but why kiss her? Was he playing with her? She shook her head. *I always see the worst in every situation.* Dan had done nothing in the past two and a half weeks to make her suspect he was manipulating her emotions. He'd saved her twice, fed her, kept her warm. In fact, he'd done nothing to cause her any pain at all. Why did she automatically assume that was his intention? A little voice in the back of her mind cried out, reminding her of the flash bang. He'd left her blinded on Nizlec Six. Ruthlessly, she shoved the memory away. He'd told her he liked her. *Maybe he really does?* His kiss certainly implied he did. Would he have kissed her if he didn't like her?

The shield over her heart faltered.

It wouldn't take much to repair his ship now. Hearing him address his CII had her aching for the loss of Mate and Zach even more. They would be okay, but she was determined not to leave them here when they left. She'd get Dan to carry Mate and she'd grab Zach's storage drive until she could return. With that resolved, she struggled back to her feet to find Dan heading toward her. He stopped a few feet away.

"Good work. D'ena is responding, but reports some of her systems are inaccessible. Think you can do something about that?"

"Get me some more power, and sure," she told him.

"Done." He walked beside her back to the ship. He didn't mention the kiss.

Neither did Toni.

*

"A-a-agent Delle?"

"D'ena, don't talk. I'm still working on those lines," Toni mumbled, her mouth full of wires. Her hands were tangled in the console's innards.

"I jus-s-st wan-ted to … thank y-y-you."

"Oh, no sweat." She rolled out from beneath the console to eye the lone active camera in the ceiling she'd managed to get working.

"I m-mean for Da … an."

"What do you mean?" Toni asked, not really paying attention to the CII's answer. She sorted through the wires in her hand. *The red one maybe?*

"For s … s-s-saving him."

"Oh, you've got it wrong, D'ena, he pulled me out of my ship. I was trapped. He saved me." She knelt back down.

"Did-d-d he? Oh I'm-m …"

"Don't speak, D'ena. Let me rework these switches so you won't be so garbled. I want to access your stored memory.

Can you try your external communications relay? See if you can get an emergency signal out. Call for help."

"We can't do-o-o-o th-that."

"Of course you can. Well, provided someone is listening." Toni changed the connection in her hand, and D'ena's response became nothing but static. *Ugh, this is such a kheghing pain in the rear.* She switched the wires back.

"—and he doesn't want that."

"What was that, D'ena?" she muttered. *What did I just change?* She tried the green wire.

"D'ena, Toni, how's it going in here?" Dan called from the *Renegade*'s entry ramp.

Startled, Toni lifted her head and smacked it against the panel. "Ouch! Khegh it!" She rubbed the blossoming bump on the back of her head as she dragged herself out once more.

"Boss! I'm back. The agent sure is good with her hands, huh?"

Dan choked on his next breath. Toni grinned at him cheekily and waited for his response. "She's never spoken like that before."

Toni shrugged. "I might have tweaked a few things."

He rolled his eyes. "Can you run a system check, D'ena? See what you can and cannot access? Ah, any messages?"

Toni wiped at the scratches on her fingers, dabbing at blood spots with the rag she'd tucked into her waistband. There was a burst of static above their heads. Toni glanced up wearily. *Not again.*

She was on her knees climbing back under the console when D'ena spoke. "Everything seems to be functioning. Diagnostics are not flagging any major issues, but then again, my diagnostics might be what's on the fritz. I have two messages, Rycee and Gall—"

Dan cut her off, slamming a hand down on the panel Toni held. He pointed at Toni and gestured outside. "I've just put another pot on. You might want to grab it while it's hot."

Messages? The CII accessed the holonet? "We should try the comms—"

"It'll wait."

"What? No, why?" Toni dug in her heels. Her stomach twisted sharply at his pause. "Are you coming?"

"Yes. I'll be right there. Pour me something, will you?"

Her eyes narrowed as she frowned. She shot a glance at the panel. *He cut D'ena off. Why?* The CII mentioned a couple of messages. Gall? Clearly smuggler stuff Dan didn't want her to hear. She hovered in the doorway but he shooed her out with a smile. "Go."

"Check the communication system is sending not just receiving. See if we can get a signal out," she said, looking at him uncertainly. She didn't want to leave. An icy cold spread across her chest. *He doesn't want me to hear something. What's he hiding?*

"Yes, I'll do that. Really, I won't be long."

Outside she hovered by the open ramp but couldn't hear anything from inside. *Get your weapon.* This was it, wasn't it? The moment he became a smuggler again, and she an agent. Why did it feel as though a blackhole had opened inside her chest? She sat by the banked fire, fingering her gun. Her tea was cold by the time Dan joined her. She tucked her gun beneath the blanket though kept her finger on the trigger and wriggled back under the shade of the tree. The moon rotated quickly here, or so it felt, and shade always crept away before she realized.

"What was that about?" she snapped.

"What?"

He had the gall to look confused. The ice inside her chest became nothing but steam as flames roared to life inside her body. It could easily become an inferno that would consume them both if she let it. "You wanted me off your ship. Why?" He grinned and held out a small package. She stared at it blankly. "What's that?"

"Open it."

"Why?"

"Shenghi, Toni, just open it. It's a thank you for getting D'ena back."

Oh. Deflating as her anger extinguished, she took the thing badly wrapped in tree leaves and tore it open. "What?" she said, staring at the polished stone in her hand.

"I found it the other day. I think it might be a natural silkcrystal. Thank you for getting D'ena up and running."

"Um." Toni stared at the stone, embarrassed over her behavior. She fidgeted on the log—every knot and deviation in the wood digging into her soft flesh. Dan sat down beside her. His leg pressed against hers, but she didn't shift away. "Thank you." Silkcrystals were insanely expensive. If it was one, he'd just given her a fortune.

"No, thank you," he whispered and moved closer. His hand rose to touch her face. "Toni."

She pressed her lips to his. *Just once, give me this.* She'd arrest him in the morning, but for now, she waited, sand hot beneath her feet. The sky a shining ball of fire above her head, but still she let Dan tug the protective blanket away. She stared into his dark eyes. He tangled his fingers with hers. His smile drawing her attention back to his mouth. She whispered his name as their lips met again. "Daniel."

*

Dan's hand stroking the length of her arm woke her. Warm breath tickled the back of her neck and she fought to hide the smile that bubbled up. She feigned sleep a little longer, wanting to enjoy the feeling for as long as she could.

"Hey."

She cracked open one eye, slamming it shut at the brightness of the early morning sun. "We fell asleep."

"You fell asleep," he whispered against her skin.

Scrunching her toes in the cool sand, she let out a moan. Rolling over, she buried her face in his shoulder and rubbed her skin against the tattoo on his chest. "It's gonna take forever to wash the sand away."

"How quickly reality sets back in."

"Oh, don't start." She raised her hand and allowed it to flop back down beside her in a demonstration of her lack of energy. Her glare quickly turned into a smile. "Hey," she said softly, looking up into his face.

He ran a finger over the scars on her neck. "Hey." He didn't meet her eyes. Leaning forward, she pursed her lips. He turned his head away. She sat back. *What did I do wrong? Did I snore?*

"Last day." His words drifted over her head as he peered into the distance.

"We weren't going to talk about it, remember?"

"Won't take long to fix those last switches."

"Not talking, not listening." She snatched up the shirt lying in the sand where they'd thrown it the night before. It was Dan's. She tugged it on anyway, uncomfortable having her body so exposed to his eyes in the bright light of morning. Her scars were horrible. Searching for her shades, she located them beneath the blanket, grateful to find her protection against the burn of the sun. When she looked back, Dan stood beside the blanket, looking out across the beach to the repaired ship. His shoulders were a tense line. Toni hesitated. *He regrets last night.* Her stomach tightened as goosepimples rose all over her skin.

"Dan?" It came out a whisper.

When he spun around he was still naked, but it was her pistol in his hand that shocked her. She stumbled back. "What?" Her foot slipped in the soft sand, and she fell.

"Toni ..."

She couldn't tear her eyes from his fingers. "Don't do this." When he didn't move, she climbed cautiously to her feet.

He fired.

Her shoulder exploded in pain. She hit the sand again, one hand outstretched as if to block the next shot, knowing she wouldn't succeed. Her mind froze even as her body screamed in terror and rage. *How can he do this?* She gaped at him. No air reached her lungs as her throat seized. Tears from the burning in her shoulder sprang to her eyes. Like a holofilm close up, all she could see was the smuggler tattoo on his chest.

She tore her gaze up. His face was an expressionless mask.

Behind him was the *Renegade*, the ship they'd been working so hard to repair, and their only way off this moon. Dan glanced over his shoulder, reading her thoughts. He looked back with a smug smirk.

"You know I can't take you with me."

She clutched at her shoulder, gasping as waves of pain sent shivers across her torso. "You said ..."

"I lied."

Hot liquid scalded her cheeks. She said nothing more, knowing from his expression she had no hope of convincing him to change his mind. *I trusted him.* Stalling would get her nowhere. There was no Mate or Zach to spring to her rescue. She was utterly alone and at his mercy. *I'm going to die.* "Why?"

"You were going to arrest me," he said.

"I wasn't." She shook her head as she said the words.

"You would. It's who you are."

"You know nothing about me."

"But I do." He pulled his trousers on, watching her out of the corner of his eye. He expected her to try and stop him, but she was practically naked, injured and in shock. She felt like a statue made of sand, and the sand had crumbled within her, leaving only a shell in the shape of her body. He was still pointing his weapon at her, so she didn't dare move. He'd shot her once—he wouldn't hesitate to shoot a second time.

At least he let her keep the shirt.

"I'll send a message out."

"You won't." She spat the bitter words in his direction and was pleased to see him flinch.

He covered it quickly and grinned. "I guess you know me pretty well, too."

Toni clenched her teeth against the pain radiating from her shoulder, clutching at the wound as if her hand could hold the pain inside. "I know *nothing* about you."

He shrugged, unconcerned by her words. His eyes grew darker. "You knew it had to end this way."

"I thought you were different." She pulled her knees up under her trembling body and glared at him with as much hatred as she could project.

He stared at her for a long time and then threw the pistol as far from her position as he could. It landed with a plop on the sand between her and the distant tree line. He walked away. "That's not all I lied about."

Her heart died. It shriveled into a dried-out ball, leaving her cold and empty.

Forcing her body upright, she stumbled over the sand toward her weapon. When she heard a thud, she turned to see a box thrown from the *Renegade*'s hatch. A second box slid down the ramp before the hatch closed tightly behind them. *Son of a she-demon*—he'd finished the switches.

The *Renegade*'s Cerenkov generator sputtered briefly and burst into flame-light. Toni turned away, dropping to her knees beside the fully charged pistol as hot sand blew over her. She didn't reach for the weapon as the *Renegade* launched behind her.

Tears hit her hands. She knelt staring at the sand beneath her knees. The grains gave her no answers. Moments or hours later, she picked up the pistol and flipped the safety on. The sun was a ball of fire above her now, burning into her sensitive skin. Her eyes ached behind her shades. *My tears are from the sun, nothing else.* That was what she had to believe. She had nothing now. Scrubbing her wet cheeks with shaking hands she stumbled forward.

Her first task was to find shelter and see what he'd left behind. She also had to wrap her wound. The risk of infection now that she was alone was scarily high.

When she reached the boxes and lifted the lid of the first one, she screamed. Bandages. He'd left her with bandages and, oh how nice, the burn kit was right beneath them. *Son of a she-demon!* Fumbling, she pressed the unit to her shoulder as fresh tears hit the sand at her feet.

*

Fire blazed high, only a few feet from where she knelt, wrapped in bandages. One arm was strapped to her side to stop it from moving. It throbbed with every beat of her broken heart.

Sitting back on her haunches, Toni flipped the final switch and two glowing eyes snapped on beneath her hands. They blinked once and then focused on her face. She smiled for the first time in days, and in a voice that croaked from disuse said, "Hey, Mate. Welcome back."

"W-w-what happened?"

Fresh tears filled her eyes. Should she tell him about the smuggler's betrayal? That she'd fallen in love? Should she tell him of the moment her heart had shattered into a million tiny pieces? "I needed you, Mate. I'm helpless without you." She stared deeply into his electronic eyes, eyes that could show no emotion yet would be there for her always.

"I am here now, Toni."

She would tell him everything, because he was her partner and she trusted him. Never again would she let someone get under her skin like Dan had done. She would become like her partner, an emotionless machine. When she got off this rock and returned to work, she'd forget all about Daniel Colten. And if she ever saw him again, she would gleefully slap the cuffs on him herself—if she didn't shoot him first.

It was time to get back to work.

Toni took a deep breath, starting from the beginning for Mate's benefit.

"So, we crashed …"

PART TWO

TWO YEARS LATER

CHAPTER ELEVEN

The sun set, and the city woke up hungry.

As the lights of the metropolis brightened, shadows crept into alleyways and emerged from dark corners, ready to conduct activities that should never see the light of day. In the heart of this darkness, evil held its breath.

Toni squinted into the murky alley light, straining to make out any detail around her. Warm blood trickled down her face. Her bruised ribcage ached with every breath she took, and luckily—or unluckily, depending on the point of view— no onlooker or startled pedestrian had yet stumbled into the alley.

Of the two men standing before her, she would have to watch the Tarrelian carefully. Her heart raced as she took in his muscular frame and giant arms. Towering over her by at least a head, he glared through tiny eyes. His face looked like he'd taken several beatings, leaving him with a flat nose and misshapen jaw. She'd caught a glimpse of the Kilmarc tattoo on his wrist with its distinctive green spiral barely exposed below the cuff of his sleeve. It was the mark of a gun for hire and when she stared into his expressionless eyes, she knew she was in trouble. Sweat broke out across the back of her neck. He would kill her without qualm.

The Tarrelian had called the other man Tubby. The first time she'd heard it, she'd laughed, given the excess body weight the man carried. She wasn't laughing now. He scowled at her through dull watery blue eyes. Her gaze flicked over his rumpled clothes. He'd probably lived in them for the last few days. That was how long she'd been hunting him.

Tubby shuffled from one foot to the other, one hand outstretched over the killer's wrist, as if he could actually stop the man from shooting her. She wasn't hopeful he'd show any mercy. Tubby needed her seal and the chip warrant for his arrest if he was to escape the spaceport's security cordon, and he could only get that if she was alive to print it, hence the tense standoff. Her stare returned to the trained killer.

At times like this, she regretted her choice in career.

Tubby stepped out from behind his beady-eyed bodyguard and grinned. "So, you're Agent Delle?" From her periphery, she saw his eyes drop to travel the length of her body, pausing at her empty holster and missing agent's star. Her skin crawled at the lingering leer. "You're a freaky looking one, that's for sure."

She didn't take her eyes off the Tarrelian, watching for the slightest twitch. Forcing her breathing to remain steady took more concentration than she could spare, but like the Tarrelian, she remained poker-faced.

Tubby shuffled into her view, his grin faded. "Did you think I'd let anyone catch me, especially a PST Agent?" He sneered when she didn't respond. With a shake of his head, he turned to the hired gun and spat, "Just lemme get the contract, and *then* you can get rid of her. Leave nothing to link me to any of this. If other agents suspect she's been murdered, they won't ever stop looking for me, ya hear?"

The Tarrelian didn't answer. His finger tightened on the trigger. Toni tensed.

"For Xendia's sake, don't do it here! I said get the contract first! If Gallian finds out, I'm a dead man." Tubby hissed, grabbing at the gunman's arm.

Gallian?

The Tarrelian stared blankly at his client's hand, and Tubby removed it slowly. Toni shifted her weight.

"Better do it here. It'll look like a beggar with a khegh load of luck killed her." The man's voice sounded rough and scratchy, as though he didn't use it often.

Shuffling back, Toni pressed up against a barrier of rotted wooden boards, hoping to feel them move, but they made a solid wall, preventing her escape. Her gaze flew in every direction beneath her electronic shades. The alley was located behind a cheap rundown bar called The Dockyard. It was the sort of place one might frequent when down on their luck, working two jobs to keep a family alive and needing to get away for just a little while. She had no faith she'd be saved by the untimely appearance of a bar patron.

Khegh it! If someone did appear, it wasn't as though they would help her. People just didn't do that. Besides, the alley dead-ended only a few yards from her current position. Crates stacked haphazardly against the brick wall opposite looked like they'd always been there. The overflowing dumpster at the mouth of the alley smelt like it had never been emptied. Ever. And above her head was an unreachable metal ladder. It disappeared up into darkness but that didn't much matter. Her breathing quickened with the realization she was trapped.

She swallowed, her mouth too dry to generate much in the way of saliva. *I need a distraction.*

Blinking rapidly, she flicked through the display settings of her tinted glasses, finding nothing until she scanned the area with the X-ray setting. The crates were empty.

A low growl rumbled out of the shadows behind Tubby. The Tarrelian twisted his head sharply.

About time, partner. Toni threw herself at the pile of crates. The gunman fired as the crates tumbled down around her. The growl increased in volume. Toni darted up, her fingers wrapped around the neck of an empty bottle. A large shadow propelled itself from the darkness. A glint of sharp teeth flashed before Mate roared into the Tarrelian's face and chomped down on his weapon, including the hand holding it.

The man cried out and dropped the pistol. He shook his arm, but her trusty C-bot locked his jaws and would not be dislodged.

Tubby stumbled back. Small whimpers ghosted from his open mouth. Mate's growls deepened as he dragged the Tarrelian to the ground.

Scrambling to her feet, Toni threw the bottle at Tubby's fat head and dove for the Tarrelian's fallen pistol. Tubby ducked, the bottle shattering against the wall, and launched himself at the weapon. He got his hand to it first. Toni knocked the weapon aside. They hit the ground hard. She wrenched her head away as Tubby swung the pistol up and fired. The laser bolt hit dirt mere inches from her ear.

Close. She grabbed at the pistol again. A scream punctured the air behind them, distracting Tubby and letting Toni wrench the weapon from his hands. She pushed the overweight man off and climbed unsteadily to her feet. A burst of laser fire caught the Tarrelian right between his beady little eyes. As he collapsed, Mate spun and howled, shattering the sudden silence. He stalked toward Toni. Tubby fainted.

"Will you cut that out?"

The howl broke off as the C-bot sat. It was now fully dark. Toni blinked to engage her night vision display and examined the familiar shaggy canine shape.

"What took you so long?"

Mate scratched at his ear with a hind leg. "Well, I assumed you had everything under control."

"Yeah, I had them right where I wanted them." At the C-bot's snort of disbelief, she laughed. "Your timing is impeccable." Raising her hand to the corner of her mouth she examined the sticky residue. *Damn it.* Searching her pockets for a cloth to wipe the blood away, she muttered, "Did you hear that? Gallian." She snatched her pistol from the dead man's belt and shoved it into her holster. "What took you so long, anyway?"

Mate growled. "It is a long run. How did he get the drop on you, Boss?"

"He just did, that's all." Toni was tired. It had nearly cost her life. *I need a break.* She felt no elation over closing this case but with Tubby's arrest, her current mission was over. *Just don't mention Gallian. Ask for a break ... No, demand one.* The invitation she received this morning popped into her mind. Yes, a holiday would be perfect. Then she could confirm her attendance at the game. A final dab at the blood on her face and she shoved the red-stained rag back into her pocket.

Brushing alley dust off her pants she ordered. "Call this in. But, uh, neglect to mention You Know Who."

Mate would send a high frequency message to Zach, who would then forward the message via forcedspace relays onto Agent headquarters.

Toni wanted a bath. She also had to call Jas back and confirm the date, and she had to get her money from Zaambuka, all while making sure he didn't assign her a new case. She spied a smudge on her pristine white shirt. Her eyes narrowed. In one move, she grabbed Tubby by the front of his shirt and hauled him to his feet. She didn't have much to call her own—her C-bot, her ship and her clothing—but she looked after what was hers. She shook him until he regained consciousness.

The gun-runner's watery gaze focused on her. "Look, Delle, don't be angry about the Kilmarc. I hired him to protect my interests. With your reputation d-do you blame me? Huh?" Tubby glanced at the bloody body. "Obviously, he's not as fast as you. I mean, he's dead, isn't he? All you have is a bloody lip and a dirty shirt—" Toni pushed him hard into the brick wall.

"Do you know," she began softly, "how much this shirt cost? It's pure rainsilk. I got it on Jamith-phi. It's tailor-made. Do you know how much time and money went into its creation?" She slammed the criminal into the wall again. He had no idea how necessary the silk was to protecting her skin.

"Listen, Delle, I'll buy you a new one. By Xendia herself, I'll buy you six. Just let me go and y-you'll get them by next week."

"Good try. Ten points for effort. But contrary to what you might have heard, I don't take bribes. Just cold, hard coin from my boss after I turn you in." *Don't ask him, don't ask.* "How is Gallian connected to this?" *Khegh it!*

His face paled. She worried he was going to faint again. She grabbed his arms. "Well?"

"Who?"

"The guns. Were they for Gallian?"

He shook his head. "I don't know no Gallian. The guns are mine."

She huffed out a sigh and gestured with a finger for him to turn around. He searched her face and complied. She cuffed him a little harder than she needed to.

"Hey, that hurts!"

"That's for my shirt. Now shut up," she said shoving him toward the alley's end. Mate fell into place beside her. Exhaustion weighed heavily; her muscles ached in places they weren't supposed to. She stretched her eyes wide and shook her head. *Yeah, I need a break.*

Tubby glanced down at the huge animal with fear-filled eyes. Mate snarled, exposing his sharp, white teeth.

"Now, don't do anything stupid, will you? Otherwise my friend here may decide he wants to play fetch with parts of you." Toni leaned close to Tubby and whispered, "He sounds kinda playful, doesn't he?"

Tubby whimpered.

CHAPTER TWELVE

"Congratulations."

Toni stared at her boss through the *Blackflame*'s viewscreen and wished she could dive into bed. Her gaze drifted to the ugly soldered tear in the wall, its familiar pattern was surprisingly comforting.

Stifling a yawn, she said, "Thanks, Boss. I trust the coin has been sent to my account?"

Zaambuka's strange gray gaze glinted over the vast light-years. If Toni didn't know him better, she'd be nervous. Too bad a glare like that was completely wasted on her. She pictured her bed and the smell of fresh linen. Imagined crawling in and lowering her head to the pillow. The fantasy made her lightheaded.

"Ta-ark Drayson is pleased with your capture of Tubby Carltiyu. He's even offered you a bonus. I told him you couldn't accept—company policy. He understood."

"So, what'd ya spend my bonus money on?"

He glared, just as she knew he would. *Wrap it up.*

"I am certain you retrieved all of the weapons our good friend Tubby was selling. And all of the money." It wasn't a question.

"There was money to retrieve as well, Boss?" She was pushing his patience but didn't care. She was weary in a way she'd never been before. The last two years had been one solid mission after another. True that her determination and, if she was honest, her desperation had fueled those missions. She'd needed to prove herself. And she had. She'd become one of Zaambuka's top agents, if not the best he had. She was a force to be reckoned with. Now she needed a break. Staring down the barrel of the Tarrelian's gun made her realize she'd tempted fate one too many times. Her mental exhaustion led to mistakes, and in her line of work mistakes wouldn't just cost her the case—it would cost her life. *Then don't tell him about Gallian.*

Zaambuka's neck muscles tensed. "Get the money in by tomorrow, Toni. All of it."

"Then pay me quicker, Ant." He actually cringed at the nickname. Warmth spread up from her belly. It clearly drove him mad every time she used it, which, come to think of it, was *why* she used it. "Last time I had to survive on my game winnings for over a month before payroll reimbursed me." And she needed that coin. She imagined rubbing her hands together. Two days, two days and she'd be at the game.

He leaned forward, his voice lowering. "Toni ..."

Her palms started to sweat. *No. No way.*

"A call came in last night. You're the only one available."

"You promised me a break. I need a break. You owe me four weeks, Ant." Her finger hovered an inch above the yellow AZ—Antonio Zaambuka—panic button she'd installed a year ago. All she had to do was press it and the call would be cut off in a burst of static, leaving him unable to reconnect for days.

"You've got a game planned, haven't you?"

How in the name of Xendia did he figure that out? She didn't bat an eyelid. "Been organized for over a year now—biggest names and wallets. I won't cancel, Ant, not even if you—"

"I owe you a break; you're right." He leaned back. "So who have you got lined up?"

"ZehBa, Jasm, and the Boppli twins. And what do you mean, I'm right?"

"Don't concern yourself with it. Agent Nar is closer." Zaambuka glanced toward her hand. It was still hidden out of sight.

Does he think I'll fall for that? She breathed deeply. *I need a break.* But apart from the game, what was she going to do? Sit on a beach somewhere? She shuddered internally. Shenghi, that sounded awful. She glanced at her hand again. *Maybe* … "How much would I get?" Her hand left the panic button and reappeared on the table beside her. Sometimes she was her own worst enemy.

"You'd get more from your"—he grimaced—"card game."

"Are you angry I didn't invite you? You're right, I'll get more from the game. And it will be entertaining. Speaking of, didn't I give you that tie?"

While she would always admit the suits he wore looked damned good, not even she could have found a tie that clashed so badly with the dark blue tones of his jacket. Not for lack of trying. The tie wasn't one of hers, but oh how she wished it was. The habit survived generations of human settlement. It should have died with the last of the original refugees. Toni was positive Antonio Zaambuka was trying to bring it back.

"Your choice in ties is worse than a Drait with snow blindness, but no, you didn't send this. If you had, I would never have worn it."

Toni grinned. "Whoever sent it must really hate you."

"A gift from Vice-President Cat Ramo."

"How can she hate you that much?"

"I assume she knows nothing about it. It's likely her aides sent it." He glanced down at the multi-colored monstrosity in disgust. Then his stare hardened—Toni's distraction had expired. "Do you recall the weapons ring you broke on Waystation EEXDU?"

"Two years ago? It was my first case, of course I remember. What about it? Dalmith is breathing ferdsk gas at the Carpathian prison colony." A wave of cold washed over her, predicting his next words.

"He escaped."

"What?" She straightened. "How? No one can escape a Carpathian prison."

"He did."

There goes the game. Her head started to pound. No, he could put someone else on Dalmith. *Don't mention Gallian.*

Zaambuka ran a hand over his closely cropped hair in an unusual display of frustration. "We've intercepted some interesting chatter, rumors that link a number of important disappearances to these weapons. All of the connections track back to one individual."

"Who?"

"Gallian." Zaambuka spoke the name without inflection, but fury barely contained showed in the way his shoulders and jaw tightened.

Khegh it. Now I have to tell him. After Toni's disappearance during the Frosk assignment last year, Zaambuka had been forced to work a case himself. Toni had returned to find the PST headquarters in chaos, Antonio Zaambuka mad as a razor bee in a tal-boar pit, and a new name added to her Most Wanted list—Gallian.

"You think Gallian has moved onto running guns?" *Shenghi! That confirmed her suspicion, didn't it?* "That's a change from his usual style. Too direct." Zaambuka was obsessed with Gallian, and Toni knew her admission was going to send her boss into orbit. After all, Gallian didn't leave evidence behind. It was why no one had caught him yet.

"Agent Darning infiltrated the lower levels of the distribution ring looking for a connection. He was to advise us of the routes the shipments were traveling so we could intercept them. He missed his check-in. I presume he has been discovered." Zaambuka paused. His eyes shifted away.

Khegh! Her boss always took the death of one of his agents badly. She understood now how personally he was taking this case. From memory, Agent Darning had a couple of kids. *I have to tell him.* "I think I can confirm your sources. Or at least add another rumor to the noise."

Zaambuka straightened. "What?"

"Tubby let the name slip. In relation to his stack of weapons."

"I knew it."

"Boss, we still have no definitive—"

"I know he's behind it."

She bit back a sigh. Her sinuses ached and she wanted to pinch her nose, but the movement would imply something else to her boss. "Who's the source of the other rumors?"

Zaambuka sighed, avoiding eye contact. "We have received several messages out of a certain smuggler camp."

A flame burst to life inside Toni. "You can't trust the word of a smuggler. If your only evidence is from those traitorous kalfj—" She sucked in a deep breath, pressing her hand to her chest. Zaambuka had betrayed her. Not just her, he'd betrayed the agents' code as well. "We don't work with criminals. This is your mandate, Boss. You drill it into us at the Academy. No blackmail, no paying contacts for information, no torture and no working with criminals. How can you ..." Her face heated, knowing she'd broken one or two of those commandments herself. Then her stomach bottomed out as she thought about what he was actually saying. She slammed her mind down on the memory, not wanting to see *his* face and rubbed at the sudden ache in her shoulder.

"I know you've had painful experiences with smugglers in the past, Toni, but the data they sent pans out. We intend to use it."

Painful experiences? Yeah, you could say that. "How can we rely on information from smugglers? They'll do whatever it takes to get us off their backs and ..." She trailed off when he didn't meet her eye. Why was he telling her this? He knew what her response would be. Her skin became clammy as realization dawned. "You made a deal with a smuggler? Who?"

He didn't so much as twitch. "I've agreed, albeit grudgingly, to allow one small group clemency for six months and a full pardon to those who assist in Gallian's capture."

"We have to find Gallian first," she snapped. Beyond angry, she knew she should have pushed that panic button as soon as she saw the look on Zaambuka's face. She scratched her shoulder. In a low voice she asked, "Which group?"

"The Cross."

"*What?*" Her cry was so loud, the sound adjusters on Zaambuka's end of the communication must have struggled to compensate given his wince. *No! Oh no!* Her stomach flipped and bile rose in her throat.

"Toni, the deal has been made."

She opened her mouth to respond but he cut her off. "You won't have to work with them. Just use the information. If you run into any member of the Cross, make no arrests. Not for six months."

Sucking in an unsteady breath, she closed her eyes. Her thoughts were a jumbled mess. *Don't let him see how much this hurts.* "What was the information?" There was no way she would ask which Cross smuggler sent the data. A shooting pain speared through her palm. She glanced down to see her fist clenched so tightly, her fingernails had drawn blood.

"Did you read the report on Doctor Rober Telksh?"

"The scientist?" Toni took the distraction, thankful for it. "He disappeared right before he was scheduled to make a big announcement on the hypersonic wave resistance mag-rifle, right?"

"That's the one."

"You think he's behind the weapons caches?"

"Sources tell us ..."

Toni grimaced again at the suggestion of smuggler supplied data.

"... whoever took him wanted the specs for these rifles."

"I thought the doc was a white coat? I mean sure, he designed an incredibly dangerous weapon, but it's a weapon for the good guys, right? What makes you link him to the shipments, other than the obvious? We didn't find any mag-rifles amongst the original haul."

"Our team discovered references to his name at one of the bust sites. Agent Delle, your priority is to find the evidence that confirms Gallian is behind these operations and locate Doctor Telksh."

See, it's nothing to do with him. "Where exactly do you suggest I start?"

"His ex-partner is a man named Roch'alie Myres."

"Ex-partner?"

"Doctor Telksh and Roch'alie Myres worked together at the Institute of Technological Research on Melbar Prime. Both men are mechanical engineers, though they have also studied biochemical mechanical dispersal systems."

"Sounds like a lot of scientific gobbledygook to me."

"The report I received suggests they designed the mag-rifle together."

She tapped her fingers against the console. "What split them up?"

"We do not know. They ended their working partnership right before Telksh disappeared."

"And you think Myres knows something. Where do we find him?"

"Apparently Myres has a bit of a gambling problem. Should be right up your alley." Zaambuka typed a command into his board. "Good luck, Toni." The screen returned to the stars of the Agents Association emblem.

Toni sighed and rubbed at her eyes. Her good day had turned to shenghi. Hot steamy piles of shenghi. A case with potential connections to Daniel Colten set her shoulder ablaze. *Why now?* It had been years since she'd even heard his name. How was the Cross connected to Telksh? Or were they linked to Gallian? That was an interesting thought. A memory from long ago skated to the front of her consciousness. Gall. Colten's CII had said the name. Gallian? Colten *had* been involved in stealing guns from Dalmith. The coincidences were stacking up to form a very nasty picture.

Mate, listening to the entire exchange from beneath the console at her feet, looked up at her tilting his head to one side. "Well, that was interesting. Now what?"

"How in Xendia should I know?"

If he picked up on her annoyance, he ignored it. Moving out from under the console, he peered at the monitor beside her hand. "Zach?"

The monitor to Toni's left blinked on to display Zach's pixilated face. Strangely, he too had remained silent during the entire exchange.

"I ain't doing this. I ain't working with the smuggler. Nope, no way."

Toni stared blankly at him, "Did you alter your voice parameters?"

"Yup!"

She scowled. "You sound like a kid."

"Incoming message. Need a clearance code, Boss. Level one prio."

Level one? "Okay, Zach, clearance code …" *Shenghi, what was the order again?* "Seven alpha WID two zeta Toni."

"Accessing." Several files popped onto the screen. As she read through the first, Zach scanned ahead. "Hey, I think we got a lead."

"Do you really think this guy Myres can help us?" Mate asked.

"Well, he worked with Telksh, so I'm guessing he knew him pretty well. You have to think Myres knows something about Telksh's disappearance. Or, khegh it, maybe *he* is behind the disappearance."

Zach's grumbling floated up from the speakers, but his face had yet to return to the monitor.

"What is it, Zach?" she asked.

"I'm looking at the holonet coding." The CII sounded upset.

"Zach," she warned. Had Colten sent the material? The possibility was there. It came from the Cross, and he *was* a member. But would he really contact the PST, given their history? It was hard to imagine. She scratched at her shoulder again. The itch was buried deep under her skin.

"I'm seeing streams from a dozen different networks and half a dozen more holonet relays. I'm just saying, Boss, I don't like it. Can we even trust this stuff?"

"I'm not saying we follow it blindly, Zach. Run a search. Let's corroborate the information if we can. Mate, help him." Toni tugged her black hide jacket tighter across her chest, feeling cold. *I don't want to see him.* She spun her chair around, glancing at the stark cockpit. *I really need to get more stuff in here. With bright colors.* If she didn't keep gaming her winnings away, maybe she'd have enough to purchase some furnishings.

Mate spoke up. "I can confirm Roch'alie Myres is on Uxt. I have three security reports here from the casino."

"Put it up." A message fragment appeared, and Toni's memories of dancing on the bar filled her mind. "The Reef, huh?" Coincidence? Too many links to her past were popping up into this case. The Cross and now The Reef? She was getting a bad feeling low in her stomach, like she'd eaten something that disagreed with her.

"I've found three reports on Myres for drunken brawling, and an arrest for counting cards," Zach replied.

"That's it?" Mate asked.

"Yep. Not much to go on, huh Boss? It's been a while since you worked The Reef."

"It's a start. Set a course for Uxt, Zach," Toni huffed sadly. "And link me through to Jas. I've got to cancel that game."

CHAPTER THIRTEEN

"Show me your modified phaser plans."

"I don't have them," Toni said, hoping Myres wouldn't be too offended by the sarcasm coloring her tone. Convincing the man she had a unique weapon to sell had proved remarkably easy. It was like he wanted to believe she had something.

Myres breathed heavily, sniffing mucus up his nose and clearing his throat with an irritating consistency. His hands trembled when he wiped at the sweat beading on his ruddy forehead. He stopped dead in the center of the dark corridor and peered furtively around. Toni would bet her next holiday pay the tunnel they were in led to a dead end. His next sniff sent twitches across her skin. "Like Xendia you don't. Come on, kid. I just want to see them."

Yeah, I bet you do.

The porous walls surrounding them seeped water, slicking the rock with a damp sheen. Drips from the roof above sounded a constant plop, plop. The whole maintenance tunnel reeked of mold and something fishy. Toni eyed the closest battery-operated lamp. It did little to fight the gloom.

"I'll make you a deal," she said, lowering her voice. Mate moved close behind her. "Tell me where to find Doctor Telksh, and if there's a new mag-rifle on the *other* market, and I won't inform the pit boss upstairs you were cheating."

"Cheating?"

Toni hid a wince at the sound of his squeak.

"There isn't a modified phaser, is there?" he asked.

"Nope."

"I should have realized you weren't a legit seller. I mean, look at you." He snorted and cleared his throat again. "A freak like you could never remain incognito."

"Freak like me," she repeated. The words triggered a memory. Colten had told her she wasn't a freak. Ha. Well, she knew he was a liar.

Myres inhaled raggedly. "Thank gods it's dark. I feel sick just looking at you."

Well, now he had her full attention.

"Don't think I won't shoot you." Her hands clenched into fists. She stepped forward, her voice cold and clipped as she demanded, "Tell me what I want to know."

He threw up his hands. "All right. What do you want?"

"Doctor Telksh's location."

"Who are you?"

"Does it matter?"

The large man grumbled and shuffled back a few steps. "I might have some information, but swear you won't—"

"I wouldn't go back upstairs if you paid me. Unless you give me a reason. Where is Doctor Telksh?"

Myres glanced over both shoulders. "That's what I want to know. That kalfj threw me out after all the years we worked together. Half those designs are mine. If he's producing a working copy of the Resonator then I want my coin. He owes me—"

"You sound angry."

He sniffed loudly. "Well, yeah, sure. What, you think I had something to do with his disappearance?"

"Did you?"

"Of course not. We were partners and he fired me. You can't fire your partner. And now he's making mag-rifles to sell? After he said he had problems with the design. Too dangerous! Then he accused me of—"

"The guns are dangerous? How so?"

He huffed. "The mag-rifles work a little too well, if you know what I mean. We could have been rich. We had buyers, you know. I had calls from everywhere. But Doctor Do-Gooder said we couldn't sell them. And the next day, he fires me. I only wish I'd made that kheghing shenghi disappear."

"Sounds like you've been keeping an eye out for these weapons."

"Kheghing right. I want to get my hands on one. If any of it is based on my design, I want what I'm owed."

"Do you know where the good doctor is now?"

"No." Myres made a snorting sound and rubbed a hand over his face.

"What about the weapons? Do you know who ordered them?"

"No idea. As I said, there were a lot of buyers interested. There's a storeroom on sub-level twenty-three that they're paranoid about. Won't let anyone near it." Myres peered around again. "Speaking of which ..."

Toni copied him, searching the gloomy tunnel for movement. Myres' behavior was starting to affect her. Her skin crawled with the feeling they were being watched. She inched closer to hear his next words.

"A big shipment departed yesterday, another leaves tomorrow. I'm meeting one of the shippers tonight. A man named Kel. Said he'd sneak a gun out for me. I could ask about Telksh—maybe he's there, you know, inside."

"Does anyone other than Kel know about this meeting?"

"No one," he puffed.

Toni glanced over her shoulder again, her neck tingling. The tunnel was empty. "Has this Kel met you before?"

"No."

"Here's the deal. You don't go to the docking bay tonight, and I won't give you up to the pit boss." Mate growled behind Myres. The large man twitched and turned his head at the reminder of her partner's presence.

She almost missed the flash of orange as Myres flung his arm in her direction.

Toni threw her head back, barely avoiding the second strike as he slashed again at her throat with a miniature phaseblade hidden between his fingers. She dove to the ground to escape the next attack. Mate launched himself at the mountain of flesh, slamming into Myres' legs and forcing him off balance. As he fell, Toni drew her pistol and fired. The shot knocked the blade from Myres' hand and took three fingers with it.

The large man screamed, dropping to his knees. He clutched at his hand and gaped.

"I don't want to kill you, but I will, understand?" Toni snapped. *What the khegh is he thinking?*

Myres' massive frame shuddered, breathing like a ship taking off.

"Make yourself scarce for a few days." She turned the pistol around so that she gripped it by the barrel. "Sleep tight," she said and hit him in the side of the head.

Myres' stunned body flopped to the ground. Toni wrapped his bleeding hand quickly—she didn't want him to die when she left him. "Mate, I hope you can get us outta here."

"Of course, Boss." With a shake of his entire body, the C-bot released a pile of dust from his coat.

"Let's go. I don't wanna have to give you a bath when we get back." She looked up and down the corridor. "You know, pal, I swear we're not alone down here."

"I do not register any lifeforms on my scanners. You must be imagining it."

*

"Kel ain't here." The guard grunted, shoving his pistol into her face.

Toni squinted at the weapon as if trying to draw it into focus. She jerked suddenly. Her hunch destabilized her stance and she stumbled back, staggering further. "What?" She threw a stammer into her voice. "But he said he'd be here. He had something for me. Did he leave it at the office?" Sniffing hard, she scrubbed her stained sleeve against her nose.

The guard didn't hesitate. "I will shoot you if you do not evacuate the premises immediately." Behind him, Toni could see another blur heading in their direction. Damned eyesight. Without her shades, the bright lights of the dock stung her eyes, making them water. She assumed it was another guard.

Pulling her sleeves down over her fingers, she twisted the material, her voice wavering, "But Kel said—"

The pistol in her face bobbed slightly. "Look, love, there was an accident, okay? Kel ain't here. He's dead." The man's face didn't twitch as he said it but his lip curled and the barest head shake gave away his real thoughts.

His glance to the nearest camera confirmed it. Kel's death hadn't been an accident.

Damn it. Toni raised her hands to her mouth. "What? Dead?"

"Just get out of here, kid. There's nothing for ya here."

She maintained her User gait until she was sure the guard could no longer see her. Straightening, she pulled her shades out of her waist band. Tapping the side, she called Zach.

His query bloomed up on the display.

Zach: Boss?

"Dead end. Literally. I was asking about a corpse. I'm heading back. These rags are making my skin burn, I need to get them off."

On the walk back to the *Blackflame*, the kaleidoscope of bright reds, brilliant yellows, and collision of blue and green coral drew her gaze to the roof.

"While The Great Lake has a long history of adversely affecting highly visual species, such as the Anu, for everyone else the underwater splendor of Uxt is the end-all, be-all stopover of the Sector."

A shock of lavender curls drew Toni's attention to the nearby tourists gathered in a loose circle.

"An incredible feat of engineering, the theme park sits atop the colorful coral rising out of an ocean, rumored to be the largest this side of the Sector-core. Near the docks at the entrance of the park, you can see through the transparent plasteel directly out onto the edges of the reef. We are beneath the coral. Astounding, isn't it?"

Rolling her eyes at the ooooohs and aaaahhs, Toni shambled past.

"Oh Xendia, they even get Users here. Look, her skin's as transparent as the roof."

"Honey, don't stare."

Scowling Toni hunched over further and tucked her hands into the sleeves of her oversized stained pullover. Stupid tourists, bane of existence everywhere.

The first thing she did when she reached the safety of her ship was change into her usual outfit (easy-to-move-in trousers, low-heeled boots and her second favorite shirt), and then fixed her agent's star firmly to her vest. The outfit said she meant business—well, all but the rainsilk shirt. She was still fuming at Tubby for the stains on her favorite shirt. Today, she wore green. She holstered her pistol at her thigh and pulled a small backpack out of storage. *Time for plan B.*

CHAPTER FOURTEEN

"Why did I think this would be a good idea?" Toni grumbled, keeping her voice low so the echoes would only travel back to where Mate crawled on his haunches behind her.

"You said it was to avoid the crowds."

"Yeah, I said that, didn't I." Prying eyes would be better than traveling the many pipes and ducts that weaved in and around the underwater air system lining the sub-level's ceiling. Her knees and wrists ached by the time Mate called a halt. Toni eyed a smudge on her sleeve as she reached for the panel Mate said was their exit point. Her crawl left her covered in dust, and itching like a crazy woman. She didn't want to think of the costly cleaning bill she'd pay at the end of this mission. *Ha!* She mentally shrugged. *I'll add it to my expenses.* She needed new shirts anyway.

Running her fingers along the panel's edge, she blinked deliberately, holding for two seconds to change the display settings of her shades and pulled her mini decoupler wrench from her bag. The bolts securing the screen to the vent walls wouldn't shift. Not even a creak. Fortunately, there was no laser-trap wired into it. She drew her pistol, twisted the base, turned her head, and fired. The adjuster connected to the grip silenced the weapon's high-pitched whine and lowered the intensity of the laser, making it perfect for melting metal catches, bolts, and the lock of the occasional bar fridge.

Unfortunately, the sustained beam quickly heated the air inside the enclosed space. After burning through all four securing bolts, she holstered her pistol and braced her slim body against the sides of the vent.

"On three," she whispered, pushing her fingers through the screen's slates.

Mate nodded.

Toni pulled her knees up for more leverage. "One," She let her breath out slowly. "Two." She breathed in again, this time deeper. "Three." And yanked.

The screen didn't budge.

Mate snorted. Toni tried again, this time harder. Nothing happened. "Khegh it!"

"Need help?"

"What makes you think that?" For a moment, she sat in the dark staring at the kheghing piece of useless metal. "Come here."

The C-bot leaned into Toni's side, his weight pushing her off her heels. Grabbing onto his fur, she pressed down on the center of his back, activating a panel only her handprint could open. A small door on the C-bot's chest swung loose. Toni connected a thin wire from Mate to the immobile screen. "On three, I want you to pull."

The wire wound taut. "Ready."

"Three."

The screen didn't move.

"Stuff this." Toni drew her pistol, twisted the adjuster to high and fired.

"I would be surprised if nobody heard that," Mate growled, winding in the wire and the screen's remnants up with it. Toni gingerly touched a cooling edge to help Mate free it and together they jammed it into the tunnel in front of them. She blinked again to return her shades to their usual setting. Beneath them lay a long, narrow room stacked high with crates. She sat back. Bright light streamed in through the hole, highlighting the amount of dust coating her partner's brown fur. She imagined she must look no better. With a sharp tug, she checked his harness was wrapped securely around his body. "Ready to fly, pal?"

"When I fly, I would rather be inside a very well-built ship."

"Then why are you with me and the *Blackflame*?" She grinned. "Down you go." Toni released the rope through her fingers inch by inch and watched him drop.

When he reached ground, she unclipped the rope via a small remote. Grabbing a pair of gloves from her backpack, she tied the rope to the panel and tugged. It held. She lowered herself down. The broken panel slipped when she was halfway. She landed hard, knocking the wind from her lungs. Rolling, she just avoided the panel and rope that slammed into the ground beside her.

"Boss?"

"I'm good." Breathing hard she flipped her shades to a scanner and checked for surveillance devices. Nothing flashed.

The large roller door at one end of the room was a concern. It would require a motor to rise. A panel next to it looked to be an infrared scanner—no doubt only the correct retinal scan or a door remote would open the door. She got close enough to check the make and model. "Maybe I can hack it." The engraved plate read Mark 70–29. She whistled. Serious security. "Yeah, maybe not. Mate?"

"I can run the calculations but it will take time."

"Don't we have access to the specs? Zach?"

Zach: Not in my database.

"Find them." In the meantime, she spun back to examine the rest of the room. Mate stalked around one lone crate. Its side was buckled, and skid marks on the floor pointed to the reason why it was not stacked as neatly as the others. Mate pressed his nose close to the ground as he scanned it. Toni noted the symbols, an X over three interlocking circles. It was supposed to contain ranic fruit.

"I do not sense a thing, Boss, and that includes ranic fruit."

Toni concurred. Nothing registered on her enhanced vision either. Moving closer, she tapped the side of the crate. It echoed. Screwing the adjuster on her pistol again, she aimed at the sealed lid.

"You do not know what is in there, Boss."

"If it was something dangerous, you'd have got a reading, right?" Patience was not one of her strong points. One of these days, it was going to get her into trouble. She fired a tight beam at the top edge of the lid. Her pistol whined loudly in the otherwise silent room.

"Of course, it could contain something I do not have the programming to scan for," he warned.

She ignored him. A moment later, she released the trigger. "Not again!" She hit at the lid with the butt of her pistol and sighed. The crate was unmarked. *What do they build these things with?*

"Maybe it is better that it did not open," Mate suggested. Toni shot him a furious glare. "Then again, what would I know?" He pointed his nose to the ceiling and at the hole above. "No security came before, presumably they will not hear us now."

"Presumably." She glanced around the room again. A large pole leaned against the wall. She carried it back to her partner. "Why do things the easy way, right?"

"Are you sure this is a good idea?"

She slid the edge under the lid and pushed down with all her weight. The lid wobbled.

"You know I would love to help you, Boss, but unfortunately …"

"Yeah, you're not exactly built for opening crates. I know." She grunted as she pressed down. The lid cracked at the corner. Anchoring with her full body weight, the seal broke with a pop. Toni and the bar crashed to the ground. The crate's lid sprang away in the opposite direction. Pain radiated up her spine from her landing. *Ow!* Blinking back shocked tears, she said, "Well, we're not dead yet, pal."

"'Yet' is the operative word."

Toni climbed to her feet and waited for approaching footsteps.

"Nothing on scanners," Mate said.

"Good." After a pause, she added, "Keep scanning." Stretching onto her toes, she peered inside. "Oh, gods."

Mate looked up. "What?"

She didn't answer.

"Boss? Toni …? Hello, Agent Delle!" Mate's voice shifted from bewilderment to concern when she didn't answer. "HEY!"

Toni spun, reaching for her pistol. "What?"

"What is in the box?" he asked in a tone just below optimal volume.

"Xendia. Just say something next time. You scared me half to death."

Mate did not reply.

"There's some sort of metallic sheath wrapped around the inside of the crate. That's what's blocking our scanners."

Mate's low growl indicated he was not willing to wait much longer. Toni lifted a long black weapon from the crate. It was incredibly light. There appeared to be a small metal box in place of the usual long-distance sight. She blinked to engage her glasses and flipped through the settings. The information didn't make any sense. She held the weapon out to her partner. "I can't get a read on this."

"I am recording a low sonic vibration."

"Suppose Telksh succeeded with the mag-rifle design? Mate, the crate is full of these things." She peered around the room, counting the number of crates. Her heart thudded painfully at the number. Someone was starting a war.

"You think he sold them to Gallian?"

"I don't know, but I'm taking one. It's been a while since I sent Ant a present." She tugged the strap hanging off the weapon over her shoulder.

"What do we do with the others? We cannot leave them here to be distributed."

"Blow 'em." Toni stared at the crate.

"Do you not think they will notice someone blew up the store?"

"We'll find out soon enough." She pulled three palm-sized globes from the inside of her backpack and ran her thumb over both buttons, debating how best to use them. Green set the grenade to explode on impact; red set the internal timer. There was no way she was letting these guns out into the public. Toni pushed the red button and lowered the grenade into the crate.

"Ah, Boss?"

"Quiet." Behind the open container, she armed two more mini-explosives and placed them between two columns of crates. Not wanting to take a chance these things might withstand the strength of the blast, two more from her bag were rolled in the opposite directions.

"Um, Boss?"

"What?" she asked, arming the last bomb.

"The door?"

Toni's head swung rapidly back and forth—there was only one exit. Without the remote or the correct retinal pattern, that door was not going to open. "Zach?"

"There is a backdoor key for military and planetary security but I cannot raise the programmer."

"Zach, in future, I want all those backdoor codes. Shenghi." She had about fifty seconds left before the first bomb exploded. *Why didn't he say something earlier? I really need to stop and think these things through.* Sweat broke out across her body; there was nowhere to take cover from the coming blast. Each grenade only contained a small charge, but who knew how the rifles were going to react to the explosion. "This won't stop them trafficking the weapons," she said, her brain working furiously on an escape. "It'll only screw with their schedule, but that's a plus at least. You know how these guys love their schedules."

She positioned herself against the far wall and crouched. Mate joined her laying down to face the wall and block her body with his more resilient form. Hopefully, she'd judged the distance correctly. "If we're going to do this, let's really get their attention." Sucking in a deep breath, she pitched the last globe with all of her strength. It hit the center of the far wall and exploded. The tremor knocked her flat. The wall blew apart.

Toni scrambled to her feet. The two agents ran for the hole, followed almost instantly by a second giant blast. Hot air rolled over them, blowing them to the ground. With her head covered by her sweaty palms, she chuckled, her cheek pressed against the grimy floor. *Guess those rifles were fully charged.*

CHAPTER FIFTEEN

Automatic fire-extinguishing systems kicked in, spraying the entire area with thick white foam. Toni's skin tingled and stung from tiny cuts and burns. Sounds were muffled, her ears ringing. Even so, she could just make out the many pairs of feet converging in their direction.

"That would be our cue to exit." Mate said.

Toni shook her head. "We've still got work to do." She pulled her trousers away from her clammy skin and swept dust and building particles from her hands. The smell of burnt wood, carbon, and foam hung heavily in the air, forcing a harsh cough from her lungs. They had to get out of here.

"I have movement coming up on all sides," the C-bot said.

She'd already spotted the bobbing lights in the distance.

Khegh it! A plan ... a plan would be icy. Eyes darting in every direction, she waited for inspiration to strike. Nothing. Her pulse, slowed since the explosion, was ramping up again as the number of footsteps increased. "Then we go down," she said.

"Down? Down where?"

"Down there." She pointed to the duct in the floor. "Unless you've got a better idea?"

"Sure, the air vents worked so well for us earlier. Why wouldn't down work too?"

"If it ain't broke ..."

She ran to the grated panel. It shifted sideways easily. *Huh, should have gone this way before.* Toni ushered Mate in ahead of her and climbed inside, sliding the panel closed behind them.

*

Toni froze at the loud clang. *What the khegh?* Signaling Mate not to move, she held the weapon on her back steady and inched closer, squishing up beside the C-bot excruciatingly slowly to ensure not even a whisper of noise. Inhaling deeply, her eyes popped wide. *Is that gravy?* Reaching the grate, she peered into the room above. Several tables were arranged along one wall. Four of the chairs were occupied by workmen. She could see their filthy boots. Toni's stomach growled, reminding her it was close to lunchtime. Her gaze flew to the man pacing the floor, his trousers oil-stained and wrinkled. He spun around to face the uniform pants and shiny shoes standing in the doorway.

Someone's having a bad day. Toni's fingers twitched where they rested on the chilly grate covering. She'd have to wait until the guy made more noise to cover the sound of her crawling past or wait until he left the room. She let out a silent sigh. The guy's voice squeaked.

"All of the crates? Who?"

Her interest was piqued. What was he talking about ... The guns she destroyed? Maybe listening in would be to her advantage. She leaned her face closer to the grate.

The security guard stepped back. "We have a blurred visual on one of the corridor feeds. Looks like a ghost."

Toni smirked. *A ghost?*

The Shouter's feet turned toward the table. "Jimb, Cherly, get out there and find who did this!"

The men didn't budge.

"Hey! I said move."

Chair legs scraped the floor as the two men pushed to their feet.

The guard stomped away.

Toni's leg was starting to cramp. She twitched and the weapon balanced along her spine shifted. She snapped her hand around its casing and froze. Had she been heard?

The two men still seated at the table, seemed to believe they were alone with the Shouter. Silently, they slid their chairs back and vacated the room. Now alone, the Shouter slumped into a chair. "How did they get into the main hold?" he muttered.

Come on, tell me more. Give me something I can use. She could spring out and encourage him to speak. Her fingers searched for the securing catches holding the grate in place.

A reedy voice stilled her hand. "Stiev, we must get the last of those rifles moving. If the squads don't receive them in time, the entire project will be jeopardized." *Khegh it.* Someone else was there. Toni twisted but couldn't get eyes on the far corner of the lunchroom.

The clack of claws preceded the Geerp into her line of sight. Toni pulled back. Urgh, she hated Geerps. Creepy little scavengers. The tiny creature rose only as high as the Shouter's knees and dragged its long limbs along the floor with each step of its clawed feet.

The Shouter, Stiev, bent at the waist. His face was pale and sick looking. "What do you know about the meeting? Why is it so important to the project?"

The Geerp shuffled forward. Its neck frill flared. "Midock."
Stiev's eyes bulged.

Midock? Come on, keep talking. A trill startled Stiev into motion. He scrubbed at his face and pushed greasy looking hair from his eyes. With a sigh he yanked a communication disk from his pocket. "Mr. Dalmith?" Stiev waved at the Geerp, waiting until it hobbled from the room before blurting, "I wasn't aware you knew, Sir—"

Dalmith! Toni could make out a buzz coming from the device but not the words.

Stiev wiped the hand not holding the disk against his trousers, leaving damp marks. "I was thinking about—"

The buzz grew louder. Stiev jumped to his feet, "Here, Sir?" The nervous man bounced on his toes. "What do you recommend?" A short pause preceded his, "Yes, Sir." Jamming the disk back into his pocket, he pulled a pistol from his belt and bolted through the door.

Toni waited a beat then lifted the weapon's strap over her head and lowered it to the conduit next to her. She grabbed her mini decoupler wrench from her bag. The bolts holding the grate secure to the duct fell, and the grate slipped. Her hand shot out to catch it. She hauled herself out and placed the panel against the wall. Mate landed with a soft thump behind her.

"Project?" she asked.

"Meeting?"

"Midock?"

"Dalmith," they said together. Mate went on. "I do not see any hidden passages or trap doors, and there are no bugs. The room is clean."

"Would've been a little late to tell me it wasn't." Toni discovered a small office at the back of the room and searched it quickly, rifling through desk drawers one by one until she came across a drawer that was locked. It didn't take long to break open. Inside she found a green notebook tablet. "Bingo!" Switching it on, she discovered columns of dates, addresses, and names—probably fake—and delivery details, most of which dated from the past few weeks. A second tablet, this one yellow, contained detailed distribution lists under the guise of urgent orders for ranic fruit. Toni matched the descriptions of several items to both tablets. Satisfaction swelled in her chest. Now they were getting somewhere.

She slid the tablets into her backpack. "I think it's time we got out of here."

The office door crashed open. Stiev pointed his pistol straight at Toni's chest, his eyes widening. His mouth twitched revealing crooked teeth. Now that she could see all of him, she noted the damp pale face, thinning hair that looked like he'd pulled at the ends a few times, and his sweat-soaked stained shirt hanging overly large on slim shoulders.

Toni immediately slouched and raised her hands. "Hey man, watch where ya point that thing. My name's Myres. I believe ya expectin' me."

"Nice try." The gun-runner gestured for her to back up. "Myres is dead."

Oh shenghi. Her breathing quickened as she backtracked. "Dalmith sent me. He wanted to check up on your—"

"Dalmith didn't send you," Stiev said. He waved his gun at her. "I know who you are, Agent." His hand trembled.

"Oh, yeah?" *Great comeback.* "I know who you are too, Stiev." He blanched at the sound of his name. *Not as confident as you want me to believe, huh?* She lowered her hands. "I also know all about the project, and ..." Stiev jerked, his pistol bobbed uncertainly. "… Midock." Toni caught a whiff of his body odor. Her eyes prickled.

Stiev stepped back, straightening his arm once more. "Don't move."

Mate was beneath the desk. Presumably the gunrunner didn't know he was there—one advantage. Provided Stiev didn't come to his senses and call for his goons, Toni could still get the upper hand.

With the barest flick of her fingers, she motioned for Mate to stay back. The C-bot shook his head. *You and me too, pal.* The pulse point in her neck thumped with the rapid beat of her heart. She sucked a breath in between her teeth.

"I don't care what you think you know, you won't live long enough to save the peace summit!"

Peace summit? The longer she stalled, the more information she got, but she couldn't wait any longer. Stiev's gun hand drooped. She twisted, dipped her knee, and drew her gun in one fluid move, pulling the trigger the instant her weapon cleared her holster. The pistol shot out of Stiev's hand. Toni was twisting before he could react and followed up with an elbow to the side of his head.

He collapsed.

"What did you do? Did you kill him?" Mate appeared at her side.

Toni went to a knee and examined the prone body carefully. "Elbowed him in the head."

Mate huffed a laugh.

She searched Stiev's pockets and found a yellow card. Holding it up, she asked, "Key to a casino locker?"

"Indeed."

Toni slipped the card into her own pocket and stood. "Time to go."

Returning to the eating area, she pulled the stolen magrifle from the duct. Cracking open the door, she examined the corridor outside. Empty. Doing her best to look as though she belonged there, she stepped through the doorway, and strode up the hall. Out of the corner of her eye, she caught a flash of movement.

Freezing, she stared over her shoulder. Nothing. Her hand tightened on the pistol in her holster as the back of her neck tingled.

CHAPTER SIXTEEN

It wasn't long before the two agents exited the lower levels of the complex and found themselves in a shuttle parking bay. The sign above the gate indicated it was a rear door out of the theme park. Gaunt figures shoved at each other as they rifled through overflowing bins. A man glanced her way and immediately turned his head. He tugged the arm of the huddled shape next to him. Eyes flashed up and away just as quickly.

Beyond the gate, Toni spied a large wheel rotating with spinning cars. Screeches of metal, the rumble of machinery, and a chorus of excited screams filled the air. The hair on the back of Toni's neck rose with the sounds. The scent of popcorn and sugar—lots of sugar—filled her nostrils. Her mouth watered.

"Were we followed?"

"I am unsure."

Toni strolled past a number of parked cruisers. When she caught sight of two workers prowling through the shuttle bay, she ducked back behind the closest cruiser. She recognized those filthy boots. Stiev's men stared intently down each row of vehicles. Toni hadn't been discovered yet, but it was only a matter of time. Glancing at the stolen rifle, she realized she'd never get it through park security.

"Mate, go back to the *Blackflame*."

"What?"

"Go back to the *Blackflame*. I'll lose our friends in the park." She pointed to the door. "I'll get them to follow me. Get those tablets to Zach. Scan the contents and get it to Zaambuka if I'm not back in an hour. Go." She strapped the rifle to his back using his harness and tied it tightly in place.

Mate took her backpack in his mouth. He dropped it on the ground long enough to say, "Be careful, Boss." His tone made it clear he did not like her plan. Heck, she didn't like being separated from him either. Without him at her side, she was missing a limb. The C-bot picked up the bag and blended into the shadows by the wall to wait for his break.

Four of the staggering, disorientated homeless people were attempting to stack a container onto a larger pyramid of similar containers. Regretfully, Toni kicked a can in their direction. It ricocheted off the wall and crashed into the pyramid's base.

The resultant noise drew the attention of everyone exiting the park and alerted security—including the two workers—to her location. One spoke into a hand communicator while the other drew his weapon. Toni jumped over the exit barriers and raced into the park.

It took a moment for her eyes to adjust to the flashing lights of the fast-moving adventure rides. Colorfully unifo-rmed employees darted back and forth before her gaze. Stiev's goons would look for movement, so she stopped at the nearest bench beside a young family. All three did a double-take as she sat down.

A little girl bounced on the knee of the woman beside Toni. The child tugged on Toni's sleeve. "Hello." Toni smiled. "I like your hair." The little girl smiled back, her front teeth missing. She whipped her head around, sending the four blond ponytails dancing wildly.

Beside the girl, an older boy with his hair tied back in two tails that exposed a bony protrusion at the back of his neck glared at her. "What's wrong with you? Why can I see through you, are you sick?"

"Mitas!" His mother shrugged, offering Toni a wan smile. "Children."

Toni shook her head. It wasn't as if she hadn't heard it all before. At least the boy was direct about it. Most just stared at her as if she couldn't see them. The mother towed the little boy around to stand on her other side and avoided Toni's eye.

The family was a good cover. When the goons headed off in the opposite direction, Toni waved goodbye to the little girl and jogged toward the stalls at the far end of the ground. Hearing a shout, she glanced back. *Damn it.*

Ducking low, she ran behind a large group of teenagers. They turned as one to watch her. How was she going to hide when her appearance drew attention like a Crellik in a bar? Pausing at a trinket stall, she glanced at the coral-colored stones and poly-gold coral shaped figurines. Who would buy this crap? Behind the table, a path of pressed dirt led between several tents.

A heavy cloud of incense hung over the area. Colors immediately swirled and gyrated around the periphery of her vision. *Whoa. Strong stuff.* No wonder the hawkers in the tents were in slow motion—the slower you moved, the steadier the colors held. Turning too fast, she stumbled into a muscular wall.

"Sorry," she muttered. The wall reached out a meaty fist.

"You should not move so fast."

Toni pulled at her arm, but it was like trying to wrench from the grip of a hover-salesman, which was to say impossible.

"Sorry." She peeked up and up and up into the eyes of a park security guard. His thick arms extended to a solid torso that melded into his head. "Ah, look, I'm in a bit of a hurry," she appealed, offering up her most innocent smile.

"No need to hurry, Miss," he replied. "Your friends will wait for you."

The guard's equally pumped partner stared blankly at her. He sniffed through a flat nose.

"I. . . I think I'm being followed. I won rather a large prize at the Jumbo wheel, you see." Toni nodded in the general direction of the main ground. "And now these guys are following me. It's really creepy."

The guard's expression didn't change. "Please point them out to us?"

She didn't have to. The two goons had been joined by another humanoid, a Roxal whose lavender skin seemed to strobe under the fluorescent lights and a ... *a Crellik?* Toni's mouth fell open. She snapped it shut. *A Crellik, here?* She'd only seen one in her life, as a small child when her father cast a Crellik in his latest holonet blockbuster. The species was rarely seen in Sector One. Standing over seven feet tall, their skeleton was on the outside of their bodies. Bony spine protrusions stabbed out through his clothing. Sharp teeth and claws completed the picture. Toni's heart leapt into her throat. A Crellik was after her.

The men separated to search the busy hall.

"Is that them?" the guard asked. He still held Toni's arm tightly; his fingers encircled her wrist and overlapped.

This time her voice wobble wasn't forced. "Yes sir, that's them."

"We will remove them from the area and inform them that harassment of our patrons is not acceptable," he said.

The guard beside him nodded and said, "Then we will eject them." His grin exposed a mouthful of extremely sharp teeth. The guard released her and advanced on the searching goons.

Toni fingered the key she'd taken from Stiev's body. Too many of Stiev's men knew her face. The locker still had to be checked, but if she was going to do it, she would need another identity, or at least another face. The Reef! She'd heard the previously PST-favored bar had changed and now teemed with all sorts of lowlife. It should be easy to hire someone there to fetch the locker's contents. She spun in a circle. *Where the khegh are those stairs?*

Hearing a commotion behind her, Toni didn't look back to see who won the fight, instead headed deeper into the park following the flashing signs toward the casino. Her heart thundered as she raced down the stairs. That Crellik wouldn't be stopped easily, not by simple park security.

The stairs ended at the entrance to a hall filled with slot machines. As soon as Toni stepped foot into the room, her shades vibrated, tickling her nose. It made sense that anti-scanning software was in operation down here. Heavily curtained windows blocked out the luminescent coral lighting the rest of the complex, plunging the room into an eerie dusk. The lack of light would work to her advantage. Breathing hard, she whipped off her glasses and clipped them to her shirt. Her tails stampeded down the stairs. She risked a quick look back. Their torn and dirty clothing blended into the long shadows created by low light and occasionally blinking fluorescent bulbs.

When she faced forward, a groan escaped her lips. The Crellik and a fat human stood at the hall's far end. *By a Mythen battletank, how many of these guys are there? Move!* Toni ran into the labyrinth of slot machines, passing unseen by the zombie-like gamblers feeding coins into hungry metal mouths.

There seemed to be no end to the maze. The hall was stuffy, and the body odor wafting from the living corpses brought tears to her eyes. The only source of light came from the screens around her, blinking in irregular bursts.

Door, door, I need a door ... She skidded to a stop. "This is ridiculous." Her chest was tight as she considered her lack of options. In front of her was a vacant seat bolted to the base of an out-of-order machine. She sprang onto the seat and pulled her body up onto the top of the machine. Since she couldn't see a way out of the maze from the ground, she'd go over it.

An exit sign beckoned her left. Chained to the ceiling were large hanging lights. Flashing signs proclaimed "JACKPOT" and "Win this hovercar!" Her feet thudded against metal as she sprinted under and jumped over the garish obstacles.

Free and clear!

Searching fingers appeared over the lip of the machine several squares ahead of her. A head bobbed into view followed by another. Within seconds, the goons climbed up to confront her. The fat human and the Crellik were way down the back of the hall, so she dismissed them from her immediate awareness, leaving only four to deal with now.

The closest goon charged. Toni kicked out, connecting with his ribcage and knocked him off balance. He fell to his hands and knees. She kicked again, this time connecting with his face. Grabbing a flailing arm, she hefted the man over the side and out of sight. Turning, she arched her body to avoid a fist thrown at her. As it flew past her nose, she pushed at the Roxal's shoulder. His foot connected with her side. She gasped as the wind was knocked out of her. Launching herself forward she took him out at the knees. He sailed over the side with a startled cry. Another goon jumped from the next row to slash at her with the knife held in his third arm.

She hit the top of the machine, hard. Thrusting up, she caught the skinny man in what she hoped was an anatomically painful place. He cried out. She launched back on to her feet and with a round house kick, took him out across the throat. Her attacker fell heavily. She grabbed his tail and tugged. He screamed as he fell over the side.

A weight hit her in the back, pushing her onto her face again. Her shoulder erupted in pain. All breath fled her lungs. She gasped, searching for more oxygen, but it was as though her lungs had gone on strike. Shaking her head to clear suddenly foggy vision, she watched the goon step closer and raise his shock paddle for another strike. The rounded edge crackled alarmingly. Toni threw up both hands, blocking the intended blow. Fighting like a drunken spacedock worker, she kicked and punched wildly, but the goon was stronger and aimed more effectively.

In desperation, she caught his belt and pulled. He flailed forward, straight into the head she slammed into his stomach. His fingers loosened on the paddle, and she snatched it from his hand, reversing it back into him. The goon shuddered as the paddle's full impact coursed through his body. With no mercy, she shoved him out of her way. He fell unconscious over the side of the machine, hitting the ground below with a heavy thwack.

Toni staggered, breathing raggedly. The last goon had disappeared. "Where …?" She couldn't waste her chance. She sprinted for the exit.

The Crellik landed between her and the final row. *Shenghi!* She increased her speed, and the second before she collided against the mountain of bones, she grabbed hold of a *Winner!* sign dangling from the ceiling.

Using the momentum from her run, she swung on the sign, lifted her legs, and planted them firmly into the Crellik's chest. At the apex of its arch, she released the sign and landed on her feet with barely a stumble. A scream split the air behind her. She didn't look back. Sliding to her knees, she hooked her fingers around the lip of the end machine, swinging off before she hit the ground running. Skidding along the polished floor, Toni slipped through the arched doorway and into the open elevator car at the end of the hall. She hit the back wall and fell on to her butt.

Panting, she stared into the eyes of the elderly man standing beside the floor buttons. The doors closed gently. "Six please," she said.

CHAPTER SEVENTEEN

The lowest level of the casino complex catered to those seeking the seedier side of life. It was also home to The Reef, a bar one entered at their own risk. Knowing the type of clientele that now frequented the drinking establishment, Toni was prepared. She removed the star from her chest and wore her pistol slung low on her right hip, the safety catch unclasped. The strength of the vibration her shades gave off as she stared up at the façade of her old haunt told her there was serious anti-surveillance equipment inside. She pulled the shades off. The bar should be dark, the protection wouldn't be needed. Heck, she could see better in the dim light anyway.

Let's get this show started. She pushed open the old-fashioned hinged doors. So far, so good—no one had shot at her. Nevertheless, she kept her hand close to her holster.

As her eyes adjusted, she noticed two things; one, Jeri was not at the bar and two, the place smelled far worse than she remembered. There was an overpowering stench of alcohol, stale smoke and week-old socks. Two years ago, The Reef had been frequented by agents, Defenders, and STCT. Now, it had become a hole—and not a safe one—full of pirates and smugglers.

In tandem, every head turned at her entry. Her fingers twitched and touched her belt. Murmurs started as the drunken patrons took in her visage. She sauntered in and eyed a familiar table, still positioned three paces from the edge of the bar. Two men were there now, but two years ago, her informant sat at that very same table, waiting for Toni to make contact. She hid a smile at the memory.

Unfortunately, memories of those days brought back things best left forgotten.

Strolling to the bar, the tacky floor tried to cling to her boots. Whispers followed her. She was used to it, but that didn't make it any easier to accept. Her skin crawled. She shot the patrons around her a narrowed stare, immediately wishing for Mate's presence. A second set of eyes was needed in a place like this. The murmur rose as conversation around her returned and the drunks went back to their business of getting drunker in as little time as possible. She recognized a face or two, people who nodded discreetly but did not approach. A rodent Testell caught her eye, flirting with a sly grin, but Toni ignored him. A barkeep appeared at her shoulder and leaned down on one of his three arms, bringing his face close to hers. "Whatya have?"

"Hosdinn on Ice. Medium rare," she answered.

With a last stare around the room, she turned back to the bar.

The barkeep returned and placed a long, purple glass in front of her. The liquid frothed at the lip, smelling sweetly of cherry and bry-berries, mixed with the tangy scent of alcoholic dinn leaves.

Toni flicked two coin chips to the scratched wooden counter and emptied her glass. The bar was busy, and it was a while before the barkeep came back. As he refilled her glass, he leaned down on one forearm. Her eyes widened as recognition dawned. *The barkeep* was *Jeri*. She jerked back. Now rotund and bald, her friend's top left foreclaw was gone. No wonder she hadn't recognized him. A beard covered the lower part of his face, and a long pistol scar stretched down the left side of it. He looked like one of the clientele.

"What in Xendia's name happened to you, Jeri?"

"So you finally recognized me, huh? Caught in a cross-fire." He paused. "You know, girl, since ya been here last …"

"Things have changed. Yeah, I noticed." She flicked her hand to the enhanced doorframe. "When did that happen?"

"New management." Jeri's southern Rikingsh accent seemed more pronounced than she remembered, each 'n' sound curling softly. "A year ago. It's gone to hell since then."

"No kidding. Listen, Jer"—she lowered her voice—"I need a job done. Simple retrieval, local setting. Anyone in tonight that can be relied on?"

"None yet. If I see one, I'll send them your way."

"We're going to need some privacy."

The big man leaned back and polished the stained glass in his hand. "There's a booth up the back if ya want some quiet."

She held his gaze. "I could do with another pair of eyes, too."

"You got it, girl."

Swallowing what was left in her glass, she headed for the back of the bar.

Toni was a step away from the empty booth when she heard the whine and pop of rifle-fire. She spun, pistol in hand, and watched the whiskerless Testell fall to his knees in front of her, the hole in his back still smoking. As he hit the ground, a small pistol flew from his hand across the floor. It stopped at the toe of her boot.

Xendia's servants! Goosepimples exploded across her skin. Her gaze darted to her friend. Jeri stood behind the bar, the rifle grasped in his lower hand still pointed at the dead man. Toni thanked him with a nod and slumped down into the booth. Her hands shook. This was why she never left Mate behind. Without the use of her glasses, she relied heavily on her partner to see what she couldn't. Without him, she was vulnerable. She forced her shoulders back and stretched out her short legs. *Don't let them see.*

If she displayed any weakness the bar's patrons would recognize a victim, and then the Testell wouldn't be the only one who tried to attack her tonight.

CHAPTER EIGHTEEN

She knew the exact moment everything went to shenghi. Her leg started to twitch and a spike of remembered pain speared through her upper arm. Massaging the muscle, she searched the bar for the source of her unease. When she saw him, her eyes sprang wide. Her skin turned to ice and she ducked low in her chair. *Don't see me!*

Raising her hand up to cover her face, Toni refused to look back at the door. In her mind, she pictured him as she'd just seen him, slouched in the well-lit doorway looking all mysterious and dangerous.

Curiosity was a curse. After a long moment, she glanced up just in time to see Daniel Colten fall into the lap of a Nymph sitting at a table in the center. The woman's pale, lime-kissed skin looked burnished bronze under the bar's lighting. The two fingerhorns on her forehead were painted with red tips. Colten leaned over to sip from her glass and whispered into her ear, brushing long red tresses over her shoulder. The woman laughed, low and throaty, before passing him what looked like a key.

Figures. Toni sighed. Colten's head shot up. He peered around as if sensing Toni's presence. When he looked directly at her, his double-take was almost comical.

Khegh it! Her instincts screamed at her to jump to her feet and flee. But she wouldn't let him drive her out of here. She could handle this. Besides, he'd probably do all he could to avoid her. Her stomach flipped as he stood. He excused himself from the flirty Nymph and walked straight at Toni, though *walked* was the wrong word. He never walked. *Stalked* was a better term. His casual air belied the alertness and strength in his tall frame. He hadn't changed much. His body was covered head to toe in black, and his hair, now long enough to fall into his eyes, was tied into a tail behind his head. Toni glared up into dark eyes and spied a hint of uncertainty. Good, he didn't know how she was going to act. Her hand twitched toward her gun.

"Caught cheating at Duilk again?"

"I never cheat." Brushing a hand over the bruise on her cheek, Toni refused to break eye contact first. He reached out to pull the closest empty chair away from the table. Childishly, she hooked her foot under the wooden frame, halting the move.

He snorted.

Hating that he made her feel so immature, she debated telling him to khegh off or just shooting him. Or ... or, she could use him. *It would be only fair, right?* She released the chair and kicked it out from under the table.

He accepted the unspoken invitation and straddled it, meeting her stare with his own. "I might be mistaken, but I'm pretty sure you swore the next time we met, you'd shoot me."

Squirming under his gaze, she'd love to tell him what she really wanted. Instead ground her teeth to remain silent.

Jeri appeared, placing two full clear glasses on the table. Toni's head shot up. "Where on Marn did you get that?"

"Consider it a gift."

"Jeri ..." Toni didn't finish the thought. Colten snatched up his glass and drank half of it down. Heathen. He should savor it. She raised her glass and breathed in the crisp scent of rain and mountain snow. Water. She took a sip and let the liquid fill her mouth. When she looked up, she caught Colten staring at her lips. She swallowed and barely held back her moan. *Beautiful.*

"I should really get into water distribution." Colten muttered, his gaze locked on Toni's mouth.

"Ha! Good luck with that. Water is too protected."

"Robbery," he murmured.

He wasn't wrong. Water was insanely expensive. Finding a safe supply was just too kheghing rare. She cradled her glass and took another sip. Jeri nodded at Toni and rested a hand on Colten's shoulder. She waved him away.

"So," Colten said, leaning back in his chair. "Why are you here, Toni? This is not exactly an agent-friendly locale anymore."

"I need your help."

He cocked his head to one side, nostrils flaring slightly.

So she still had the ability to surprise him. Good. *I don't want to do this.* She reached into her vest pocket and pulled out a yellow card, placing it in the center of the table. Colten stared at it.

"Don't get any ideas," she said, suppressing a grin. *Okay, that looks pretty bad.* "I need you to open a locker for me—I'll pay."

"A locker?" He looked up, his intense gaze fixed onto her face. "You want me to open a locker?"

She eyed him carefully. "And bring me what's inside. You owe me." She watched his face for any reaction. Her shoulder ached, and it was everything she could do not to clutch at it.

He didn't blink. "I owe you?"

"You think you don't?"

"I didn't kill you."

She hissed, a flame igniting in her chest. Words stuck in her throat, but she managed to get them out. "You do this for me and I won't arrest you."

He leaned back, a smirk playing at his lips. "You can't. PST waived the charge."

"That wouldn't stop me and you know it. Listen, it's not difficult. Just go to the lower park storage bay, open the locker, and bring me back whatever's inside. The number is on the tag." She tapped on the key.

"Why don't you do it?"

"Long story."

"Your stories always are."

She sucked in air slowly, struggling to hold onto her temper. "Something important is in that locker, and some big, very ugly gentlemen know to look out for me down there. I won't even get close to the main bay. They don't know you. I'm pretty sure they don't know which locker I'm after. All I need you to do is empty it and come straight back to the *Blackflame*. I'm sure even you can handle that."

"How do you know the key is for a locker here?"

She held up an identical card. "Booked one when I arrived."

"All right," he said.

"Look, it's not that hard … Oh, you said yes? I mean, good. The *Blackflame* is in Bay Seven." *Gods! Stop it.*

"Fine." Colten stood. "What's so important about this locker? What's in it?"

"I don't know, but it's something to do with why the Cross got a temporary pardon."

He pocketed the key and sauntered toward the exit. As he passed the Nymph, he winked. The woman tilted her head and blew him a kiss. When she glanced at Toni, her face lost all expression.

Honey, you can have him. Of all the people to run into here, why him? Toni should have picked someone else. She couldn't trust him. What had she been thinking?

The truth of the matter was she hadn't been thinking. His appearance had driven all rational thought from her mind. Giving him the key had been instinctual. *See! I need a break. Look at the mistakes I make when I'm tired.* A storm was becoming a tornado inside her belly.

She could feel the Nymph's eyes on her back as she left the bar. Toni dismissed it when the doors swung shut behind her, her mind now focused on how to deal with Colten without shooting him.

CHAPTER NINTEEN

"Ah!" Toni fell into her chair and tapped her fingers against the armrest, glaring around the inside of the *Blackflame*. Her eyes traced the soldered crack in the wall, memories surfacing to suffocate her.

"Zach, what time is it?" she demanded.

"Four minutes since the last time you asked."

"Khegh it. He should be back by now. It was just a little locker, for Xendia's sake!" She threw herself out of her chair and stomped to the nav-link.

"Boss, if you do not sit down, I will shoot you in the knee," Mate growled. "The smuggler has no doubt got into and out of plenty of trouble without your help. I am sure he is fine."

"Of course he's fine. Scum like that always survive."

"Zach!" Toni snapped. Inwardly, she smiled. Both at the sentiment and the tone.

The CII had changed his voice again. He now sounded *older*, his words clipped and proper, like an old, two-dimensional holo-actor. It made his attitude against Colten sound even more judgmental. And he wasn't wrong to think that way.

Zach didn't like Colten, neither did Mate, and they had their reasons—as did Toni—but Zach made it clear he was particularly aggrieved Toni asked Colten for help instead of shooting him. The CII was taking out his bad mood on her. "You should not have requested his assistance."

"I had no choice." *Liar.*

Mate, as usual, stayed well out of the argument. He lowered his head to his paws and closed his eyes. Though he was not looking at her, she felt his disappointment. It radiated from him, hot enough to scald her skin.

"Of course you had a choice—how many degenerates were in that establishment? There were many others you might have chosen, why *him*?"

"How else was I going to get to that locker?"

"Bribed someone? Asked? There are so many ways. You chose him because you wanted to."

"Zach!" she snapped, scandalized. Heat flooded her entire body. She couldn't look at the CII, instead stared at her feet. *You know he's right.* Running into Colten was surprising, yes, but she needn't have prolonged the encounter.

It was the best option—the only option. But even she refused to listen to her excuses. Fed up with Zach's attitude and her own internal arguments, she paced again. This was what *he* did to her. Made her second-guess every decision. It was infuriating, but she refused to delve deeper into why that hadn't stopped her asking for his help.

After she received the contents of the locker, she'd get rid of him. She couldn't re-open the same damned wound or she'd never heal. Flutterwings danced in her stomach. Pressing her hand to her skin she told herself she was just hungry.

"Call him."

"No answer." Zach immediately replied.

"What? What do you mean no answer? Try again."

Panting noises burst through the speakers and a familiar groan filled the air. "Colten?" Toni jumped to her feet.

"What?"

"Are you running? What's going—" Gunfire sounded in the background. "Colten?"

"It appears they know about the locker. Hang on."

Toni paced the length of the room—all eight steps. Mate and Zach remained silent. They all listened as the smuggler's breathing grew quicker. There was a thud, like a heavy door slamming shut, then another groan.

"Colten?"

"Yeah, I'm here. You weren't kidding. These guys are kheghing determined."

"Where are you?"

"Hiding in a stairwell."

"What?"

"Walked into an ambush."

Feeling cold, Toni crossed her arms. "Why are you grunting?"

"I can't walk through the casino with blood dripping down my arm. Lucky me, the flooring in this area is a lovely deep burgundy. I've got a few minutes' peace. But I gotta keep moving. I can hear them at the other end of the corridor."

He's been shot? Two sides went to war inside Toni. She bit back every comment hard enough to taste blood. Before she could say anything, he hung up on her. *Son of a she-demon!* She checked her weapon was fully charged and ran toward the door.

"What are you doing?" Mate snapped, stopping her before she could smack her hand against the release.

"To rescue his ass. We need what is in that locker." Shenghi, she'd forgotten to ask if he'd even reached the locker.

"Not like that you are not."

Zach popped up beside her. "Your image has been flashed to the security teams."

"Khegh it!"

"They're saying you're an escaped criminal with a history of insanity, warning people you're telling your victims you're an agent."

"For the love of … right, I can't go out—"

"Boss?"

Toni stomped toward her costume cupboard. At least Jas's birthday gift would finally be of use.

*

Patrons screamed and scattered, the smart ones ducking under nearby tables as shots grew louder. Through the hysterical mass, Toni spied Colten heading her way, followed by goons—several of whom she recognized from her own escape—and plenty of casino security guards. A red globe next to Colten's head exploded. He ducked as the blood-colored shards sprayed over him.

She had to shout to be heard over the noise. "Stop sightseeing and get your butt up here."

He searched over his shoulder.

"I said *up,* you idiot."

Colten grinned as he caught sight of her.

Yes, I'm on a winner platform sitting in a display Cadford hovercar—just like a kheghing prize. "Need a lift?" She felt her face flush. Fortunately, the layers of toned foundation caked onto her face would hide it. She flicked the brown wig's annoyingly long strands off her shoulder and blinked down at him. "What are you waiting for?"

He clambered over the lockout fence and under the sign. Toni pushed the passenger side door open.

"Nice dress."

"Shut up," she snapped, glaring daggers at him. "The locker?"

"Got it."

Huffing out a relieved breath, she ducked under the dashboard. Two bolts ricocheted off the windshield and shattered the blinking sign beside them. Ignoring the noise, she sorted through a ball of wires. "Not that one," he said.

"Khegh off."

"Not that one."

"Shenghi, Colten, I know what I'm doing." She tugged a red wire clear.

"Not that one," he repeated.

"Fine." She pulled the green wire instead, wrapping it tightly around an already cut silver wire. The repulse-engine roared to life.

Toni slid into the driver's seat and yanked her troublesome skirt aside to stamp her foot onto the accelerator. The hovercar shot forward, severing the wires securing it to the platform and flew out over the main casino floor.

"Hold on!" she cried, yanking the wheel hard to the right. The hovercar nearly stalled as it turned ninety degrees and hurtled toward the exit. Colten bounced against the door, hissing in pain.

"Go higher!" he shouted as they skimmed too close to the Duilk tables. Cards and chips were sent flying under the vehicle's repulsion field.

Twisting the wheel, Toni tapped rapidly at the control board's touch panel. Antigrav lifts patched into the underside of the craft generated a burst of power, thrusting them up fast. She cut the lifts back to half and flew out above the crowd.

The hovercar's back window exploded, sending her ducking for cover. Colten's face pressed close to hers.

"No rear shields," she answered his unasked question. She wrenched the wheel hard one way and back the other, weaving between large signs and advertising boards. Stamping on the brake, she nearly sent herself and Colten flying through the front screen. Only their belts stopped them. "Oh, khegh it."

Beside her, Colten sucked in a sharp breath. Her eyes snapped to his and then flew in the direction he was staring. The theme park's giant entrance doors swung closed ahead of them, heavy doors that could not be opened again without three men to crank the giant wheels on the ground. Toni punched the accelerator and wished she could close her eyes.

"Hold on!"

"Are you crazy?" he bellowed.

"No!" She jumped on the brake again, swinging the car sideways. Before he had time to react, she withdrew a long black object from the rear seat and shoved it into his hands.

"What the hell is this?"

"The door remote." She grinned wildly. "Open the kheg-hing window and shoot the damned door."

CHAPTER TWENTY

"What? It can't blast through that, that's reinforced plasteel and crete-brick!" He held the weapon across his legs and in the crook of one arm, the other hung loosely from his shoulder.

"Where's your optimism?" she asked, increasing the forward shields. Adrenaline flooded through her. She was hyperaware of the man in the seat next to her as he unwound the window. He stuck his head though only to pull back when a bolt exploded against the side lens. She shot him a glance, worried he'd been hit. He gave her a strained smile. There was blood on his shoulder. *Shenghi!* He *had* been hit.

The car rocked wildly. Before Toni could stabilize it, the back wheel clipped a large promotion sign, which crashed to the ground, hitting another as it fell. The second sign clipped another, and then another … Steel panels cascaded to the floor, sending electronic sparks all over the Park. She glanced at Colten. "Whoops."

He grinned and leaned through the window again. The casino entrance was deserted. Everyone appeared to have scattered into the Park. She heard him take a sharp breath and then silence. He pulled the trigger.

The mag-rifle let out a high-pitched squeal and a whoosh exploded from the barrel. At first it seemed as though nothing happened. Then the doors dissolved, melting right off the hinges.

Toni gasped. *Xendia!* No wonder Zaambuka wanted information on these things. She checked the rearview screen. Goons and park security lay unconscious on the floor.

"What is this thing?" Colten shouted, shaking the weapon with his working arm.

Toni didn't answer. Instead she slammed her foot onto the accelerator and flew them out of the Park.

*

Toni peeled the blood-stained jacket from Colten's tense shoulders. At least she tried to. The material was stuck to the wound, and she had to tug at it gently to remove it.

"Ahh," he groaned as she picked at the tacky leather.

"Sorry." She bit back a smile. Karma was such a bitch.

"Sure you are."

"What?"

"Nothing." He pulled the bag over his head and dropped it at her feet. "The stuff from the locker."

"Great." Toni grabbed the bag.

"Wait a minute, what about my shoulder?"

"What about it?" She stared at his pained expression. "Damn it, Colten, this is important." Being this close to him, her skin soaked in his familiar warmth. Her belly flip-flopped. *Stay cold and impersonal. Don't let him see he still affects you.* His scent wrapped around her and clogged her nose. *Get rid of him!*

"Hey, you asked for my help."

She stared, contemplating the irony and debated throwing his own words from two years ago back at him or telling him to toughen up. Several other phrases came to mind about what he could do with his arm, too. "You didn't … Oh, for Xendia's sake." She stomped away to fetch her medical box.

In the *Blackflame*'s cockpit, she sagged against the control console and released a heartfelt sigh. Dipping her head, tears prickled in her eyes. She blinked them back. *Stop this!* Huffing out a breath, she caught sight of her disguised visage in the mirror. She ripped the wig from her head and snatched up her skin spray. It took only seconds to remove the heavy foundation. The redness in her face rose in welts around her hairline. She scratched at the bumps on the side of her nose. It was certainly good to be herself again. A pep talk to her reflection sent her back to Colten, the aid kit in her hands. "Take your shirt off."

"Well, now, I don't know whether this is the time and place for that," he drawled. His gaze crept over her skin. Toni twisted away, warmth flaring from her collar. She caught Mate staring at the smuggler. The C-bot sat on a cushioned passenger seat beside the door. She didn't see Zach.

Toni gave her partner a desperate look before turning back to the injured man. *I don't want to do this.* "I can't look at the wound with your shirt on."

Colten ground his teeth and reached for the waistband of his pants. The blood-stained shirt got stuck halfway over his head before he froze.

She watched in silence. There was no way she was going to help. Not until he begged. A soft mutter came from under the black material.

"Sorry, what?" she asked.

"A little help?"

With a sharp move, she jerked the material from his fingers. Holding his shoulder steady, she peeled the material from the wound. Clammy dark skin radiated heat. It spread over her fingers and up her arm. *Xendia!*

"Ah, careful," he gasped.

Lifting her hands from his bare shoulder, she cursed silently. Unwanted memories threatened her focus. She remembered the feel of his body against her and the safety of his embrace. Swallowing hard, she leaned forward to examine his arm. Luckily for him, the bolt had gone right through. The exit wound on his back looked pretty torn up, but the entry on his chest was reasonably clean. The bolt had hit his body just above his Cross tattoo.

She wanted to shove the kit into his hands and tell him to fix his injury on his own—after all, she'd had to. Huffing out a breath instead, she set about cleaning the wound, finding several antibiotic sprays and cleaners in her kit.

The scar across his stomach caught her eye. She pressed her lips together tightly to stop the question emerging. It was none of her business. He twitched again, and Toni's shoulder ached in sympathy.

She held the palm-sized bone regenerator to his shoulder. The demand to know why he had abandoned her on that moon danced on her tongue but she couldn't ask it. He was a smuggler and a liar—that was all the reason he needed.

"Is this a private party, or can anyone join?" Zach asked popping up on the screen to her right.

"Hey, you must be Zach. I've heard a lot about you." Colten's voice sounded strained.

"Smuggler, that looks like it hurts." If a computer could generate a voice that sounded happy, her CII was using it now.

"Stop squirming," Toni snapped. With one hand, she searched for the mu-knit unit. Colten twisted, trying to face the closest screen but she forced him back and pressed the device over the hole in his back to reknit the muscles. "Hold still!"

"I'm not moving," he said through clenched teeth.

"Right."

Zach appeared on every screen. "I don't understand why you're treating him here, Boss. You got the bag. Dump his ass out the ramp and let's go."

Colten held out a hand. "Whoa now. Calm down, Zach." His pleading gaze fell on Toni. She stared blankly at him, refusing to budge.

"For what it's worth—"

"It's not."

There was a long silence. Toni plucked the healing unit from his chest. It looked okay. She slapped an accelerant patch to the new skin and wound a flexible bandage around his arm and shoulder. With one arm around his chest, she tightened the bandage.

His heart was pounding when she pressed her ear against his back. Her own heartbeat increased in response, and her face flamed. She straightened, closing the kit with a snap and stalked from the room, returning to throw an oversized white poly-cotton shirt at his face.

"Time to go, Smuggler. The door's that way."

"Zach's right. You can go, Colten. Thanks for the help." Toni emptied the contents of his bag onto the table, all the while keeping him in her periphery. She refused to turn her back on him.

She found several prints of a dark-haired woman with pale skin who looked maybe ten years older than Toni. In each print, the woman's face looked serene, staring off into the distance as if she could see a future no one else could see.

"Vice-President Cat Ramo." Zach said.

"I know that, Zach." Toni examined the pictures with care. Everyone in the Sector knew of the Vice-President. Last year, when Xhonda Ramo resigned her position as President, she'd publicly encouraged her daughter to enter the Senate. Marcus Hemalter had been elected President, much to the dismay of many. He'd barely shown his face in public since, canceling event after event and avoiding holocameras completely. Cat Ramo was the real face of Sector One politics. Toni figured it was only a matter of time before Ramo was elected to the top job, but she had big ideals, and even bigger shoes to fill.

"Gorgeous, isn't she?" Colten said, staring over Toni's shoulder.

"Door," she stated, pointing to the exit.

He ignored her, leaning sideways to eye the images on the table. "I never really thought about it, but wow, she's incredible."

"Yeah, she's all right," Toni was irritated both by Colten's reaction and by her reaction to his reaction. She tried to ignore him as she sorted through the rest of the bag's contents. Pausing, she fingered a small projectile weapon. It looked like a bow, but the trigger and projectile chamber looked different. She'd not seen it's like before.

"Look familiar?" she asked, holding it up.

Colten shook his head.

Left on the table was a piece of plastipaper. Toni flattened the scrunched material. The only thing on it was a name scrawled in ink: *Jase Balandez.*

"Balandez?" The high pitch of Colten's voice brought her gaze snapping back to his face. He looked at Toni though wide eyes. "Balandez is an assassin. Specializes in targeting the rich and famous. I hear he commands a huge performance fee." Colten took the small bowcaster from her hand. "This is the sort weapon he would use."

"They're going to assassinate Vice-President Ramo?" Toni whispered.

"Why?" Mate asked.

"I don't know. Ant might," she offered. "But it has to link back to the distribution of those Resonators." She gestured to the bow. "This is clearly intended to carry some kind of explosive projectile."

"What's a Resonator?" Colten asked, handing the bow back to Toni.

"The mag-rifle I gave you."

"They're shipping those? To where?"

"They're being ..." She wanted to say *smuggled* but stopped herself, just. "... distributed underground. I have a delivery list, but no idea where they're being made, or what they're being distributed for."

"I'll contact the Cross, get them looking for the source."

Toni forced herself not to respond. The Cross probably knew more about the Resonators distribution than anyone.

"So, what now?" he asked. "I assume you'll warn the Vice-President, but are we going after the Resonators or Balandez?"

Mate growled, the sound so deep Toni felt it in her feet. Zach reappeared on every screen. "You're not coming."

"Zach," Toni warned.

The CII ignored her. "You're not invited, Smuggler."

"Zach," Colten tried to reason. "*She* asked *me*."

Toni shook her head. "I said I'd pay you for a single job. Which you completed. Thanks for your help, but the PST will take it from here." She had to hold her ground. His presence would distract her from the mission. She'd end up spending her whole time watching over her shoulder, wondering when he was going to shoot her again. *Hm, Mate's right. I do have trust issues.* But were they *issues* if it had legitimately happened? Toni could never look at Colten and not remember the heartache and physical pain he'd caused.

"What?" He examined her through narrowed eyes.

"This is an official operation, Colten. You've been very helpful, and I thank you for that, but I can handle it from here."

Mate stood near the wall, backing her up all the way. Zach grinned and bounced from one screen to the next.

"Wait a minute, Toni, I'm involved now. This is personal." He gestured to his injured shoulder. "These guys chased me, shot at me! I'm involved. I can help you."

Her breath puffed out of her. *Are you kheghing with me?* Why on Marn did he want to help—unless … Did he actually feel guilty?

Use him.

"If you really want to help, see if you can track down the origin of those Resonator shipments."

Colten climbed to his feet, moving straight into her personal space. She backed up, but he followed. Leaning into her body, he hissed, "You're shutting me out, Toni. I'm involved now. It's too late to back off."

Mate growled a warning. Colten didn't move.

"No," she replied. Her heart rate skyrocketed. She licked her lips and swallowed. "I won't work with a smuggler." What she really meant was that she wouldn't work with him. She pushed him away.

"You're still angry? Well, get over it!"

"Get over it?" *He actually dared to say that! Khegh-loving ass!* "You shot me and left me stranded!"

"I had my reasons and if you'd just let me explain—"

She didn't care about his reasons. She didn't care about him. Storming to the wall, she put space between them before she did something she couldn't come back from, like shoot him. "Just go."

"Those goons tried to kill me. I want to even the score."

"This is not a game."

"You think people trying to kill me is a game?"

"No." She pressed her lips together, exasperated.

"You won't work with me?"

Is he serious? "No."

"Then I'll find Balandez without you." He snatched up his jacket and the empty bag.

"What are you going to do?"

Colten turned in the doorway. "You'll figure it out." He walked right up to her. She stepped to one side but couldn't help the shiver that ran through her body when he pushed up against her. He spoke in a low voice. "You need to trust me."

Toni didn't reply. She hit the hatch release and watched him storm away. When he was halfway across the docking bay, she shouted, "You taught me not to trust you. You've got no one to blame but yourself." *Asshole.*

He didn't turn.

Damn him! Toni slammed her hand against the catch to close the ramp, wishing she could get him out of her heart just as easily.

CHAPTER TWENTY-ONE

The *Blackflame* streaked away from the bright lights of the casino complex. As they cleared Uxt's atmosphere, Toni told the CII to contact Zaambuka. She wasn't sorry to leave Uxt, but was happy with how she'd handled her meeting with The Smuggler. For two years she'd been afraid of how she'd react if she ever saw him again. She'd proven she could maintain control. He had no power over her now. She swallowed hard. The little voice in the back of her mind laughed hysterically. She ordered it to shut up.

"What's taking so long?" Mate grumbled as he paced the floor at her feet. It seemed as though her anger had infected her partner as well.

She couldn't concentrate. Colten's words replayed over and over inside her head. She drummed her fingers on the console, knowing she was too wound up. She needed to calm down and figure out what she was going to tell Zaambuka. The screen melted into the PST logo and then dissolved into …

"Oh, my gods." Toni ducked out of her chair.

"Not one word."

She exaggerated a wide-eyed look of horror and turned back to the screen, covering her eyes. "Let me guess, it's another one sent by the Vice-President's staff?" Toni burst out laughing. Zaambuka brushed his hand down the tie's length. "They really don't like you, do they?" She dropped her hand, chuckling sporadically. Her body relaxed, the momentary jocularity going a long way to settling her nerves.

"I don't want to hear it," he muttered, but Toni couldn't stop herself.

"I have to find out where they get them. I wonder if they're designed specifically or are an off-the-shelf variety."

"Toni." Zaambuka's glare was hot enough to melt metal. "I assume you've contacted me because you have some information?"

"Oh, yes, I do." Her demeanor became all business. *Don't mention The Smuggler.* Her fingers tingled. She clasped them tightly together.

"Go on."

"We have two computerized dispatch tablets in possession and have located and destroyed a shipment of Resonators, a big shipment. I have a sample. It's been tested, and it's effective, to say the least." Her stomach flipped just thinking about it. She scrubbed a hand over her face.

"What a coincidence. I received word this morning that a powerful weapon was fired in the main casino on Uxt, causing untold damage. The perpetrators haven't been found. You wouldn't happen to know anything about that, would you?"

Toni smiled. "That's not all."

"What do you mean?"

"Do the words Midock, secret meeting, a master assassin named Balandez, and Vice-President Cat Ramo mean anything to you?"

Zaambuka muttered under his breath.

"From what I've discovered, they intend to assassinate the Vice-President on Midock using some sort of untraceable dart—filled with what I don't know, poison I suspect. The suspect is Jase Balandez. What I don't have is a motive or evidence of who masterminded this plot."

"I can give you the motive." Zaambuka leaned back in his chair and interlocked his hands in front of him.

Oh no, lecture mode. She slumped back into her seat.

"What do you know about the current political situation?"

Toni waved her hand around. "That I don't care about it. You know I steer clear of politics, Ant."

Zaambuka ignored her. "At this very moment, the APE Senate is in the middle of negotiating an alliance with the UPC, the United Planets Confederacy."

"The President is behind it? I don't think I've seen an image of him on the holonet for an age. Are you sure he's not dead and Ramo's running the show? It sounds like the kind of project she'd initiate."

"I thought you stayed clear of politics?"

"Doesn't mean I don't hear gossip."

"Toni."

She waved a hand. "So, an alliance with Sector Two. I've flown to the border but never through Confederacy space." You didn't just fly into another Sector without permission. It was a fast way to get shot. "That's Gendix, Hemell, Ziim, Djpitt and the Anderee systems."

"As well as the Cryy'v-eft, the Shayshall, and the Teriniz zones."

Toni shook her head. "That many systems must add up to over a third of the populated space."

"If the Confederacy allies with APE, well over half the galaxy will be governed by a peace-focused collaborative political party. And yes, Vice-President Ramo is the campaign's spearhead."

Toni tapped the tips of her fingers together. "I still don't see where the assassination comes into it other than to get a lot of negative publicity."

"The Ascendancy."

Toni sat forward and leaned her elbows on the console. "Sector Three?" She remembered stories her grandfather told her when she was little, of pirates and smugglers and of Sector Three. A place filled with ghosts.

In reality, she knew little about the Ascendancy. Its borders were tightly controlled.

"Yes. The Ascendancy is consolidating their control over Sector Three and are starting to expand. The area is deep on the other side of Confederacy space. They're taking down independent border worlds with deadly force. Vice-President Ramo is aware of this incursion and wants to be prepared in the case of full-scale invasion."

"Invasion? That's jumping to forcedspace, isn't it? They'd have to overrun Confederacy space to get anywhere near Sector One's borders." This was insane. It would never happen. The Sectors were too established, too regulated to degenerate into war. The public would never go along with it. Toni shook her head. *Those Resonators though ...*

"Perhaps not. The Ascendancy strictly controls their communications network. Our security specialists suggest it's impossible to predict the Ascendancy's strengths and weaknesses without regular updates. We don't even know who's coordinating their attack."

"So if Ramo is taken out of the picture, the entire peace alliance will collapse, making us vulnerable to an Ascendancy invasion force? You're stretching the threat a bit, aren't you? Ramo can't be that pivotal. She's not even officially in charge."

"Ramo's leading opposition, Senator Kalzee'tiam is a Protectionist. He and his followers believe in tightening our borders and strengthening our armies against both the Ascendancy and the Confederacy. If Vice-President Ramo is killed, her supporters will lose their loudest voice in the Senate. If her supporters were to join 'Tiam's party, he'd control the majority Senate. He'll demand the entire project be scrapped."

Toni rolled her eyes. "Surely Ramo's supporters are more loyal than that. Don't they believe in the alliance?"

"They do, but without a leader as gifted as Ramo, many would settle for the APE to continue on as they are now. And besides"—Zaambuka leaned forward and rested his hands on the panel before him—"I have suspicions Kalzee'tiam has been bought. He's received information from someone trying to influence his position. I've had him under unofficial investigation for the past year, and he's good. I can't find direct evidence linking him to the Ascendancy, but someone is pulling 'Tiam's strings."

Let me guess. "Gallian?" This is ridiculous. The strings were barely tangible.

"I fear so. Toni, if Ramo dies, 'Tiam will reject the peace alliance. If he has been paid off by someone with loyalties to the Ascendancy …" Zaambuka didn't finish. Toni understood the implications.

"But what does Gallian have to do with the Ascendancy?" This sounded like nothing more than conspiracy talk. Was

Zaambuka so focused on capturing Gallian that he was seeing connections that weren't really there? Gallian was an obsession—it colored her boss's judgment.

"We don't know that he does."

"Are you suggesting two separate factions want to disrupt the summit? For completely different purposes?" Now it *was* sounding like a conspiracy.

"I don't know."

Do I go along with this? She gave the idea some thought. Could it be a coincidence? But what was Gallian's motivation? Why disrupt the peace process? If Gallian knew of the Ascendancy's plans, he could be taking advantage of the timing. It certainly wouldn't be the other way around. It *was* possible he knew, but how?

"So, these underground weapon shipments? You think they're part of this plot to undermine the alliance project. I mean, if they intend to attack the Confederacy while representing the APE, then the APE and UPC will never ally. Maybe the Ascendancy is attempting an underground coup, and using Gallian to do it? Organizing a private army, maybe?" It was only Toni's respect for Zaambuka that allowed her to give this scheme airplay.

"It's possible. We need more information. The summit is in less than a week."

"Follow the shipments or hunt down the assassin?"

"Do you have a lead on Balandez?" Zaambuka straightened.

"No, but I can make some calls."

"Then focus on the shipments. You have the tablets, pick a target and find out what's been planned. Destroy all the deliveries you find. I'll put a team on Balandez."

"Gotcha, Boss." Good—that was the tangible threat. The rest was pure guesswork. The thought of standing around playing bodyguard 28/6 was just boring enough to send her over the edge. Before signing off, she grinned. "When you warn the Vice-President, thank her for the tie. Perhaps you can get the manufacturer's name for me?"

"Toni …"

With a smirk, she closed the link. "Zach, have you scanned those tablets?"

"Yup. Closest target is Telber. Interestingly enough, that's closer to the Sector core than Border Space."

"Then that's our destination."

With a fluctuation of the *Blackflame*'s shields, they disappeared into forcedspace.

CHAPTER TWENTY-TWO

The fight was dirty but brief. Toni dragged the heavy body back into the enclosed washroom and started on the fastenings holding the man's jacket closed. Mate was at the end of the platform keeping an eye on security. There was *a lot* of security.

Toni dressed quickly in the stinky uniform, muttering under her breath as she did so. "Oh my *gods*."

Zach's text bubble blossomed on her shade's display.

Zach: What?

"I don't think this guy has showered for a week. His shirt *reeks*." Given the height difference between her and the guard, Toni was forced to tuck the pant legs into her boots and fold the material of the sleeves over several times. Hopefully no one would look too closely. Of course, that was a ridiculous thought—given her genetics, she would stand out regardless. Still, it might buy her some time. She tied her hair back and tucked it under the guard's cap. Immediately, her skin began to itch, not liking the rough fabric at all. She groused inwardly. Tonight, she'd have to soak in a bath of her special salts and liberally spray her allergy diffusers.

They'd arrived on Telber in the earlier hours of the capital city's morning. As soon as they touched ground, Zach hacked the arrivals database, and between him and Mate, tracked several unusually large shipments of ranic fruit to this train station.

"Original, are they not?" Mate said in response to Toni's question about the ranic fruit. It worked in their favor that Stiev and his distribution buddies kept the same routines and the same cover stories.

According to the records, the ranic fruit crates were delivered to this train yard twenty-one standard hours ago and loaded onto three separate trains bound for Ganick City.

Toni had never been to Telber before. To familiarize herself with the terrain, she had Zach prepare a brief analysis. She hated homework, but for missions such as this one, the more she knew, the better. Zach displayed numerous maps of the largely mountainous planet and explained most of the cities were built deep underground. The planet's extreme tropical temperatures made the surface too uncomfortable to live on. Toni couldn't get over the size of the giant Truby trees that grew everywhere. The trunk width on an average Truby was the length of a star-roller, and they grew to at least thirty-five hundred feet.

She quickly realized there was no safe way to travel over-ground and limited travel by air, restricted by the height and width of the Truby trees. The inhabitants found it easier to transport items of worth between cities via long underground trains. The tunnel maps were incredibly intricate. As she traced her fingers along the paths, she snorted. The tunnels looked like the veins beneath her skin. They wouldn't be able to land in a city travelport without coming across one of the many train hubs tasked with running vital supplies between the cities and the giant storage facilities at each mountain. Which, as it turns out, was exactly where she needed to go.

On arrival at the platform, Toni and Mate were forced to turn back at the sight of heavy security. They had to find another way in, which led Toni to the guard change rooms.

She scratched at her neck scars and walked briskly along the platform toward one of the waiting trains. It looked like it would be departing shortly. Gusts of metallic air pressed against her as she walked the length of the train. The three rear cars appeared designed for storage, large and bulky. They had plenty of room to carry the fruit crates. She counted four cars to each train, designed to carry passengers. More trains waited on nearby platforms.

Toni passed two maintenance workers crouched at one of the train's repulsor ports. They didn't look up as she stopped beside them.

"Morning, Miss," one said. He didn't move his outstretched leg, so she just stepped over it.

By climbing over the two men, she made it clear she was not sneaking around. It was a way to maintain anonymity while being obvious about it. The maintenance men would only remember her as a rude member of the security team.

Sliding into the car, she moved swiftly along the inside corridor. The train floor trembled beneath her feet, forcing her to sway as she walked. At the sound of voices ahead, she ducked into a nearby compartment. It smelled moldy. She dreaded to imagine what was stored inside. Pressing her ear to the wall, she waited.

"We're running thirty behind. Patch the kheghing thing so we can get moving."

"Sir, if we rough patch it, we run the risk of popping it out during transit. We could end up halfway along the wet zone with no way to repair it if it blows."

"How long for a full repair?" The voices trailed off as they moved away. "We must arrive before the woman—"

"Politicians. Getting rid of her won't change nothing. I just can't guarantee …"

Toni slipped out of the door and continued down the corridor behind them.

Zach's text bubble appeared at the lower corner of her display.

Zach: Sounds important. Think the woman they're talking about is the Vice-President?

"Yup." Toni had no idea if there were more security or maintenance on the train but it sounded like at least some of the crew knew what the crates contained. She had to stay quiet, but that didn't stop Zach from texting.

Zach: I can't see ranic fruit being on the urgent list for any community.

"Yeah."

Zach: Be careful, Boss. If they know what's being transported, they'll be keeping a close watch on it.

Toni slipped through a door between the car she was on and the next carriage, closing it softly behind her. Her blood thrummed as she crept to the large window overlooking the passenger car. "*Oh shenghi.*" The words were barely a whisper emerging on the breath of her exhale. The carriage beyond was full of uniformed men and women. They sat strapped to their chairs or milled about the carriage, talking quietly to one another. She did a quick headcount. "Too many." She backed away slowly.

Zach: What?

With one last glance through the window, she darted back along the train corridor.

Zach: What?

"Too many," she said. She had to get off this train.

Zach: What is too many, Boss? Too many guns? Did you see the guns?

There were at least a hundred soldiers sitting in that car. If the train had three more passenger cars and they were all full, then that was four hundred soldiers on this one train alone.

If each of the three trains carried the same numbers …

"They are starting a war." It didn't make sense. Telber was a relatively peaceful planet. Why stage a coup here? Messages kept popping up on her display.

Zach: What?
Mate: What?

Toni didn't have time to explain. She ran for the end of the train. "Mate, I need a distraction."

Within seconds of her order, a loud rumble filled the air. The entire train carriage jolted at the sound of the first explosion. Windows rattled within their rubber seals, and the whole carriage vibrated ominously. There was a moment of silence, then came the thundering sound of feet running in the direction of the explosion. Toni could smell smoke.

When the sound faded, Toni ran.

Reaching the end of the train without issue, she tugged open the rear access door. Gray smoke surrounded the front of the train. She slipped off the rear carriage and over the damaged repulsor still waiting for its patch. Her heart thudded as she searched the area for anyone looking in her direction. She had to be careful now. Anyone catching sight of her would wonder why a guard was headed away from the explosion instead of moving toward it.

"What did you do?" she asked.

Mate: Do you really want to know?

"Nope. Meet me at the café on the corner, near the supermarket."

Mate: Yes, Boss.

Toni kept her walk brisk and her head straight, reaching the wall unseen. She made her way quickly down the stairs, hoping to be mistaken for a guard on a mission. Her luck held until she hit the last door.

A fresh-faced young man in the same uniform as the one she'd stolen stopped her at the gate. "Madam, did you hear the train rail popped a holding bolt and exploded?"

"What? Kheghing hell," she replied. "Look, I'm sorry, kid. I really need to get through."

"But, Miss, they said to hold the doors."

"Of course they did, but my orders were given to me before whatever happened out there happened." She stood ramrod straight and glared at the young man. He looked uncertain. She could use that. Moving into his personal space, she growled directly into his face, "Now, soldier."

"Orders, Miss?"

"Are from Him. Are you stopping me on His order?" *There was always a Him people were scared of.*

"No, no, Miss." The young guard shuffled back and held the door open for her.

She nodded sharply. "Thank you."

*

Mate tilted his head. "What do you mean?"

"I mean there were over four hundred soldiers on that train." Toni slumped further down on her little metal chair. The shadow of the café's outside wall chilled the air around their corner table. With great pleasure, Toni had stripped out of the guard's uniform, leaving her in her decidedly wrinkled shirt and trousers. The hot manna juice she'd ordered was doing nothing to calm her nerves.

"Soldiers?"

"Uniformed."

"Local army?" Mate sat close to her leg. He rested his head against her knee so they could talk quietly.

She scratched his ear and stared blankly at the digital reader she held to maintain her cover as a woman enjoying leisure time. Zach, still active on her glasses display, grumbled nonsensical text bubbles, but had yet to add anything of value to their discussion, so she ignored him. She glanced up into the overcast magenta-colored sky. It was going to rain. She could smell it in the air.

"The big boss said to destroy all the shipments we find," Mate reminded her.

"Not a chance. There were too many. Did I mention they were an *army*?"

At last, Zach cut into their chatter.

> Zach: I've broken into the freighter company's communication server. There's a conference center in Ganick City booked for a company's retreat. It's described as military boot camp exercises. That's where they're going to strike from.

"Company training?" Toni's mouth dropped open. She hurriedly took a sip from her mug to cover her lapse, staring blankly into the distance. Chatter from the café's patrons formed a wall of noise around them. Training exercises? *They think that's going to work?* She considered the paperwork required to get that many people into a city as large as Ganick. It explained why they were in uniform. She figured training was as good an excuse as any. Problem was, she couldn't deal with those sorts of numbers alone. Handling this would require a full scale STCT deployment. She needed to contact Zaambuka. If this was happening in each of the locations they'd identified, a uniformed response was required to combat it. A war, either way. What a mess. How had things reached this stage already? The waitress dropped a tray with several mugs on it. The clatter drove Toni's head up. Her heart thudded loudly at the sudden sound.

"So we are not going to try?"

"What?" She looked down at the C-bot.

"We were ordered to destroy the shipments. We have just found a big shipment."

"One that's going to be split over half the kheghing planet after it reaches Ganick City. Do you have a plan for that?" she asked.

Zach: Um, actually, Boss. I do.

Toni made eye contact with Mate. "Shenghi," she whispered.

*

The explosions were glorious, though Toni and Mate didn't get to see them.

Zach's plan, as he described it, was not all that complicated—for the Computer Intelligence Interface at any rate. First, he hacked the train network. This took some doing, as the security levels on the coordination servers were quite stringent. When he gained access, he initiated a series of emergency drills to remove any "live eyes" watching the system. This evacuated three city control centers and removed any on-site monitoring of the real-time data.

He also needed to remove any technical support; that was a simple matter of slipping the Deathknell Trojan in through their firewall and setting it to flood the network with self-replicating viruses.

He didn't tell Toni where he got the viruses and she didn't ask.

With the IT teams busy trying to isolate and flush the various systems, Zach spoofed the live data on the three freight lines. In all the technical chaos, he only made a few minor tweaks.

It was at this point that the important work began.

The changes wouldn't raise any alerts and, with luck, as he explained it to Toni, when the kheghing thing went haywire, the viruses would be blamed for the incorrect track signals.

Zach told her he altered the running instructions for the three trains. He flipped a few intersect points to red when they should have been green, and reversed the green ones back to red. Then he wiped his intrusion from the network. In fifty-eight minutes and twelve seconds, he was out and reporting his success.

> Zach: Line M, Line Y, and Line E left the Mountain Sevger station at twenty-five past the standard. At the junction where Line M should have deviated right, oh dear, look at that, it switched to the left track. That won't end well. The faster moving Line Y's change looks to have gone unnoticed as well. What awfully unobservant train masters they have working today. And here we are, slow little Line E, moving at a bit of a limp, it seems, has finally crossed the track where it should have turned left. Dear, oh dear.

"Zach, really?" Toni grumbled.

> Zach: Wait for it …

The CII sounded almost gleeful—if a CII could feel glee. "Zach."

> Zach: All three trains have collided, and, oh …

"What, Zach?" Toni demanded.

"Zach?" Mate questioned.

> Zach: It appears your experiment with exploding the mag-rifles on Uxt was not so much an experiment as it was the way these weapons usually react to fire.

"Big boom?" Toni asked, her voice low.

> Zach: Yes.

An army couldn't fight without weapons. Zach had neutralized one battleground, but the fight was far from over.

CHAPTER TWENTY-THREE

"Are we close to the Hideaway?" Toni asked. She rocked back in her seat, unable to sit still. Her skin still itched from the mission on Telber. She scratched her arm, avoiding the red marks that indicated how long she'd been uncomfortable.

Zach popped up on the screen at her elbow and shot her a quizzical look. "Ah, Boss?"

"I know I'm not meant to know about it. I'm not asking where it is. I'm asking are we close?"

She glared at the two tablets on the table. Having spent several fruitless hours trying to decipher the data, she was close to throwing the damned things. It was all coded. She'd been able to decipher eleven of the seventeen locations but had no idea about the rest. One word she did translate was *Quarter*. A word she knew from her own secret communications with Jas. It was used to describe the Cross.

Her first thought was to call Colten to help break the rest of the code. She had a nasty argument with Zach over it. When she finally convinced him to place the call, she bit her lip, praying he wouldn't answer. He didn't. She didn't leave a message.

The only option now was to contact her best friend.

From early in their relationship, they'd established an unbreakable rule that Toni would never use Jas's job against her.

That promise was about to be broken.

Jas, because her location was a closely guarded secret, never received calls, only placed them. Usually, Toni would have Zach send out an alert and Jas would call her back. Toni had never attempted to discover Jasmine's hidden base. Until now.

Given the importance of these shipments and the possibility of galaxy-wide acts of terrorism, she was willing to break that rule. Zach had his doubts.

"I can send a signal. Ask her to call."

"Are we close?"

"Boss, I can't—"

"Who are you loyal to, Zach?" Mate demanded from the floor.

"It's not that." The CII glared at them both. "I made a promise."

Toni debated altering Zach's programming to force him to tell her the coordinates. It was only a brief thought, gone quicker than she could blink. It would be tantamount to betrayal, a version of mind control. She'd never do that to him. "Okay, send the message."

Zach looked relieved. In moments, it was done.

"Call coming in," he announced.

So they *were* close. "Connect it."

The CII's face disappeared, only to pop up on a smaller screen behind Toni. Jas appeared and demanded, "Is the game back on?"

Toni grinned. Jas had a one-track mind. "No, actually I'm calling because I need your help." She explained about the Resonators, the shipments and the train full of soldiers. Then she told her friend about the green tablet.

"You think he hired smugglers?" Jas's ears flicked back and her hand fidgeted where it rested on the desktop. Toni recognized the tell. She'd seen it before. The other woman was worried about something, or someone.

"I know Stiev contacted you, Jas. I recognized the Cross codeword."

"Are you asking if I'm helping to start a war?" Jas's wide-eyed stare contained a hint of hurt. Her ears lay back against her head.

Toni was quick to reassure her. "Xendia, no. I just want your help to break the rest of the code. The trigger point is in less than five days."

Her friend didn't move. Toni narrowed her eyes.

"I swear it, Jas."

The screen went black. Toni spun around in her seat. "What happened, Zach? Did we lose the connection?"

"She cut us off."

"What will we do now?" Mate rose up onto all fours. He shuffled closer and pressed his body against Toni's leg. Absently, she ran her hand over his furry head.

"Call Zaambuka. If he can prepare the teams, they can be on-site as soon as an attack is launched."

"We cannot afford to wait for the attacks to happen, Boss. People will die."

Toni's stomach turned cartwheels. "We have eleven of the locations and we shut down Telber, but—"

"Call coming in," Zach announced.

"Put it up."

Jas reappeared. "Okay, I've thought about it. Zach?" The display split in two as Zach joined the call. "Bring the *Blackflame* here."

"Are you sure, Jas?" While she was excited to finally see her friend's secret base, she didn't want Jas to second-guess or regret her decision later.

"Yup. I need to see the tablet. The actual tablet. There will be more in it than you can read. Zach?"

"The course has been plotted. I will ensure the Boss does not see the coordinates."

"Oh, Zach," Toni grumbled to the sound of Jas laughing in the background.

*

Zach commandeered the *Blackflame*'s controls and kept every internal screen black during the descent. Severe turbulence was one thing, not being able to see the landing was another. Toni peeled her fingers from her seat arms and shot the CII a nasty look when they touched down.

He ignored it.

Her body quivered, a reaction to the loss of control. She sucked in a deep breath and stood on wobbly legs.

Stepping from the *Blackflame* with Mate at her heels, she stared around in wonder. "Where in Xendia's name are we?"

Mate shook his head. She couldn't spy the source of the dim light. Pulling off her shades, she examined the rough-cut rock walls enclosing them on all sides, and ... *Are they stalactites?* The rocky spikes looked sharp. It was like the best kind of magic trick. But there was no smell of water or damp dirt. No echo either. *A façade?*

Jas waited at the base of the *Blackflame*'s ramp. Her caramel skin shone where it was exposed by a pink flowered dress flowing over her body. "Surprise!"

"You can say that again. Here." Toni handed her friend the problematic tablet. Toni wasn't the sort to hug, but it was good to see her friend again. It had been too long.

Jas scanned through it. "Yeah, here it is, just as I suspected. Come on."

The two agents followed the smuggler down a short corridor into a room covered in screens. "Wow," Toni mumbled.

"It's something, right?"

"It's something." Had Jas seduced Zach to her side by promising him retirement in her systems? The room was a terminal geek's nirvana. The buzz and vibration from the spinning discs and flashing lights was mesmerizing. Giant servers filled every available floor space and massive air conditioning vents poked out of the ceiling like rodent holes. Toni only wished she'd brought her jacket. Her nose began to drip from the cold as soon as they stepped inside. She tugged her sleeves down over her hands. Jas had to have installed a ship CII—who else would be able to keep track of all the data?

When she asked, the other woman smiled. "It's a secret," was all she said. Her ears were pricked up. It only made Toni more curious.

"Stay here. I'll be back shortly." Jas took the tablet and disappeared, leaving Toni and Mate to wander the room. Minutes later, the woman returned with the tablet and a small slip of paper. On it were six names.

"You're not going to tell me how you did that, are you?"

"Nope."

"Secrets?"

"Something like that. Listen, do me a favor? Go to Kyth-tact first."

Toni stared at the names in her hand. "It's not the closest planet. Why Kyth-tact?"

Jas shook her head. Her ponytail flicked back and forth like a whip. "I can't tell you why. But I'd really like you to go to Kyth-tact first."

Toni had a choice. Take her friend at her word—she'd never lied as far as Toni knew—or not, and risk losing the valued friendship. Something had Jas worried. "All right."

At Toni's agreement, the tension dropped away from Jas's body. Her ears twitched. Yes, she was definitely worried about someone. All of the blacked-out screens burst to life, scaring the bejeezus out of Toni. The servers lit up like celebration fireworks had gone off and the noise in the room became almost unbearable. A digital face appeared and bared his teeth.

"Cos, no," Jas snapped.

"Emergency call."

Jas pushed Toni toward the doorway. Many of the screens filled with static and then cleared. The whine and pops of laser fire came through clearly, bursting through the speakers at a high enough volume the place vibrated. A male voice screamed. Toni's heart leaped into her throat at the horrendous sound. Eyes wide, Jas raced back to the central chair and grabbed her headset. She shouted into the attached microphone. "Charls? Charls??"

A face appeared. It was a young man streaked with blood, the whites of his eyes shining, pinpoint pupils darting in every direction. His breathing was short, his voice high-pitched and tense. "We're under attack."

"Get to safety," Jas ordered. Clipping the headset over her ears, her hands flew over the panels, typing quickly. A number of screens dissolved into streams of digital coding. It looked like Jas was running a trace.

"We can't," he shouted. "The whole world is under attack. There's no way off."

Toni and Mate stayed out of view, but listened as the young man began to shout a long list of names. Jas switched on her headset and the speakers shut off so abruptly Toni was stunned at the sudden silence left behind. Her chest felt unbearably tight. *What the khegh?* Moments later the screens dissolved into static.

"Cos, get him back." Jas threw the headset off. Her ears rested flat against her skull.

"Negative."

"What—"

"No signal."

Jas turned horrified eyes on Toni. All the agent could do was shake her head and ask in a soft voice, "Where was he calling from?" She kept the quiver from her voice, barely. *How many people were on that planet?*

"Could be any one of three planets. All border worlds."

"He didn't tell you? What was that list he gave you?"

"I can't—"

"Say," Toni finished for her, frustrated. "Jas, I'm just trying to help." *You need it. Tell me!*

"You can help by going to Kyth-tact."

Toni could recognize a lost cause for what it was. Reluctantly, she nodded.

Jas gave Toni a quick hug. It startled her enough that she didn't move to return it. Jas backed off. "Be careful out there, huh?"

The agents returned to the *Blackflame* in a solemn silence. Toni held the last of the locations in her hand. She had to get them to Zaambuka, but it felt wrong to just leave after what they'd witnessed. She clenched her fists.

Zach told her they would be unable to make any calls until they were clear of the Hideaway. The take-off was as harrowing as the landing. Toni clenched her eyes shut and held on tightly, but couldn't get that young man's face, or that scream, out of her mind.

Back in space, Zach jumped from one screen to another, almost as if he'd had too many stimulants. He didn't seem to notice Toni and Mate's silence.

"Boss," Mate said. "We cannot just act as though we did not see that."

"I know," she said, staring into the distance. "But what can we do? If she won't give us the—"

"Quick question. Did you meet him?" Zach interrupted, bouncing into her line of sight.

"What? Who?" All Toni could hear were the sounds of explosions and that hideous scream. She bit her bottom lip, crossing her arms tight over her chest.

"Cos. Did you meet him? Isn't he ah-maz-ing!"

Toni glanced down at Mate. He looked up at her and cocked his head. "Cos?"

"*Did you see him?*"

"Oh, Jas's CII?" Toni felt the hint of a smile dance at her lips and fought showing it.

"Yesss!" Zach's digital eyes looked soft and wistful.

"I'm not—"

"Oh, come on."

"Yes, Zach," Mate cut in, letting the CII off the hook. "We saw him, but we were not formally introduced.

Zach giggled for a moment and then became serious. "You can call the big boss now, Boss."

"Dial it, and punch in a course for Kyth-tact."

*

After a short silence, Zaambuka's response was swift. He ordered Toni to proceed to Melbar Prime.

"I'm already headed to Kyth-tact."

"Kyth-tact?" he clarified. His eyes narrowed. It was the only part of him that moved.

"Yes."

"Melbar Prime is closer."

"Yes, it is."

"Explain?"

Toni tapped on the console, staring down at her fingers to avoid his stare. "My informant. I can't tell you any more than that." She flicked up her eyes. *Oh, khegh it. He's going to reach through the screen and throttle me.* Zaambuka actually turned purple. To distract him, Toni reported the planetary attack they'd witnessed. She heard Zach's quiet gasp in the background.

Zaambuka was silent for a long time. "And you don't know where he was calling from?"

"Only that it was a border planet."

"I'll look into it. Do you believe it is connected?"

"A border planet attack just as a political summit is to vote on an alliance between Sectors? It would have to be a massive coincidence."

"Without knowing where—"

"I know, Sir. Is there any way to increase Sector patrols?"

"I can reinforce the Defender teams at the Sector One/Two border, but without knowing the exact location of the incursion, that leaves a lot of space to cover."

Toni groaned. "Yeah, it does." She picked at her nails.

"We need more information."

She looked up. "I shouldn't have even seen—"

"Is there anything else you can tell me?"

Toni sighed and shook her head. "Nothing official. It could have been anywhere. The call was definitely made via a planet line, but the view was limited. There was smoke everywhere." She heard that scream again. But she'd heard something else as well. "I could make out the sound of ship-based weaponry, but saw no confirmation. Mate recorded the partial list of names the kid was screaming, but we have no idea what they refer to. Could be people, or coded locations, even ships. Really, it could be anything."

"Contact me as soon as you reach Kyth-tact."

"Yes, Sir."

CHAPTER TWENTY-FOUR

The *Blackflame* flew into Kyth-tact's orbit a day later.

From above, the planet looked like a dry ball of leather. Cracked and scorched, with crumbling mountains and numerous desert regions, each more dehydrated than the next. Toni had no idea what she was looking for. Jas had given her nothing to go on, but as the planet was one of those listed to receive shipments of Resonators, maybe it was a staging area. Perhaps a central point for delivery where the crates were then transferred to another ship, bound for ... *where?* That was the question.

"If the shipments have been redistributed, how will we discover where they went?" Mate asked as they circled the Northern Hemisphere. Toni flew a wide orbit of the planet, observing all of the ships that had arrived and departed over the last few hours. It was the only area of Kyth-tact to see any movement. She figured this indicated the location of the docking port, but there was no beacon or signal received when they broke through the lower atmosphere, so she couldn't be sure.

"Do we go down?" Zach asked.

She eyeballed the CII's screen. "Might as well. We're not going to learn anything further from up here."

"We should be cautious, Boss. There is no beacon or transponder on the entire planet. Given the lack of governmental oversight, this could be a trap," Mate said from her knee.

That was a fair point. This far out from the Sector core, there was really no way to enforce APE regulations, especially when a planet was not officially settled. A person could get away with anything provided they didn't draw attention to themselves and avoided STCT or agent flybys. It was a hole in the system the current President had opened with his cutbacks. It would take something catastrophic for that to change back. Perhaps it was why Ramo was being targeted.

"What did Jas say about avoiding that mountain ridge again?"

"Only to avoid the left side."

"Well, what does that mean?" Zach asked. "Which mountain ridge?" The CII disappeared off the screen, replaced by a map of the region they were flying over. There were mountains everywhere.

"Presumably that one," Toni said, pointing to the long canyon between the two mountain ranges. It dead ended where the mountains joined together. The only way to fly into the docking port was along that corridor. The terrain was too steep to come at the docking port from above, except if you flew straight down. If you tried that, there would be no way to stop before you hit the ground, unless you crawled down at a speed barely above the pull of gravity. Going that slow would give any land-based weaponry easy target practice.

"Well, doesn't that look cozy?" Zach said.

Toni wasn't overly impressed either. She rubbed at the spot of her throbbing shoulder. There was no way to go down without making the *Blackflame* a target. Unless ... "Zach, how long would it take to hack our own registry details and create a fake ship identity?"

"Not as long as you would think," he told her with a digital grin.

"Can you link up to Cos? Have him confirm a Cross identity for the *Blackflame*?"

"Absolutely, Boss."

"This is not a good idea." Mate warned.

"It's the only option we have," she told him. Several minutes later the '352 Jackdes Hegnforth lightship model sixteen, newly designated the *Tear of Fire*, began its descent into the docking port.

"That's a lot of guns," Zach commented as they flew along the mountain corridor.

"Yeah." The number of guns Zach's scanners picked out of the camouflage made Toni's right eye twitch. *This really is not a good idea.* She'd have to keep her wits about her on the ground. This level of security could only mean one thing—illegal activity was going on here. A lot of it.

Toni ceded flight control to Zach while she applied a heavy coat of toned foundation. She pulled out her trusty brunette wig and contacts, and became Seli Mendel, a sly and dangerous smuggler.

Then she faced the hardest task of all—convincing Mate to stay behind.

"We can't attract too much attention. I'll have my shades, and you and Zach can follow everything from here. We have to be sensible about this."

"I am not comfortable with you going out there alone," Mate stressed.

She wasn't either. Her skin already itched from the makeup, and she couldn't wait to rip the damned wig off. She felt sick to her stomach, but was determined to go in alone. "That's the deal, Mate. You're only going to put me in more danger if you come with me. It's bad enough that we don't have time to repaint the *Blackflame*. But a '352 Jackdes Hegnforth lightship model sixteen flown in by a woman and a canine robot? I'm not famous Mate, but agent rumors get around criminal types. It'll trigger suspicion. Enough that they might see through the make-up to who I really am. I can't take the risk."

"I don't like it either, Mate, but if she needs you, you can get out to her pretty fast. It's not a large area. And as a smuggler, at least it won't be suspicious if she goes in armed to the teeth, right?" Zach said.

"Right," Toni agreed. The weaponry currently hidden all over her body was not only extremely uncomfortable, but also kheghing heavy.

"Jas should have told you what we are here to look for."

"Well, clearly the Resonators, so let's start with that."

"Boss, I am receiving a message from the master-house. The dock master is advising we should make our way to the open land in the center of the port. I need you at the controls," Zach told her.

The CII had flown the re-designated *Blackflame* as close to the right-hand mountain ridge as he could, but as they approached the docking port, the mountains closed in quickly, creating a number of physical hazards. Toni dropped the *Tear of Fire's* speed further and carefully weaved her ship under a massive rock archway formed at the end of the corridor.

They shot out into the dead-ended canyon. Toni pointed the *Tear of Fire* toward the open space marked with a black cross as directed and let the ship jolt down hard onto its landing struts. "Zach, while I'm out there, see what you can access? I want to know what's really going on here."

Resting her hand on the butt of her holstered weapon, she strode casually down the ramp, whistling loudly and off-key. In deference to the blasting sun she wore a large, battered hat over the brunette wig and had pulled on her long-sleeved jacket. It was kheghing hot outside. As soon as she stepped from the *Tear of Fire's* air-conditioned goodness, she broke into a sweat. She couldn't stay out here long or her make-up would melt.

"Hey, love. What're you doing here?"

Toni spun at the voice of the woman who stepped from beneath the *Tear of Fire's* landing struts. *How did she get under there?*

"Well, hey there," Toni drawled, in her best Ralish accent. Way back in her younger years, Toni, along with her brother and sisters, had been forced to sit through many of their mother's language and elocution lessons. Toni's mother was a second-class holo-actor whose fame was in steady decline. Fortunately, Trina Delle's acting lessons had come in handy over Toni's career. The ability to alter her accent was not quite as much fun as Zach playing with his voice controls, but it did help her sink into her assumed character.

The woman was shorter than Toni, blonde and overweight. She rocked from side to side as she ambled forward. Toni couldn't see any obvious weaponry on the woman, but assumed she was armed. Toni's skin crawled with the feeling of being watched. She fought to keep her breathing steady and not to peer back over her shoulder.

"Can I help ya, love?"

"Yeah, hey listen. I was told I could, ah, pick something up from here."

"Really? Who told ya that? There ain't nothin' on this rock worth pickin' up. Look around you, kid. This place ain't nothin' more than a dump."

"Well, a friend of mine sent me here." *That much was true.* "And I was told this was where to go, if you know what I'm saying?" Toni couldn't tell if the other woman was buying her act but she really needed to get inside before her disguise started to drip down her face.

"Ya name, hun?"

"I'm sure that doesn't matter, does it?" As soon as the words were out of her mouth, she felt the tension in the air grow thicker.

The woman didn't move but Toni sensed movement out of her periphery. She glanced over her shoulder at the old man who appeared in her shadow. He was tall and skeleton thin with a pointy chin and little eyes.

"Mic, we expectin' anyone?" the woman asked.

Mic scratched at the side of his balding head with something metallic and answered with a simple drawn out, "Nope."

The woman gestured to Toni. "Looks like we ain't expectin' ya, hun."

Toni shuffled sideways and threw another glance over her shoulder. She was close enough to the *Tear of Fire* that Zach could drop the railgun into place, should she give the signal, and she was seconds away from giving it. "That's weird. Stiev said to come straight through. Tight deadline and all, what with the rush on, ah, ranic fruit." *This had better work.*

The woman tilted her head. "Ranic fruit, ya say?"

"Yeah, odd, right? But whatever." Toni kept her shoulders low and her stance open. Her fingers itched with the desire to draw her weapon.

"Mic?"

"Yup."

"Take the girl out back." The dark gaze of the woman lightened suddenly and she relaxed, making Toni aware of just how tightly the woman had been holding herself before.

"Sure?"

"Mic, ya stupid shenghi-loving Naftet, get moving. The girl ain't got all day." The woman glared at the old man over Toni's shoulder. "Now, you fool!" Turning back to Toni, she said, "It's all right, love. We have to be careful around here, you know what I'm saying?"

"Oh yeah, hey listen …" Toni took a few steps forward, partly to get away from Mic—she didn't like the unknown man so close to her back—and partly to draw the woman into her confidence. "I know there's stuff going on, and I'm not going to ask about it. Now that Kel's gone, I don't want to know, you know? I've got a job to do."

"Don't we all, love? You got a name?"

"Seli Mendel."

"Well, call me Debi."

"Nice to meet you, Debi." Toni slumped her shoulders and shifted until she could eyeball the old man behind her and keep the woman in her sight at the same time. "And you too, Mic."

The old man looked close to wilting. He pointed to a small building. "Over there."

"Chatty fellow, aren't you?" Toni said, throwing a wink his way.

Mic flushed red.

A text bubble popped up on her shades display.

Zach: Careful, Boss. That takes you out of our line
of sight, I don't like it and Mate's having a fit.

Toni tapped the frame of her shades as acknowledgment. Before she followed Mic, she tried to strike up another conversation with Debi. It would be better if she could keep both of them in view. "Khegh it! It is hotter than a fire-pit out here. How do you stand it?"

"Awful, ain't it? But ya get used to it. Mic, take Mendel out back. There's enough cool air there that a delicate thing like you should be able to breathe a little easier."

"Well, thank you kindly, but please tell me you're not staying out here in this heat?"

"I'll be fine, girl. Ya get used to it. Mic, get ya lazy ass moving."

Toni mumbled to Zach to keep an eye on Debi.

"What?"

The old man was watching her with a strange expression. "Oh, I was just grumbling about the heat," she told him, flapping her jacket dramatically. "Seriously, how do you live out here?"

"Don't." Mic pointed to the building they were walking toward. "Live in there." The master-house looked no bigger than a small shed and was full of holes. Toni couldn't see how it could possibly be better inside, so she was doubly surprised to see a large, black door dug into the wall at the back of the shed. The blast of cold air that was released when Mic remotely opened the door sent a welcome shiver over Toni's body.

"Oh, thank gods. I was beginning to think this place was just a little backwater, but here we have signs of civilization at last," she said to alert her worried partners. "Secret passage way into the mountain, huh?"

"Yup." Mic grinned, exposing blackened and rotten teeth. "Crates are through there. Not many left."

Hmm. She had a choice now, step into the mysterious secret lair or stay out here in the overpowering heat. She knew what her body wanted to do. She also knew what her partners would say. The two desires didn't match.

"After you, sweetie," Toni said and tapped on her glasses as soon as Mic turned his head. She was okay—for now.

"You got a mag-lift, or a trolley?" she asked, following the sweating man through the large door. As soon as she crossed the threshold, her glasses buzzed and jolted on her nose. *Shenghi.* That's what she'd been afraid of. The doors acted as a signal blocker. *Khegh it.* She let out a soft sigh when the doors didn't automatically close behind her and seal her inside. Her gaze darted over hundreds of barrels. Each stamped with the circular ident and logos for water. *Water?* Toni inhaled the beautiful scent of mountains and rain. *So many barrels?* In the corner she spied a tank. It was a stockpile! She closed her mouth with a snap. This had to be what Jas wanted her to see. Where were they going? Someone was making a khegh load of coin. In a different corner, she spied three familiar-looking crates. *Only three?*

"Truck's back there," Mic grunted.

Toni followed the old man behind the barrels and walked straight into his sawn-off blaster.

"You ain't no smuggler," he said. "Your skin's runnin'."

Toni looked down at her hand where she'd wiped it against her thigh. Yup, the toner streaked with the sweat coating her fingers. Translucent skin gleamed around her wrist. *Khegh it!* She raised her hands. Her heart thundered as her breathing spiked. She was alone in here with this man. He was old. She could take him out before he shot her. The gun didn't waver. *Probably.*

She swallowed around a dry mouth.

"When Debi gets in here, she ain't gonna be happy with you. And she ain't gonna take that bad mood out on me. No more, you hear? No more." He glanced over his shoulder fearfully.

Wait, what?

"Cover it! Naftet hurry!"

Watching the nervous man twitch, Toni rubbed at the toner, smoothing it into place over her exposed skin. Mic grabbed a rag poking out of his back pocket and threw it at her, gesturing for her to wipe her fingers. It was an awkward move because he didn't remove the weapon pointed at her. When he deemed her covered, he gestured toward the truck. "Get going."

It was hard to breath. "You're still letting me take the crates?"

"Get going," he said again.

Toni raced to the truck. She had no idea what was going on, but knew when to cut and run. She clambered into the driver's seat, and Mic appeared at her side. "No names, kid. But we got a mutual friend. Tell Darning's family that he's dead."

She closed her eyes. *Oh shenghi.* Mic was Agent Darning's contact, and he'd now confirmed Zaambuka's worst fear. Darning had been murdered. "How did you—"

"Kid," he grunted and pointed to her hand, the betrayal of her own skin. "Be quick. I ain't wanting no trouble with Debi. She can't find out who you are."

Nodding, Toni started the truck's repulsor engine. Emitting a roar, the rear of the truck rose several feet off the ground. It didn't take long for Mic to load the crates.

He activated a remote and the side wall of the warehouse opened onto the port's landing strip. Toni threw the truck into gear and buzzed the engines lightly. As the doors opened fully, her glasses activated with several vibrations.

Text messages burst onto her shades display.

Zach: Where have you been?
Mate: Are you well?

"Fine," she told her partners. "Coming out now." Toni turned to Mic. Speaking quickly she asked, "Do you have any records? Where did the rest of the crates go? And what about those barrels of water? Who are they for?"

Mic thrust a piece of greasy paper onto her lap. "Get outta here."

She revved the truck again and inched the big vehicle out the warehouse. The *Tear of Fire* waited in the distance. Debi stood outside the closed ramp.

Zach: She tried to get in, Boss. I think she was going to use an explosive next. Oh, and Boss. They've got insane encryption here. I've only just broken into their logs.

"And?"

Zach: Just an old Sunchaser berthed there. I am working on the designation but it looks like they've been wiped by a professional.

"Keep trying, Zach." So they were also flipping ships here. Quite the operation.

Zach: Boss!

"What?"

Zach: There's a Stargazer here. It looks like the *Renegade.*

Colten? Toni scowled. One step ahead of her, as usual. She peered over her shoulder. "I wonder where he is?"

She drew the truck to a halt right in front of Debi.

"Mic. Kid." Debi glared at the old man over Toni's shoulder.

"Ma'am." A glance at her wrists ensured they were still covered, but Toni knew she had to get out of the sun. She held up a hand. "Ah, I'm going to need access to my ship to load these—"

"You ain't on the list," Debi said.

"What?"

"I checked." The blonde woman raised a sawn-off blaster identical to the one Mic held and pointed it straight at Toni.

Khegh it.

Zach: I can drop the guns in a micro-second, Boss.

"Hold," she muttered. If he dropped the guns, it would put her right in the line of fire. She had to settle this herself or get the woman to move first. "Checked what?" she called out.

Zach: Mate's ready to move, just give the word.

Toni remained silent. *Not yet, Mate.*

"You ain't on the list," Debi repeated, stepping forward. She charged her weapon with a sharp move of her wrist. Toni dove out of the truck as the first shot exploded where her head had been. She looked up to see Debi sink to her knees, a bleeding hole right through her chest. Toni gaped and then, realizing what had happened, glanced over her shoulder, expecting to see Colten with a smug expression on his face. Mic lowered the blaster in his hands.

"Well, khegh it! That ain't been the plan," he grumbled.

Toni rolled to her feet. "No, Mate, wait!" she shouted knowing the C-bot would be racing out to help her. Mic didn't raise his weapon again but he did look at her and shrug.

"Thank you," she told him.

"I ain't here, Agent. I'm back inside and I saw nothin', you got that? You did this, self-defense, all right?"

"What? Oh, yes, sure. You were not here."

"Well, go on. Get." Mic headed into the warehouse as if nothing had happened. Toni glanced at the body of the woman lying in the dirt at the base of the *Tear of Fire's* ramp. This entire morning had not gone as she'd expected. She glanced around again. No sign of Colten.

*

Zaambuka called just before they entered forcedspace out of the Trayner system. "I need you on Midock, Toni. Keep the Vice-President alive at all costs. Find and neutralize Balandez. I'll contact Ramo and let her know you're on your way, along with two additional Sentinel teams for added security."

"What about the shipments?"

"I've got them covered. New information has come to light and we have to act on it immediately. I need someone I trust to handle Midock."

"I have a new list of planets from Kyth-tact."

"What makes you think this information is . . . ?"

She held her boss's gaze as regret curled in her belly. "I have confirmation Agent Darning is dead."

"What? Did you see—"

"No sir. I encountered his contact on Kyth-tact. He gave me a list. It's a different list to some of the planets from the tablet. He told me to let Darning's family know."

"That's not proof."

"I know, Sir. But the guy just saved my life. I think he's telling the truth."

Zaambuka was silent while he absorbed this information. "And the list?"

"Zach is sending it to you now."

"Do we know what's going on out there?"

"No, Sir. They're border worlds, human settlement worlds. It may be connected to the attack Mate and I witnessed."

"Interesting. That might also tie into the information I've just received from an old friend. Very well, send the list and I'll put some agents on it. I need you on Midock."

"Yes, Boss."

"Be careful."

"Worried about me?"

"No. If Ramo dies, so does intergalactic peace."

"Well, it's nice to feel appreciated." The screen blacked out. Toni turned to Mate. "You heard the man."

Mate backed himself under the console to her left. At her order, a lead shot out of his neck and into a socket above his head. Zach appeared on the screen above him.

"I've calculated the nav for Midock," the CII announced. "But what about the *Renegade*? The smuggler must be down there somewhere. Boss, I didn't even get into the other hold. It was locked down tight as a forcedspace surfer."

For a brief moment, she thought about returning to the planet to look for him. Debi had been ready to shoot Toni. Then her shoulder began to throb, reminding her. Colten had left her behind on that moon. Had known she was hurt—after all, he'd shot her. Hadn't cared. Glaring at the soldered tear in the wall, she shook her head. "Send Jas a message. Tell her we found water barrels on Kyth-tact. Let her know one of her people is on the ground. Next stop, gentlemen," she said, "Midock."

"Boss?" Mate began. She stared down at him and said nothing. He settled down at her feet. "I hope we will not be forced to listen to any speeches. I hate political speeches."

Toni fired the *Blackflame*'s engines and they burst into forcedspace. She grinned down at the C-bot forcing Colten out of her mind.

"Maybe they'll have snacks."

CHAPTER TWENTY-FIVE

The *Blackflame*'s TAFF klaxons jolted Toni from her restless sleep. She scrubbed at her eyes and peered up at the viewscreen.

"What the …?"

"What's happening?" Mate asked, padding into the cockpit.

Zach answered both startled agents. "We've been pulled out of forcedspace."

"Only an Anti-Ticyon stream can do that," Mate stated.

"Exactly." Toni pointed. Stars appeared in their fixed positions as the *Blackflame* was dragged from its course into normal space. In front of them sat an ATS freighter.

Heart pounding with the certainty that it was already too late, she threw the control stick hard to the right and fingered the deceleration sequence. Reversing the pattern a split second later, the *Blackflame* paused, turned one hundred and eighty degrees and flew back along its own flight path. Toni quickly strengthened the rear shielding. "Shenghi!" She ignited the *Blackflame*'s forward thrusters and dove under the three battleships that appeared directly in front of her.

"They're blocking us in. Holonet communication is down. There's no way to send a signal to headquarters," Zach reported.

Damn, damn, damn! Toni dodged the *Blackflame* in and around the three large Padotel battleships. They identified themselves on her screens as *Incinerator*, *No Quarter*, and *Dayraider*.

"There is a direct hail link from lead ship, Boss," Zach announced.

"Give me a minute and then put it on." She turned the *Blackflame* again, jigging hard left and then right as the three ships closed in on either side. The ticking clock in her head was speeding up. While the *Incinerator* tailgated, the *Dayraider* and *No Quarter* boxed her between them.

Who the khegh are they? Pushing the *Blackflame* faster, Toni managed to pull slightly ahead. She couldn't jump to forcedspace as long as that ATS freighter flooded the area with Anti-Ticyons. They were stuck here for the duration of the battle. Her stomach whirled. Her skin felt cold and clammy.

"Lightship *Blackflame*. This is Captain Soogin of the Redflag seventh squad battleship, *Dayraider*. I order you to shut down your TAFF generators and prepare to be boarded." The man's plummy voice boomed from the ship's speakers.

Like hell, I will. Bile rose in her throat. Someone had sent mercenaries after her. Colten? No, that didn't make sense.

Toni cleared her throat. "This is Agent Delle of the PST. You need to back off. I am on an official mission—"

"Shut down and prepare to be bordered."

Blowing out a sharp breath she activated the mic again. "I refuse to shut down my engines and allow you to board. Khegh off." And with that, she flew the *Blackflame* straight up. The three ships shadowed her every move.

"Zach, reinforce the rear shields." Though she was a decent pilot, she could recognize a lost cause when she was inside one. *Is this it? Is this how it ends?* Laser fire rocked the *Blackflame* sharply. Without looking, she sensed Mate move into his hub under the console. Zach's calculations of the distance required to exit the Anti-Ticyon blanket scrolled down her right-hand screen. *Come on, come on.*

Mate initiated the *Blackflame*'s targeting program and fired back.

Laser fire exploded against the *Blackflame*'s rear shields in reply, rocking the ship further. Emergency lighting flashed. Toni fought to keep her little ship out of the enemy vessels' range, but loss was inevitable.

"We can't take too much more on ..." Zach broke off as enemy lasers targeted the shields again. Fire exploded against the rear stabilizers. "Shield four down to fifty percent." The *Blackflame* rocked, despite the wild maneuvers Toni made to avoid the beams around them. *One chance. We need one little chance.* Her heart thundered as the truth sunk in. She bit her lip and glanced at her companions. They were likely to survive explosive vacuum. Certainly more likely than she would. *Will they miss me?*

"Shields at twenty percent. Next shot'll take 'em out."

"Zach?"

"We have another ten light years before we can jump."

"Won't make it." Sucking in a deep breath, Toni ordered the CII to transfer all unneeded power to the front shields, including the power from their rear protection.

"This is not going to end well," Mate growled.

"Mate, as soon as we're in range, lock onto the *Dayraider* and fire all guns, three second bursts, two seconds apart. Aim the TAMM torps, but don't fire until my mark." She gripped the stick with a trembling hand.

"Yes, Boss."

She threw the *Blackflame* into a wide arc, inverting the ship, and applied speed. Flipping the *Blackflame* over again she pointed the ship's nose straight down, stamping onto her boost accelerator. Her body moved sharply. The *Blackflame* jumped forward. Mate fired everything at the ship that fell into their firing line. The *Blackflame* spun hard to face the opposite direction, looped up and came head-to-head with the *Dayraider*.

Toni ignored the *Incinerator* and *No Quarter*'s presence over them and lowered the *Blackflame*'s nose to skim the *Dayraider*'s hull. The *thump thump thump* of her pulse beat a rapid yet steady rhythm in her ears. She focused on the sound, letting the blaring alarms fade away.

Laser fire blossomed off her front shields. The *Blackflame* hugged the undercarriage of the larger ship. Emerging from beneath, Toni pulled back on the forward thrusters and spun the *Blackflame* into the *Dayraider*'s rear. When the torpedo tubes were angled at her attacker, she cried, "Now!"

"Firing one, two, three and four."

In battle, Toni envied her robotic friend's calm.

"Lasers!" she demanded as the first torpedo exploded against the *Dayraider*'s shields. The torpedoes themselves didn't do much damage, but the lasers fired immediately afterward penetrated the shield as it wobbled. The Redflag officers attempted to stabilize the shields, but Toni's laser fire had hit the rear shield generator.

Internal gravity support and the rear torpedo launcher, both located close to the *Dayraider*'s shield generator, exploded along with it, blowing a hole the size of the *Blackflame* in the battleship's hull. Pressure ripped the *Dayraider* wide open.

Toni's mouth dropped open as the damaged ship exploded.

The *Blackflame*, too close to the dying ship, was thrown back as the shockwave rippled outward. The *Incinerator* was caught in the *Dayraider*'s death throes. Heavier than the *Blackflame*, it was unable to maneuver away in time. The *Incinerator*'s shields buckled under the intense bombardment of the metal and plasteel bulkheads that once made up the Redflag's lead ship. Toni gasped as the *Incinerator* emulated the *Dayraider*'s fate and also exploded.

Her body was a tense spring poised for sudden release. *Icy.* "Good shot, Mate!"

"Yeah, nice one, Mate," Zach echoed.

The C-bot looked up at them both. "I planned that, of course."

Toni's laughter sounded a little hysterical. *We might actually get out of this.* "We've still got one to go." She pulled the *Blackflame* around in a wide loop and lined it up with the *No Quarter*.

Her ears rang with the alarms as the *Blackflame* stopped dead in space. Vibrations in her feet increased as she revved the generators well past their safeties. Flutterwings in her stomach invited friends. Goosepimples broke out across her neck.

"Two more ships have emerged from forcedspace," Mate confirmed. "The lead ship has captured us in a holding beam."

All breath exploded from her body.

"It's a class nine battleship, Boss. There ain't no way we're gonna break free from it," Zach warned.

"Well, we have to try." She reached for the thruster controls. Before she could act, the *Blackflame* bucked and every cockpit panel sparked and shrieked. Zach disappeared from the screen. When he came back, he was smeared over it, as if someone had rolled his face with a crop-crusher.

Mate dropped to the floor, sparking and jerking wildly. His operational lights flickered and then died.

Toni's heart froze. *No!* She slammed her hands against the lifeless panel. "Damn it, they have a plasma cannon!" All she could do was watch her ship draw steadily closer to the battleship. With her instruments damaged, they were utterly helpless. She glanced down at the still form of her partner. Memories of the last time she lost her friends hit her. *I can't do this without them.* Tears prickled. She sniffed and blinked back the haze. Mate and Zach should be okay. Plasma charges wore off after a while. They'd probably need some level of repair, and she hoped whoever found them would treat them with care.

She set the *Blackflame*'s internal security system and quickly added a few additional layers to protect Zach's profile. Her attackers might take her, but they would not take her friends without losing someone in the attempt.

Minutes ticked by. Toni turned her attention to her partner. If she could bypass some of his protocols and cut down on essentials, like his verbal programs, she might be able to reactivate him.

She felt the moment the *Blackflame* was sucked into the battleship's docking bay. Her skin tingled as the vibrations stopped. Reconnecting the last switch, her partner's eyes flickered and focused on her face. Mate opened his mouth but no sound emerged.

Her voice wobbled. "Sorry, pal, it was the only way to get you reactivated in time. Listen, we were shot with a plasma cannon. The *Blackflame*'s inoperative and we've been dragged into the battleship's dock. I'll do what I can to distract the welcoming committee—it's me they want. Activate security protocol Theta and get Zach back online. With our systems down, I can't even get off an emergency signal. We're on our own. While I'm gone, repair what you can to get the

Blackflame up and running. With any luck, I'll be back soon." Without Mate and Zach's help, that was unlikely. Knowing it was the last time she'd see him opened a chasm in her chest. "I love you, Mate."

She caressed his head and blinked back hot tears. One escaped to slide down her nose. She sniffed and reached for her pistol. If she was going down, she'd go down fighting. "It's better that you stay here," she insisted, guessing what was going through his circuits. She didn't want him to witness her death. *I won't live without him.* Sliding her shades onto her face, she realized the plasma cannon had shorted the display. *Khegh it.* Raising her pistol, she sucked in a deep breath and tripped the system to open the door.

Outside, mercenaries had gathered and were preparing to hack the door. At the sight of the lowering hatch, they ran for cover.

Triggering the lock to seal behind her, Toni gave a crazy yell and ran down the ramp firing at anyone who moved. She got in several good shots and three men fell.

Before she reached the ground, multiple stun beams converged and cut her down.

CHAPTER TWENTY-SIX

Eyelids heavy, Toni twitched at the dagger-like pain digging into her brain. *I'm still alive?* It felt as though someone had smashed a brick against the side of her head. After a moment, she gave up trying to force open her eyes and concentrated on her facial muscles instead. They were weirdly stiff and sore. Her head pounded, and her body ached as though she'd been hit by a dozen stun blasts. She assumed she had. She was also swaying. *A boat?* Something hard dug into her stomach. She could hear footsteps, slow and methodical. Each time a step sounded, her body swayed. *Oh, I'm being carried.*

She struggled to lift her body but her arms wouldn't move. By flexing her fingers, she discovered her hands were chained behind her back. Cold metal bit into her wrists, tight enough to cut the blood flow to her fingers.

Her transport didn't appear to have any trouble carrying her weight. Boots rang out on the metal floor, four at a time—*four footsteps?* The sounds echoed around whatever space they were moving through.

Her transport stopped. Toni listened as two of the feet shuffled back and forth before the sounds of buttons were punched into a touch pad somewhere to her right. She listened carefully. The different tones made a pattern; two short and low, then one long and low, followed by three short and high. The swoosh of a door told her the panel had been a door lock.

They passed through three more doors and a crowded corridor before they stopped again. Another door, heavier than the rest, groaned open. Lifted off the solid shoulder, Toni was thrown to the ground. She stifled a cry as she landed on a cold, unforgiving floor.

Through the haze, she heard a husky feminine voice. "What is this? I was promised a single. I refuse to pay full price for shared accommodations." Toni tried to place the accent but it was unfamiliar to her.

"Quiet," snapped the rougher, male voice, probably her guard.

"Oh, you're leaving? But I get so few visitors."

"Now I've brought you permanent company."

Toni opened her eyes, blinking rapidly when they watered under the harsh overhead light. With blurry vision, she glanced at the two beds bolted against the far wall and metal toilet in the corner. The voice belonged to the woman, beaten and bloodied, lying on one of the beds. Her hair hung limp and her shirt was ripped down one sleeve, exposing an intricate armband clipped around her bicep.

Toni had no more time to examine her roommate before the guard dragged her to her knees. Her heart beat frantically against a chest that only felt pain. Giant hands encircled her wrists and, with a tug, removed the chain. She was pushed back to the floor where she lay still for a moment, just breathing.

"Could you remind room service I like my eggs over easy?" the woman on the bed asked.

"Want chips with that?" the second guard grunted.

Toni rolled to look up at the large Dobers standing in the doorway. She'd worked with Dobers before. Bodies of pure muscle wrapped around sensitive organs. They carried themselves stiffly—no neck. The two guards stared at her mouthy cellmate with no hint of expression. Interrupting before her new roommate could answer, Toni offered, "If I may? I'd like fried chey and sausages on toast, sprinkled with rim salts and a glass of tilmile-pine juice." Her voice sounded croaky and died out on the last word. What she wouldn't give for a glass of water right now.

"Sure," grunted the front guard. He scratched his head, ruffling the white streak in his hair. The man beside him snarled out a laugh, exposing sharp teeth, and slammed the cell door shut. It locked loudly.

"I wouldn't recommend the service here," the woman commented after a moment of silence. Deep lines around her mouth and eyes made Toni believe the woman was older, but the way her face lit up with her laugh belied that impression. Something in the way she pronounced the 'w' sent a spark of recognition through Toni. Sector Two?

"I'll be sure to take it up with the manager." Toni pushed herself up from the floor. "What exactly will we get?"

"Something mushy, disgusting, and tasting of cardboard. Name's Berni."

"Toni." She shivered in her thin shirt, wondering curiously when her jacket had been removed. Her shades apparently hadn't made the trip to the cells with her. She stretched her legs and hobbled around the room. "How long have you been here?"

"Two days. I don't remember much, and I don't want to."

"Nice place." Toni wondered why she'd been left alive. Whatever the reason was it couldn't be good. She had to get out of here. Examining the cell closely, she noted one door, no windows, and the bright overhead light came from three large panels above her head—nothing to shatter. There were slits at the top of each wall. She presumed these led to more cells much like this one. She pressed her ear to each wall in turn and could just make out the sound of movement behind the back wall. Leaning closer she heard a pained groan. *We're not alone.*

For now, Toni turned back to her cellmate. "I hate to ask this, as you seem to have made yourself quite comfortable, but when did you last redecorate?"

Berni grinned. At least Toni assumed she did. In this light, with her sensitive eyes and at this angle, it was hard to tell. "Listen, you're wasting your time. I've already checked the place over."

"It's my time to waste."

"So it is."

A little longer spent searching for weaknesses, Toni was forced to conclude the other woman was right. There was nothing here she could exploit. She crossed her arms, wishing again for her jacket.

"So," she said, sitting down on the free bunk. It was as hard as rock. The mattress, if it could be called that, was barely thicker than her finger. "How'd you get here?"

"Long story, but as I seem to have a captive audience, I'll start from the beginning." The woman laughed loudly at Toni's exaggerated groan. Berni's posture was tense. Portraying a calm and relaxed nature didn't hide her wariness. And pain, if the bruises were any indication. *Be careful.* This woman might be on the lookout for a vulnerable cellmate. Khegh it, she could be a plant. Toni wouldn't provide her with any weakness. *Play it friendly—just not honest.*

"Okay, the short version, then. I made a mistake. Delivered some merchandise for a client, got a little nosy, and my client took exception. Seems he decided I was to be removed from any future action."

"I see."

"Jumped in my own ship, if you can believe that. I managed to lock myself in, but that wasn't as successful as I'd hoped." Berni struggled to sit up. As she did, her torn shirt fell open just above her left breast, exposing the mark on her skin.

Toni sucked in a sharp breath. *Be very careful.* "You're a Cross?"

"What's the matter? The Cross steal from ya?"

"You are a Cross?"

"So?"

Toni swore again. "So, the *merchandise* your so-called *client* hired you to *deliver* was actually smuggled goods?"

"What's your problem?"

"You don't know who I am?"

"Should I?"

"Agent Toni Delle, with the PST."

Berni straightened, an expression of surprise crossing her face. "I should have guessed. There can't be too many women who look like you in the galaxy. You're Dan's Delle, aren't you?"

"What?" Toni stared at the woman in disbelief. "Dan's Delle?" she repeated. "I was never *Dan's* Delle." Fury burned in her belly.

"Not the way he tells it, love," Berni replied with a grin.

I will kill him. Slowly. Toni was so angry that for a moment she couldn't speak. With no way to vent her fury, she slumped onto the empty bed and threw a hand over her eyes. If this woman knew Colten that intimately—enough to discuss Toni in such detail—then Berni definitely couldn't be trusted.

"Sooo." The smuggler stretched the word out to fill the charged silence. "You're an agent? In that case, I might as well tell you that the *merchandise* I delivered was a shipment of weapons. Some sort of anti-government thing."

"How do you know that?"

"I might have snooped."

"Really?" Toni didn't even try to keep the sarcasm out of her voice.

"After I landed on Jantiea to pick up the initial shipment, I might have followed the supplier back to his boozed-up bunk house. You know, just to get a feel for things."

Toni turned her head to eye the other woman. "Felt wrong transporting merchandise for someone you didn't know, did it? However did you force yourself to go through with it?"

Berni smirked. "Funny. You letting me tell this story, or what?"

"Sure, I haven't got anything better to do." Huffing out a breath, Toni wriggled back on her bunk to get comfortable—it wasn't going to happen.

"So, the guy was a tallish, skinny looking thing. Dark-haired, but slimy—you know the type? I followed him to this rundown old hotel and found him meeting with Michaels—oh, you wouldn't know him, he's a smuggler from the Ten Line gang—a real khegh-loving ... Well, anyway, a real sleaze, and believe me, I know. I dated him once."

Toni shook her head. "And the part where you found out about the secret evil plan?"

"Getting there. Gosh, you are impatient, aren't you? No wonder Dan has a thing for you."

Toni glared at that but it just bounced off the other woman's emotional shields.

"I overheard Kel on his communicator, talking to some guy named Dalmith. He starts listing off all these locations and numbers. So I was confused. I thought I was the only one making a delivery and here is this guy talking about more, a lot more. So I figure they're working several gangs—all different pilots—each with no knowledge of the others. That's not normal, you know? So once I was safely in space, I checked the contents of the crates, and, well, there you go. Clearly, planets are being secretly armed. That's not a good thing, right?"

"You think?" Of course, Dalmith was involved. Escaping the Carpathian prison was just a start. He'd immediately returned to his old ways.

"I don't smuggle guns." Berni winced and added softly, "I can't smuggle guns."

"I'm heartbroken," Toni snapped. Her body itched with the need to get far away from this woman as she could. *She knows him.* Trapped in close proximity, the only thing Toni could do was mentally distance herself from the conversation. She lay down and rolled to face the wall.

*

Toni slept for a while, waking with a jerk from a nightmare involving a lot of white sand when the guards returned. The sight of the two Dobers filled her with trepidation. Her belly ached from hunger and her eyes hurt from the constant light, but neither mattered when the cell door flew open. Her heart quickened. One guard carried a tray while the other kept his weapon primed on both prisoners. Neither woman moved. Toni focused on the guards' actions, hoping to find a weakness she could exploit. *Not that they were doing much.* If their movements were repetitive, maybe she could find a way to take advantage. The guard with the tray, the one with the white streak in his hair, walked two paces into the room.

His partner kept a clear view of the cell. White Streak placed the tray on the floor and took two steps backward. The cell door slammed shut. *Khegh, they're too alert.* Not once had they turned their back on their prisoners.

After the tray was removed, Toni broke the silence. "So, what are you, Colten's ex-girlfriend?"

"Ex-partner, actually." If Berni was surprised by the question, she didn't show it.

Toni looked the other woman up and down. "I can see what he … saw in you." If this woman was Colten's type—tall and voluptuous—no wonder Toni hadn't been able to keep his interest. Anger swelled in her chest like a live beast, snorting and pawing at her skin, desperate to get out. Toni locked eyes with Berni and was startled to see amusement in them.

"We were the best."

"I'm sure you were."

"Dan said you had a temper."

"What else did he tell you?" Toni had to get out of here. Not only was she locked in a cell with a Cross, but a Cross who was *his* ex-partner. And an ex-partner who wanted to talk about *feelings.* Somehow, Toni didn't think her day could get any worse. She rolled over on the grubby mattress and placed her head in her hands. Her shoulder ached in memory.

Her worn mattress dipped as the other woman sat on the end of her bed. Berni tapped Toni's leg. With great reluctance Toni opened her eyes, blinking up at the cell ceiling. Without her shades, she noted the green of the chelix gas mixed with the mercury gas inside the fixtures. In the rear left hand light, the mixture was off. The green was darker, almost emerald.

"What are you staring at?"

"The rear light gas mix is more chelix than mercury."

"What?" Berni lay down beside Toni on the bunk, almost lying on top of her. Toni scooted back, shooting a glare at the woman. It made no impact. "I can't see it. There's no color at all."

"I can."

Berni hitched up on one shoulder. "What?"

"I see stuff. Good eyes." It was an internal joke. Berni wouldn't get it. Toni's eyesight was terrible without her shades, except in useless circumstances such as this.

"Explosive?"

"Unfortunately, no."

Unable to think of a way to escape, Toni was bored. She turned to look at the other woman. Berni was staring at her. "What?"

"How is Tone these days?"

"Tone?" Toni didn't raise her head. Her thoughts were circling around her partners. Had Mate managed to get Zach up and running?

"You know, Antonio? Still Head of the PST?"

"You know Ant?" *She called him Tone?*

"Ant? How cute. Yes, I know him. In fact, we were once quite close."

Toni stared at her cellmate. She didn't want to ask, really she didn't. Although imagining her boss's face when she mentioned the smuggler drove her to find out more. "Tell me about … Tone?" she asked sweetly.

"You two wanna cut the chatter and let a guy have a little peace?" shouted a voice through the back wall.

Toni's eye's popped wide. She looked at Berni and saw a surprised expression that probably echoed her own. Toni rolled off the bed and moved closer to the wall. Her heart thumped unevenly. She pressed her ear to the cold surface.

"Dan?" Berni called out.

"Bern? I'm glad to hear you're not dead," the voice called back. "Jas sent me after you. She was worried when you activated the emergency messaging system."

Him. Toni would recognize that voice anywhere. Her day, in a matter of seconds, had gone from worse to a total disaster. She smacked her forehead against the wall several times.

"Who's in there with you, Bern? I can hear two voices, but I can't pick 'em."

Berni leaned close to the wall next to Toni. In a sing-song voice she called, "Oh darling, it's your worst nightmare."

"What is?"

"Two of your ex-girlfriends trapped in a tiny room together."

"Well, that doesn't narrow it down, Bern," Colten replied.

Berni laughed, and even Toni struggled to keep a smile off her face. *Don't flatter yourself.* Aloud, she called, "Colten, I told you to stay out of my case!"

"Toni?" There was a long pause. "I thought an ex and Berni together would be bad, but *you* and her …"

"Sounds like your trip here wasn't via the Princete cruise." Toni told herself she didn't care if he was hurt, but her practical side suggested an escape with three would be easier than with two. An escape with two and an injured third? Not so easy.

"No. The manager of this proud establishment wanted a chat with his new tenant. I guess he didn't like the answers I gave him."

"No doubt this *manager* will want a word with me eventually," Toni muttered.

"Probably," Berni agreed. "He's already had a *chat* with me. Left me this lovely fashion statement." She gestured to her shirt sadly. "I paid good money for this."

Unlikely. The shirt looked like a cheap knock-off. Toni slumped down onto her bunk, knowing she should try to catch some sleep if she was about to get dragged off for interrogation. Just the thought of it clenched her stomach. She didn't want to think about it. Flashes of what could happen popped into her mind anyway. Her nausea increased. *Block it out.*

"Toni?" Colten called after a short while.

"What?" She lay on her side, facing the back wall. Her eyes were closed, and she was trying to imagine somewhere warm that didn't involve sand.

"You were followed on Uxt. That's how they knew about the locker."

"Who?"

"The Nymph with the red hair."

Toni immediately pictured the woman Colten tried to seduce at The Reef. Vague impressions of red hair flashed through her mind. "Kheghing hell, I think I saw her several times ... Wait a minute, you mean—"

"Yep, she starred in my interrogation."

"That bitch."

"I got her number, remember?"

Berni snorted.

Toni rolled onto her back and closed her eyes. She napped for a while, surprising given the tension twisting her body. Her empty stomach woke her by complaining loudly.

"She's awake," Berni called.

"Hey, how'd you get caught?"

Like she wanted to answer that. Though boasting about taking out two battleships would probably heal that embarrassment. No. *You don't boast about something like that.* Unlike the many embellishments Berni put into her story, Toni kept hers brief. "Pulled out of forcedspace by an ATS. You?"

His story was just as short. Debi had taken him out on Kyth-tact where Jas sent him after Berni. He wasn't sorry to hear the dock master had met her end in a nasty way.

"You mean you walked straight into it?" Berni paced the length of the cell. "I thought I'd taught you better than that." Stopping to stretch one long leg behind her back, she raised a brow at Toni's look but didn't comment.

"I had other things on my mind," he called back. "Toni, you have to get out of here."

Really? "Any thought as to how I do that? I'm meant to be on Midock protecting the Vice-President. I'm doing a fabulous job of that."

There was a pause before he said, "I forgot."

"Yeah, well, if she dies—"

"Someone's coming," Berni interrupted.

Measured footsteps approached. The cell opened and the two guards stormed in. Grabbing Toni none-too-gently by the arms, they dragged her into the corridor.

"Have fun," Berni called before the cell door slammed shut behind them.

CHAPTER TWENTY-SEVEN

Toni dropped to the floor when the guards released her, her heart racing. She drew in a breath and climbed to her feet. *Don't show any fear.* "Nice place you have here." Expecting the Dober to knock her back to the floor, she slouched her shoulders. When he didn't move, she peered around as though visiting the local zoo. There was a camera mount in the corner of the ceiling, and several darkened panels in the walls. *Screens or cabinets?*

Two men and a woman waited patiently for her.

Oh Xendia!

It was impossible not to react. Her mouth dropped open. *Zaambuka? Zaambuka here and …?*

The posture was different. The blank expression on the man's face sent a shiver down Toni's spine. She steadied her body but couldn't tear her stare from his face. The mouth, the hair, the eyes … oh the eyes. The same and yet … there was no response, no twitch of recognition.

"Sit down, won't you?"

There it was. The difference. Too high and nasal. *Not him.* But so close. Brothers? They had to be.

Toni needed to breathe, needed a moment to think. She started walking. *What the Khegh is going on here?*

The woman Toni recognized as the Nymph from The Reef sat regally in one corner, a slight smile lifting her lips into a sneer. The other man was grinning at her as if he'd won the holo-lotto. Dalmith's scalp was fully bald, his once neat beard bushy and unkempt, as if he were overcompensating. His muscles had muscles now. He grabbed for Toni when she stepped too close and she skittered back at the suddenness of his move. He was covered in tattoos, and not the pretty picture kind. They were thick, black marks that circled his muscles, making them seem even larger. He froze when the Zaambuka lookalike raised his hand. So, he was in control. *Who is he?* Toni continued to circle the room as if she owned it. Her belly flipped. Fear tightened her chest. She hoped the tremble in her hands had gone unnoticed by her captors.

"Good evening," Toni said as she passed the Nymph. The woman was disinterested in Toni's examination, instead eyeing her fingernails, gleaming silver in the harsh light.

"I'd like to complain about the state of your guest rooms. Your staff were not at all pleasant, and room service was over three hours late." Toni might as well get this party started. She stopped in front the suit and looked him up and down. The fabric looked expensive. *Same likes.* It was eerie. She glanced at Dalmith. He vibrated with barely contained anger.

Not-Zaambuka glanced at the guards positioned on either side of the door and waved them out. "Sit down, won't you, Agent Delle?"

"I'm good, thanks for asking," she replied and sucked in a short breath. *There's no air in here.*

Not-Zaambuka stared directly into her eyes and stepped forward, looming over her. She could count the number of hairs in his plucked eyebrows. Waiting a beat to see if he would say anything else, she reluctantly lowered her body into the empty chair placed in the center of the room. She crossed her legs.

"Agent Delle. My name is Gallian. I'd like to ask you a few questions."

Her heart stopped. *Gallian?* Zaambuka lied to her. He had to know Gallian personally, if they were family. *Why had he never said anything?*

"What did your friend find in that locker?"

Toni watched Gallian through hooded eyes. There was an air of danger surrounding him. She had the feeling she wouldn't get away with any of her usual baiting tactics here. He wouldn't rattle easily. A voice in the back of her mind told her she wouldn't like it when this man became angry. They were so similar and yet so different. Zaambuka had never scared her like this man's very presence did.

Dalmith moved to stand behind her. His silence was getting on her nerves. Before the Carpathian prison, he'd been impossible to shut up. His silence was far more ominous. The longer he remained out of her sight, the greater the tension in her shoulders grew. Gallian leaned down into Toni's face. The cloth of his trousers brushed her knees, and it was all she could do not to flinch at the contact. She felt Dalmith's overheated presence press close to her back. Looking up into his eyes, she schooled her face to remain stoic and breathed as normally as she could manage. Her head swam. *Gallian and Zaambuka?*

A giant hand landed on her neck. Thick fingers dug into her skin. She chomped down on her lip, refusing to cry out as the fingers squeezed. Dalmith pulled his hand away and then slapped her across her face. Her head snapped back, her face burning with the strength of the blow. She gasped, holding back tears.

"Oh we're going to have a lot of fun, Agent." Dalmith's breath ghosted across Toni's neck.

Gallian clucked his tongue. "I will not ask you the question again." He turned to the Nymph. The woman held a force-syringe. The tip glinted.

Toni's heart skipped.

"I will get answers from you, Agent Delle. If you prove resilient to Ralinna's drugs, then I will allow Dalmith to continue with his exercise. I understand agents are well-trained. We could be here for a while, wouldn't you say?" Gallian strolled to the wall furthest from Toni's chair. She watched as he pressed one of the panels and a small cabinet opened beneath his palm. From inside, he removed a decanter and a glass.

Dalmith pinned Toni to the chair and began to laugh, his sour breath hot in her face as the sting of Ralinna's needle dug into Toni's flesh.

CHAPTER TWENTY-EIGHT

Toni flopped around on the bunk, unable to find a comfortable position. Her arms felt like plasteel, her stomach did the Chalinga, and her head pounded as though a hovercraft compactor had crushed it before molding it back into shape. Moaning pitifully, she buried her face in her arms. Light flared behind her eyes like a thousand pins. Playing over and over in her mind was Gallian's face morphing into Antonio Zaambuka. To block her mental anguish, she focused on the conversation between the two smugglers.

When their words became clear and she understood what they were saying, she rose onto her elbows and raised her voice so the fool in the next cell could hear her. "That's a stupid idea!"

"Toni, khegh it. It's the only way."

"For you, maybe."

"Hey, hey!" Berni interrupted, her voice loud enough to be heard over their argument. "Give it a rest, you two." She lowered her voice once she had Toni's attention. "Enough planning for now. I'm bored. You're awake. Why don't you tell me how you and Dan met?"

Shenghi. "Ask him." Hadn't Berni said she knew *Tone.* She'd been interrogated by Gallian—why hadn't she said anything about their appearance? Toni's spiraling thoughts returned at the press of Berni's thigh. The woman shifted on the thin mattress.

"I did ask him. He wouldn't tell me."

Toni laughed, though it hurt to do so. "Wouldn't tell you?"

"No. I couldn't get it out of him."

"Then what makes you think I'll tell you?" She rolled to face the smuggler. She didn't want to give voice to what Colten had done to her—it messed with her need to pretend it never happened.

"I reckon it would really tick him off if you did tell me."

Toni snorted, groaned, and rolled back the other way. No matter which way she moved, parts of her ached.

"What's going on in there?" Colten called when they both fell silent.

"Nothing," Berni called back. She dropped her voice again. "Go ahead."

Oh why the khegh not. "He's a smuggler. What is there to say? I questioned him on Nizlec Six. He got away from me there, but I followed him to the Shetii System and shot out his TAFF drive. He hid from me in the lower atmosphere of the second moon around Jatele, you know it?" Berni nodded. Just thinking about it brought sharp cramps to Toni's empty stomach. *I was such a fool back then.* "Those stormfronts played havoc with my sensors. I saw an eddy hit his ship, and some sort of electrical discharge hit me. I lost power. We both went down. I ended up on one of the islands. I thought I was alone, but he found me after the crash. I dropped the bounty. End of story."

Her mind flew to her missing friends. Had Gallian's mercenaries found Mate? She imagined a technician somewhere pulling Zach apart. Her heart ached for her electronic partners. The smuggler's questions reminded her of how very alone she was.

"There has to be more to it than that," Berni demanded.

"That's it." *You're not going to hear the rest.*

"How long until you were found? The second moon of Jatele is uninhabited, isn't it?"

"We salvaged enough parts off my ship to repair his."

"How long?"

"Three weeks."

"Three weeks?"

Toni closed her eyes and clamped her lips shut. Her refusal to answer further questions was obvious.

Either Berni didn't get the hint, or she didn't care. "So, what happened?"

"We …" Toni paused trying to think of the best way to put it. "… worked together." She said the word *together* with such distaste that Berni dropped the subject. For about two minutes.

"Yeah, but—"

"Look, I was injured, barely conscious most of the time. We got the ship repaired and then he left."

"But you don't exactly like each other now. So, what *really* happened?"

"He left me behind," Toni admitted after a long silence. Her throat tightened at the thought of this woman knowing her pathetic story. This normal-skinned woman who *he* had chosen to work with when he'd told Toni he always worked alone. Another lie.

Toni forced herself to remember how long it had taken to rebuild the shattered emergency communication radio with her one working arm, wrapped up like a mummy to protect her skin.

To remember the pain that made her sick every time she was forced to use her arm to collect enough wood for the fire that ultimately allowed the searching agent team to find her. It worked, and her anger burned away any lingering emotion.

She could still feel the smuggler's stare on the back of her neck. When Berni spoke, her words were soft, as though she hardly believed them herself. "He left you?"

Toni didn't answer. She wondered if Berni would think differently of Colten now or if she'd support his decision.

"He's an ass. He shouldn't have left you alive."

"What?" Toni rolled over instantly and pinned the woman with a glare. "What did you say?"

"Bern, what are you talking about in there?" Colten called from the next cell.

"Your friend seems to think pissing me off is the right thing to do. Maybe she thinks I'm in too much pain to do anything about it," Toni called out.

Colten fell silent.

Berni stood. "You're an agent, I'm a smuggler. We ain't gonna be friends."

"Not seeing a problem with that right now."

"I'm just saying. Did you think three weeks playing house was going to change him? He is who he is. And look at you. You don't exactly blend in, if you know what I'm saying."

Oh, she knew alright.

"He has a type, sweetie. And you're not it."

Toni barely hid her flinch at the smuggler's poisonous words and climbed to her feet. With one step, she stood toe-to-toe with the woman. "He lied to me. He shot me."

"He missed."

CHAPTER TWENTY-NINE

Three Dobers burst into their cell. "All right, just relax," White Streak ordered, leveling his pistol at them. Berni didn't move. She didn't even glance in their direction.

Toni lay slumped against the cell's bed cataloguing each guard's stance. Her face stung where the smuggler had hit her. What was probably blood rolled down her nose. "Bitch."

"Really?" Berni drawled. Toni jerked her arm back when she sensed the woman standing over her. Berni grabbed Toni's shirt and dragged her to her feet. Toni hung heavy in the woman's grip. Out of the periphery of her vision she could just make out the guards surprised expressions. Berni drew back a clenched fist and drove it into Toni's stomach. Her breath burst out of her. Toni doubled over, clutching at her belly and groaning weakly. She spat on the floor. The liquid speckled with red. *Great.*

Swaying, Toni dropped to her knees. Berni dug her fingers into Toni's chin and shook her fist. "Watch what you call me in future, Agent."

Sagging forward into Berni's one-handed grip, Toni guessed the smuggler's next move as her fist flattened into an open palm. The slap snapped her head back sharply. The smuggler punched her again.

Khegh it all to hell. Hurry up, boys.

"Jah, what do we do. Let 'em fight?"

"Break it up," White Streak—Jah—snapped, waving his pistol around.

About damned time.

Colten called out, "Ah, let them go. This has been building for hours. You should have heard them half an hour ago. Shenghi, even *I* learned some new words."

"Shut up!" Jah snarled. Colten fell silent.

At this rate, Berni was going to cause some real damage. *Come on boys.* Jah snapped his fingers at the thin Dober behind him. "Tige, get her out of here. Mah, help him."

"Khegh off." Out of the corner of Toni's now blurry vision, she could see Berni struggling against the hand that clamped onto her arm. Mah grabbed the smuggler's other arm and yanked the woman backward.

Jah bent down in front of Toni. Without Berni's hold, she let her body sway and collapsed into the Dober's legs.

"This is none of your business. Let me go!" Berni fought wildly behind him.

"If I were you," Colten's voice piped up from next door again, "I wouldn't get involved."

Toni sagged heavily in Jah's grip. She waited until the guard's attention switched back to Berni before she flicked her fingers. Berni's struggle became more vicious, but instead of pulling away from her captors, she pushed into them with a loud battle cry.

At the sound, Toni straightened and pushed into Jah's knees. The quickest way to drop a Dober was to get them off balance—their thick bodies didn't adjust well to a sudden change to their center of gravity. The injuries Berni had inflicted may have been mostly superficial, but the wounds from Dalmith sent ribbons of pain radiating through Toni's body as her hand connected with the guard's face.

When Toni regained her feet, Berni shoved further into Tige, pushing them both into Toni's path. Toni stumbled back as the Dober cried out. Berni slammed a heel into his toes again. Wrenching her arm from his grip, Berni spun and hit Mah in the face with both fists.

Toni stopped paying attention to the other woman's fight, suddenly busy with her own, wrestling with Jah over his pistol. Using her shoulder to twist his arm against its natural bend, Toni reversed her pull and shoved the weapon to the side as his finger depressed the trigger. A tile on the ceiling exploded. Toni kicked out, her foot catching the side of his knee with a crack.

He lost balance. Toni twisted and kicked out again, this time aiming at his jaw. She caught his neck instead. He collapsed, coughing harshly and clawing at his throat with his free hand. Toni wrenched the pistol from his hand and smashed it across the guard's temple. As he fell, she turned to the other woman, ready to shoot if required.

Berni still struggled with the remaining guard. Tige lay crumpled at her feet, clutching his face and moaning softly. Berni shoved at Mah and lashed out. Her fist was caught in mid-air. The guard spun her around and pinned her arms to her sides in a bear hug.

Gasping as air was squeezed from her lungs, Berni stomped on his foot and rammed her head into his chin. She twisted and punched Tige, who was climbing unsteadily back to his feet, in the face. He fell back as Mah grabbed at her again. Berni writhed but was held fast. "Are you just going to stand there watching, Agent?"

Toni, panting lightly, shrugged. "I'm good."

Berni slithered within Mah's sweaty arms, turned, and headbutted him with all her strength. She stumbled, sucking in great gulps of air as he fell to his knees beside her. Berni grabbed his head and kneed him in the face. He fell back, but didn't collapse.

"Seriously?" she gasped. "Just go down!" She looked at Toni. "A little help?"

"Doesn't look like you need it, but if you insist." Toni slammed the butt of her pistol into Mah's head. He collapsed as the younger Dober, his underdeveloped neck ridge an indication of his lack of maturity, rolled to his knees. Berni jammed both hands into Tige's neck. He lost consciousness and slumped to the floor beside his partner.

The smuggler looked up, smiling. "Who would have guessed we'd work so well together?"

The idea of it sat like a stone in Toni's belly. "Don't ever say that again," she said. "Did you have to hit me so hard?"

Berni stared at her. "Well, what are you going to do?" Her look was a familiar one. Determined yet intense, and it didn't quite hide the fear deep inside. It was the same look Toni saw every time she looked in a mirror.

She sighed loudly, her shoulders drooping. "I'll drop the bounty."

Berni grinned, pausing only long enough to grab the weapons off the two guards. She shoved one into her waistband and powered the other.

Toni spun on a heel and limped out of the cell.

"Hey, how'd it go?" When no one answered, Colten called again, "Ladies?"

CHAPTER THIRTY

Toni peeked around the corner. Releasing a silent sigh, she crept back down the corridor toward the smugglers. Her leg ached—all of her did—but sore muscles didn't stop her brain from functioning. "We need to check this out," she hissed.

"We can sneak past," Colten mouthed.

"Why is he there?" Toni whispered back. They hadn't seen any guards anywhere in this prison section. So why was this one standing outside that cell door? Colten tilted his head. His eyebrows met in the middle of his forehead.

She walked two fingers through the air. "I'm checking."

"What?" His hiss filled the hallway. She waved him away.

Rounding the corner at a brisk hobble she dropped the surprised guard with one shot. It sounded far too loud in the constricted corridor. As he collapsed, she limped to the cell's door and triggered the open sequence. Nothing happened.

"Need a hand?" Berni appeared at her shoulder. Toni shrugged—she wouldn't say no. Berni aimed low, Toni went high. They fired in unison.

Smoke filled the corridor and swept into the cell. Through the haze, she spied movement on the sole bunk. Smoke curled toward the vents in the ceiling and as the room cleared Toni stepped over the door debris to approach the prone figure. He tried to sit up. A groan burst from his cracked lips. His hands wrapped around his stomach. Toni was concerned at the sight of blood staining his collar. His breathing sounded ragged, irregular, not a good sound. She brandished her weapon. "Name?"

His voice was weak but she was able to make it out. "Rober Telksh."

"Doctor Telksh?" She holstered her weapon and blinked the lingering smoke out of her stinging eyes.

"Yes." The battered man coughed weakly. "Who are you?"

Toni grabbed his arm and pulled him to his feet. "I'm one of the good guys. Come on, we need to get you out of here." Telksh wobbled, his face losing what little color it had.

"Wait. There is a poison …"

"Now's not the best time. Come on, Doc."

"No, wait, you don't understand—"

"Let's just get moving. You can tell me later."

Colten stepped into the cell. "Whatcha doing, Toni?"

"Would it shock you to know I was told to find this guy?" She hauled Telksh up as he collapsed. Slinging his arm over her shoulder, they limped toward the door. "Help me." Colten took the doctor's other arm.

There was a pale tint to the Doc's skin Toni didn't like. Sweat beaded his neck like he was in a sauna and he favored his right side. She hoped he'd not given up all his secrets to Gallian—he'd clearly been put under a lot of pressure to do so.

Toni was trying to hide her own limp, but from the look on Colten's face she'd failed. Her leg ached painfully and her eyes were killing her. It was damned bright on this ship.

"We're expecting company, Colten, Move," she said, encouraging the injured doctor to hustle up the corridor. "Why have there been no alarms?" It had been a while since the fight and their escape. Their pistol fire hadn't exactly been quiet or subtle.

Berni fell back to cover their escape without a word.

Toni couldn't believe her luck. She'd found Doctor Telksh. Truth to tell, she'd only remembered Zaambuka's order to "save the doctor" as she'd hobbled down that damn corridor. It was pure guesswork Gallian might have him here on the ship. When she'd spied that guard stationed outside the cell, the order came flooding back, as did her anger at the man she'd always trusted. Pushing that emotion to the back of her mind, she knew she had to focus. Get the good doctor off the ship without getting them all killed, and get to Midock before anyone died. Piece of cake.

"Agent, I must tell you about the poison."

"What poison?" she finally demanded.

"The one they made me make. It is deadly in only the smallest dose."

She thought of the dart weapon that Colten had found in the locker on Uxt. "Can you make an antidote?"

"I already have," he gasped. "I designed them together. I just need the ingredients." Though he struggled to breathe he kept walking. Toni was impressed with his determination to continue on despite his injuries.

Okay, she really had extraordinary luck; she had the doctor *and* the antidote. Squinting along the corridor ahead, she hoped they were headed in the right direction. Her throbbing leg threatened to derail her progress. It crossed her mind Dalmith might have caused some real damage during her beating. *Where is Dalmith?* She eyed the long corridor suspiciously, expecting the monstrous man to be lurking in wait. Her strength ebbed with every step, the adrenaline from the earlier fight dissipating fast. She forced one foot in front of the other and struggled to keep her pistol raised without letting her arms droop. The corridor was awfully quiet.

Where are all the guards? Their escape seemed too easy.

"—synthesize it. It won't take long."

The doctor's words served to get her thoughts back online. "Good," she replied and turned her head to find Berni lurking a few steps behind. Toni waved a hand until she had the woman's attention. "How do we get out of here?"

"Why ask me?"

"You've been here the longest." A wave of dizziness hit Toni so fast she nearly keeled over. Slapping a hand against the wall, she forced her shaking legs to hold, yanking Doctor Telksh and Colten to a halt. As the wave passed, she swiped a hand over her sweaty face.

"Toni?" Colten's brows knit together looking her up and down. He focused on her leg.

"I'm good," she said. He watched her for a moment longer. "Get going," she snapped. *I can do this.* With a grunt, she straightened.

Colten returned to his previous conversation, but kept a wary eye on her. Her skin tingled wherever his gaze lingered. "Berni's never had a good sense of direction, I wouldn't ask her which way to go."

"Wait," Berni stopped. "I do recognize where we are." She crept up to the group. "I was awake when those dumb guards dragged me down to the cell. We came through here and around that corner to the left."

They hobbled to the corner and stopped. At each junction, they found a sealed door blocking their path and, so far, each had been dealt with easily. The doors quickly disintegrated under the force of their combined weaponry.

Toni searched over her shoulder, the hairs on the back of her neck quivering. Why hadn't they run into anyone? Every time a door exploded, an alarm must have sounded in someone's office, somewhere. Each time the smoke cleared, she half expected to find an entire squadron of armed guards waiting for them.

This access door looked different. Rounded edges sealed into the wall around it. Perhaps it indicated the last exit out of the prison wing?

Colten handed the wounded doctor fully over to Toni. She sagged under the man's weight. The two smugglers agreed this door would fall like all the others and raised their pistols.

"No, wait!" Toni lurched forward, knocking Colten's weapon aside, dragging the poor doctor along for the ride. He grunted into her ear but didn't complain. She could smell blood.

"What?"

"Look." Squinting up at the top of the door, she pointed out several strategically placed pinpoint ports in the frame.

"If we'd fired, the damned thing would've fired back and fried us." Berni whistled, standing beside them.

Toni felt Colten's stare. She didn't acknowledge it.

Handing Doctor Telksh over to Colten, she leaned forward and examined the lock, pressing her nose so close to the panel she nearly touched the glass. It looked like a Mark 70–29 security system. She recognized it as the brand she'd come across in the warehouse on Uxt. Lights flashed on the number pad. *Huh?* Toni's sensitive eyes reacted immediately to the signal; she'd be the only one capable of seeing it. *Zach?* Her eyes snapped up, searching for the closest camera port.

When she looked back down, the pattern ran again. Toni copied the long combination into the panel.

Mouth dry, she stared at the door as if she could will it into accepting the code. Seconds passed like light-years and then it let out a sharp beep. *Now we get laser-grilled?*

The door beeped a second time and swooshed open.

"How the …?"

"Don't ask." Toni led the way through the door, staying well clear of the smugglers to hide the tremble in her hands. *Zach?* Was her CII functional? The idea that he was and had hacked the prison's system filled her with hope. That explained the lack of alarm and guards. They might just get out of here after all.

Behind her, she heard Colten mutter, "I told you she was good."

CHAPTER THIRTY-ONE

"Where is everyone? This is a battleship, an active battleship. The place looks deserted."

Doctor Telksh spoke up, his voice faltering. "The *Capacitor* has a limited flight crew."

"Hey, wait," Berni called. "I'm pretty sure we turned right at the docking bay here, so I guess we turn left." Toni gestured for her to lead the way.

The two smugglers walked side by side, Dan leaning down to listen to Berni speak. Toni's chest spasmed. Probably an injury from Berni's beating or the earlier interrogation. She stared at them balefully. Berni was a beautiful woman; Toni was just a clear-skinned, scarred freak who had no claim on Colten. The accusations Berni had thrown replayed in her mind, and Toni knew the other woman was right. Colten would never choose someone like Toni, so fundamentally wrong that even her parents hadn't wanted her.

The ship's hanger opened out into a large storage bay piled high with crates, maintenance tools, and shipping containers.

With a thundering rumble ending on a clang, the heavy plasteel door rolled shut behind them. They turned fast, pistols raised high to find four men in battle gear standing behind them, weapons steady on the injured group. Toni turned, finding more guards, soldiers, and members of the flight crew blocking the bay's other end. Every face a sneer, every weapon signaling death.

Beneath the sudden silence, Toni could hear the hiss of a hydraulic pump, a low hum rising up from the floor, and the rapid breathing of her companions. The smell of her own body clogged her nose. There was no way out. They were caught.

"Well." Berni's voice echoed. "Now we know why we made it this far."

One of the guards, a Ghil with a jutting jaw, laughed, thick and phlegmy. "Why should we go all the way to get you when you came straight to us?"

"Do I have time to fix my face?" Berni asked Colten.

Toni raised her eyebrows. *Really, she has time to banter?* Why he'd ever worked with the woman, Toni couldn't understand. Berni was clearly demented.

"You look stunning, darling," Colten murmured back. "Three, two ..."

Berni turned back to the guards and fired at the nearest man.

Shenghi! Toni dove to the floor as gunfire erupted all around them. Out of the corner of her eye, she saw Colten push the doctor toward the pile of multi-colored containers stacked against the wall.

Holding her breath, Toni crawled for a large machine parked near the wall and ducked behind its extended grav lifts. Berni joined her, hissing loudly as she clutched at her arm. It smoked where a bolt had caught her across the muscle.

The hanger was filled with the sound of pistol fire, calls for assistance, and cries of pain.

Toni breathed carefully through her mouth, but it did little to lessen the effect of ozone, burnt skin, and melted plastics. She coughed uncontrollably on her next inhale. Beside her, Berni hacked, bending over and holding her nose. If they didn't escape their present predicament, it would be all over for them very quickly. They'd pass out from lack of oxygen, and that was if they were lucky.

She leaned into the smuggler's side and grabbed her arm. "Some party." Berni popped up and fired randomly over the machine's engine mount. Toni examined their temporary protection, coughing into her sleeve. The machine was a tow projector, one used in large ships to move heavy containers and crates around. It was extremely solid and well-shielded. Toni raised her head and fired three shots. She ducked back down before seeing if they'd hit home.

Past Berni's shoulder, Toni could see Colten using the large containers stacked against the wall as cover. Enemy fire exploded around him. Next to Colten, the doctor lay huddled on the floor, avoiding the firefight as best he could. How on Marn were they going to get out of this alive?

Berni laughed with wild abandon, firing steadily.

My gods, she's having fun. Toni fired off another few rounds, breathing shallowly and growling at the recoil in her hands. "This is ridiculous!"

"What is, being shot at? Or that we don't actually have a plan to get out of here?"

All of it. Toni's heart pounded. *We have to get out of this kill box.* She fired again and cursed loudly. "This kheghing pistol. Gods, I wish I had my own back. This one pulls to the right something awful." Toni hit the offending piece of metal against the panel in front of her angrily. With all the noise in the bay, she could barely hear it. She ejected the power-clip and reinserted it. The pistol lit up again in her hands.

Berni ducked as more blasts hit the cross beam above their heads. Sparks showered down over them. "While this is fun, we need a plan."

The machine they were using as shelter gave Toni an idea. She looked at Berni, raised her eyebrows, and pointed up.

Berni's eyes widened, but she nodded and took the weapon Toni handed over.

Under the cover fire supplied by Berni's two pistols, Toni clambered into the tow projector's control booth. From up high, she could see the odds were not in their favor. Colten appeared to be holding his own, protecting Doctor Telksh and firing randomly over his crate cover, but Toni could see guards steadily encroaching on his position. She'd better move fast. A moment later, she jumped back down, hitting the ground and rolling quickly.

A loud rumble became audible above the noise of the firefight. It grew around them like an approaching thunderstorm. With a wave in Colten's direction, Toni motioned for cover fire. He obliged, shooting wildly. Tapping Berni on the shoulder to retrieve her weapon, Toni pointed and then sprinted away as the massive machine let out a blart and rumbled forward on its heavy treads. Berni was hot on Toni's heels. The laser fire around them lessened, the guards and the ship's crew turning their fire on the approaching machine instead.

Huddling behind a number of large crates with Berni, Toni peered around, searching for Colten. The smuggler had Doctor Telksh's arm over his shoulder and was lumbering in their direction. They made it halfway across the hanger when the projector smashed into the heavy plasteel door and tore through it like paper, trampling over the guards in its way. It shuddered to a violent stop part way through the door. Then it exploded.

Pieces of metal and shards of glass sprayed the area with a deadly rainfall of hot death.

Toni's ears rang with the sound of the blast. She blinked rapidly against the stinging smoke and surveyed the bay, tasting acrid ozone in the back of her throat.

Berni, on her knees from the force of the blast, shook her head and poked her fingers into her ears to clear them. Doctor Telksh was curled into a ball beside Colten. The smuggler lay in the middle of the hanger.

Toni ran toward him. "Dan!" she cried.

He didn't move.

CHAPTER THIRTY-TWO

Dropping by his side, she touched his shoulder gently. "Dan?" He jerked away from her, shaking his head, his gaze unfocused. He probably couldn't hear her. That blast had been loud where she'd been standing. It would have been worse out in the open. Blood leaked from his ears.

"What happened?" he shouted. As he raised his head, his hand snapped to his neck. She wrapped an arm around him and helped him to stand.

Smoke billowed from the explosion, blocking her view. It began to dissipate in long trails, drifting up off the ground as the hanger's exhaust fans kicked into overdrive.

Tears blurred Toni's vision. She blinked them back and clutched Colten's arm when he swayed suddenly. His first steps prompted her to sidle close and wrap her arm around his waist. He was pure heat where she pressed against his body. "We gotta move," she shouted into his ear.

"What the hell did you do?" he asked, his voice still too loud.

She shot him a look that asked "Do you really want to know?" Peering around, she examined the damage. It looked as though the projector had blown a hole the size of a small lightship through the plasteel door, trapping the guards between it and the projector. The guards hadn't fared as well as the machine. Handing Colten over to Berni, Toni proceeded alone toward the wreckage.

A single shot blast sounded behind her.

Toni spun, holding her weapon aloft and watched an armed guard collapse. The hole in his head still smoking. Her heart jumped into her throat. *Shenghi!*

Dan lowered his weapon. Berni had supported the smuggler's body; her hand steadied his aim.

"Now we're even," he called to Toni.

In response, she aimed her pistol directly at him and fired.

Berni flinched, twitching them apart. The shot flew between her and Dan and slammed into the mercenary creeping up behind them. Both smugglers looked back to Toni who shrugged, "Now, you both owe me."

He gestured to his ear as if he couldn't hear her. She turned her back on him to climb through the hole in the wall into the adjoining hanger. Her hands trembled from the two near misses. Seeing Dan's body—Colten's body, khegh it! He was back to being *Dan* in her head. *Why fight it?* Seeing Dan's body lying so still after the explosion frightened her to the core. Her breath caught when she'd reached his side, shaking fingers searching his neck for a pulse. His first move sent a wave of relief through her. For a moment, he'd looked at her with a gaze full of emotion. Then he'd opened his mouth. The accusation in his tone stung. She'd been trying to save their lives and get them off this kheghing ship but ... *Whatever, Dan. You're welcome.*

She trained her weapon at the two guards seated at the control panel. "Your choice."

One twitched toward his sidearm. She fired and swung back to the other man. He raised his hands. She motioned for him to get out of the chair. He fumbled at his belt. She shot him and focused on the monitors.

It appeared Zach *had* hacked the system. The CII's happy face icon with the devil horns blinked randomly over the positive shield indicator. It told her that though the shields showed as active they were in fact inoperative. *Clever, clever little CII.*

Inching open the access door, her jaw dropped at the sight beyond. *Exactly the hanger I want!* She shot the Ghil standing at the base of the *Blackflame*. It took three bolts to drop him.

Dan and Berni hobbled into the bay. Doctor Telksh—moving under his own steam—trailed behind them.

Berni surveyed the bodies. "Nice work."

"Thanks. Doctor Telksh and I have a date on Midock. I'm pretty sure if you leave a note, the guys here will let you borrow one of their shuttles." Toni keyed her security code and spoke into the *Blackflame*'s voice lock.

"You're just leaving us here? Shenghi, Agent, you're a piece of work," Berni snapped. "Look at him."

Karmic justice, Toni figured. She actually did think about leaving him behind.

Dan didn't look like he had much left in him. Blood soaked his shirt from his head wound, streaking his face like something out of a horror holoflick. *Khegh it!* "Come on then," she snapped.

"Where have you been?" demanded Zach when the hatch dropped. Toni ignored the CII and helped Berni settle Dan on her small sofa. His feet hung off the end. Blood soaked into the fabric. She'd have to replace it now. She stared down into his face and didn't know what to say. Her throat tightened and it was hard to swallow. If only he was someone different. If only she was. *Let him go.*

Doctor Telksh swayed alarmingly. Toni lurched up to grab him. Her hands clashed with Berni's. "Help me get him down the hall to my room."

"Yup."

Berni stopped Toni just outside the door. "Don't forget, you dropped the bounty."

"How could I forget?"

Hunting for the aid kit, Toni shoved it into Berni's hands. "Sort them out." She turned her back on the woman's snort and headed for the cockpit. "Where's Mate?"

"Here," Mate's distorted voice rose from the floor. Zach fired up the engines as Toni dropped to her knees beside the C-bot. She hugged him tightly, throat thick with emotion. "Good to see you," she whispered. His limbs twitched but he didn't rise.

"And you."

Toni dragged herself from the comfort of his familiar form and sat down in her chair.

"Drop the lower gun," she ordered. Taking over the controls herself, she fired a sustained blast at the *Capacitor's* shield control room. It exploded. The outer dock shield disintegrated. Air, and any item not tied down, was immediately sucked toward the breach in the ship's hull. The bay's giant door slammed shut behind them, a last-ditch attempt by the *Capacitor's* crew to save the ship.

Toni flew the *Blackflame* out of the hold, cleared the *Capacitor's* gravity well, and jumped into forcedspace.

CHAPTER THIRTY-THREE

"Should not the Doctor be working on the antidote?"

"I told him to get some rest first. He's pretty banged up. Seemed to think it wouldn't take long and that I have what he needs in the hold," she told Mate as she poked around at his insides. The pulse looked to have fried several of his primary switches that she was now working on replacing. It was slow going but it helped keep her mind off her guests.

"How does Doctor Telksh know what you have in the hold?"

Toni shrugged. She hadn't asked. She eyed the closed cockpit door—the door she never closed. She wasn't hiding. Her mind laughed at her naivety. "Zach, how did you get into the *Capacitor's* systems?"

"Remarkably easily. Invite sent to all inboxes. Eventually someone clicked, someone always clicks. I tried to do more."

"You gave me the code to that final prison gate, Zach."

"Well, you did tell me to get the backdoor codes, Boss."

"And you redirected the guards and brought down the shields. You did plenty."

"I couldn't help you."

She rubbed at her face, hiding emotions that were still too close to the surface. "You ..." She wouldn't convince him. Better to give him another job instead. She climbed to her feet, leaving Mate's side panel gaping. "Zach, call Zaambuka."

There was a pause, and then Zach said, "Mary Jeller reports he is not available."

"Put her on." The screen near Toni's elbow flickered. Mary Jeller, Zaambuka's assistant, appeared. As usual, her hair was immaculate and her sheer black shirt perfectly pressed. Crimson lips pursed as she stared at Toni. "Yes, Agent?"

"What do you mean, he's not there?"

"Exactly what I told your CII, Agent Delle. Commander Zaambuka is not currently in the office."

"Well, where is he?"

"I'm afraid that's classified."

Toni frowned at the woman. "Sorry, what?" She and Mary Jeller were not exactly on friendly terms. Nor did they pretend to be. Toni had known Zaambuka's assistant too many years to be impressed or intimidated.

The feeling, as Mary often confirmed, was entirely mutual, telling her Toni's cases generated more paperwork than the rest of Zaambuka's agents combined. Mary made it clear she did not appreciate that extra paperwork, nor did she like working late. As a result, both women were often short in their communications with each other.

"Commander Zaambuka is not available."

Toni huffed out a breath. Her leg ached, and a sharp pain kept stabbing at her left eyeball. The instant she'd stepped inside the cockpit, she'd blissfully wrapped her spare shades around her eyes, but the much-needed protection did little to soothe the pain in her head. The best cure would be sleep, and a lot of it. The old snalot stalling was not helping.

"This is urgent."

"And?"

Toni held back a scream, barely. "Fate of the universe urgent."

"Yes, yes, urgent, urgent. I get it, Agent Delle, but he is not here."

"When he gets in, tell him I'm on my way to Midock."

"Weren't you supposed to be there yesterday?"

Toni scowled at the woman's blank expression. "Just make sure he gets the message."

Closing the call, she vented loudly. Sucking in a deep breath she held it for a moment and then released it slowly. "Zach, find a livestream of the Midock summit." Her aches, bruises, and sprains needed time to recuperate, but she didn't want to rest. With Dan on the sofa in the main room and Telksh on her bed, there was nowhere to go, other than the floor. She knelt back down beside Mate and gingerly shifted the wire leading to his hind legs.

"—to vote on the alignment of the Allied Planets Executive Party and the United Planets Confederacy against a common enemy. A remorseless enemy. A bloodthirsty enemy. An enemy determined to enslave, decimate, and destroy."

Toni lifted her head to eye the screen. The speaker was a handsome bald black man. The pop up ident across the bottom of the screen named him Prince Chrismatt—leader of the Confederacy. "As many of you know, my home world is located close to the border of Ascendancy space. I have witnessed neighboring worlds lost to the Ascendancy's encroaching armies. I have comforted families who have lost loved ones to the ships that advance across our borders. I have held my own grandmother through her gut-wrenching sobs when we were notified of my brother's death at Ascendancy hands."

Listening with half an ear, Toni's mind drifted back to Dan and her reaction to seeing him lying so still in the hanger. Anxiety yes, but also a sense of loss.

How could you lose someone you never had? Perhaps it was more the death of a dream? Toni had never experienced anything like Dan before, and her emotions were wrapped in colored glass—the slightest shift and they would shatter.

She opened her eyes on a heartfelt sigh. *Don't think about it anymore.* Easier said than done. Her brain tortured her again with the look on his face, still dazed from the explosion, as if she was the only person he'd wanted to see. *Stop it!* She focused on the mini chip gripped between her fingers—the sides were burnt out. *Khegh it! Do I even have any of these?* As she climbed to her feet, she eyed the orator.

"The Ascendancy has strength in numbers, a well-trained battle force, and an unquenchable desire to rule. They will not stop, they will not hesitate, and they will not retreat. When we are gone, who will stop them?" Prince Chrismatt certainly was a charismatic speaker.

"Well, there's a sight for sore eyes."

Toni's eyes snapped over to find Berni standing in the doorway. When had she opened the door? "What is?" *How long has she been standing there?*

"The Prince. Chrismatt."

"You're from Sector Two right? It's a long way. Why'd you leave?"

Berni didn't answer. She stared at the screen and listened to the speech, muttering. "Handsome fella."

Toni had certainly noticed. He offered a smile, full lips curling to expose straight white teeth to the crowd. His deep voice carried over the agitated room, instantly hushing the crowd. "Only together can we fight this unrelenting encroachment on our territories. Only together can we defeat these twisted, dark souls working to pit us against one another. Do not wait until they have destroyed us before you decide to act.

"I have the support of my government and of my people to make this offer here today. Align with us against the Ascendancy. Stand with us, side by side and say *no more*. I support an alliance between us. I thank the spirits of Trelner who protect us in this time of uncertainty and I pray that they guide us here today to make the right decision."

The spirits? What a shame. Toni didn't go for the religious types. As Prince Chrismatt stepped away from the podium, the Great Hall exploded into a cacophony of voices. Toni turned back to Berni. "He seems genuine."

"He is."

"The audience are responding," Toni said referencing all the applause. They were quiet as they watched for a little longer. "Why didn't you tell me about Gallian?" The question had been sitting on her tongue for hours.

"What?"

"Gallian and Zaambuka?"

"Ah, yeah. Well, I knew you'd have to see it to believe it."

"You could have warned me."

In reply Berni said, "Look, I know you're not going to trust me, but you should know, The Underworld—that's the group on Marn—have been invited to take advantage of the Vice-President's assassination. They were told to start an attack to coincide with the riots and to poison the water."

Toni's mouth dropped open as the implication set in. *Khegh!* Marn was the main supplier of drinking water to Sector's One's Army. If Berni was telling the truth, someone *was* starting a war. It made sense. Attack the supply systems of the enemy and you hobble them before firing a single shot. Doctor Telksh's poison? Toni swore under her breath and sat up. "How do you know this? It seems a little coincidental that you just happen to know the bad guys' plans. Are you working for them?"

Berni glared at Toni, her jaw clenched tightly shut.

Toni stared back, waiting.

"I pieced some of it together from what I overheard, guessed at some, and heard the dock master discussing locations to the bad guys who dragged me out of my ship."

"Dock master?"

"Overheated hole called Kyth-tact."

"Humph, I know it. So that's your only evidence? Supposition and hearsay?"

"Look, I don't care if you don't believe me. That's not my problem." Berni spun on her foot and stormed out.

Whether the information was accurate or not, Toni had to get it to Zaambuka.

She followed the smuggler out, wanting to speak to Telksh and search for a replacement chip otherwise Mate's legs were not going to work. Ignoring the smuggler snoring on the sofa, Toni made her way to her bedroom. It was empty. Where could the Doctor be? Conducting a thorough search Toni worked her way through each room until she reached the rear storage cupboard. The small one located above the hatch leading to the lower hold and engine room. The sound of glass clinking together drew her attention to the ladder. The two smugglers were back in the main room, so who was down there drinking? She feared she'd located the missing Doctor. The climb was uncomfortable but Toni managed it through gritted teeth. "What are you doing down here?"

Telksh nearly dropped his drinking glass. "Oh good, Agent. When will we arrive?" He tugged at the edge of the stark bandage wrapped around his forehead. He tipped the glass he held into a smaller one in tiny increments until he seemed pleased with the result.

"Five hours, give or take. Doc, can the poison you created be used to taint water?"

He nodded. "It was designed to be activated when placed in water."

"How much did you make?" she asked leaning on the table.

"One small vial."

"What about a large body of water? Would a small vial be enough to poison a water supply, such as a reservoir on Marn?"

He froze. "Agent, what are you saying?"

She held his stare and didn't respond.

"Agent, we must go to Marn. The poison I gave that man must not be used."

"It was only a single dose, wasn't it?"

"Yes, but dispersed in water, it will infect every molecule, regardless of the size. Xendia! I've been used to kill millions."

Toni eyed the contraption Telksh had set up on her small work bench. "What is this?"

"I'm synthesizing the antidote. Agent, please. We must go to Marn. There is a limited window of opportunity. We dare not dally."

"Can you make enough?"

"Only a small amount is required—the same size as the vial of poison."

Toni held her hands up. "Listen Doc, my orders are to go straight to Midock. The Vice-President's life is in dan—"

"You don't understand, Agent. The attack on Marn will go ahead regardless of the Vice-President's condition. It is clearly the real purpose of Gallian's scheme. Can't you see that?" The sheen on Telksh's skin could indicate a fever, but it was hard to tell. His reddened face grew brighter. He huffed out a breath and practically stamped his feet. It might just be anger.

Khegh it! "Okay, listen Doc. How long is this synthesizing going to take?"

"Several hours."

"Right then. We're heading to Midock, but as soon as we arrive, I'll get you set up on a ship straight out to Marn."

He was shaking his head before she'd finished speaking. "Agent, you must reprioritize—"

"Get it done, Doc. I'll get you there, I promise, but I have my orders." Hopefully she was making the right decision. She'd never disobeyed a direct order and she wasn't about to start now. Gallian's face appeared in her mind, reminding her of Zaambuka's lie of omission. Was her boss a conspirator to Gallian's plot? Maybe she *should* reverse her course. If Marn was the ultimate target, what was she doing heading to Midock? The summit would be crawling with security. She wasn't needed there. Come to think of it, just as she was making headway with the Resonator caches, Zaambuka pulled her off the guns, ordering her to Midock. *Is he the real enemy?*

Toni bit her lower lip as she climbed up the ladder. *Why the khegh can't I reach him? Where is he?*

She didn't know what to do. *Focus on what you can do. Fix Mate.* She could discuss the problem with her team. Mate would know the best course of action.

It took only minutes to find the chip she wanted in the top storage cupboard. *What about another agent?* Huh. Why hadn't she thought of that before?

Colten's snores were growing louder. When they cut off suddenly, her heart lurched. A snort started them up again.

She paused on her way past. His bruised face looked painfully swollen with dried blood around his nostrils and ears. He had to be uncomfortable lying like that. The sofa was not big enough. She stilled her trembling hand before it landed on his shoulder and forced her feet to return her to the cockpit. "Zach, get me Agent Nar."

The screen blinked on and Agent Nar's grizzled face appeared. He grinned tiredly at Toni through the light years separating them. "Agent Delle, you missed Trena Gelin's celebration day."

"I know. I was in the middle of a firefight; I would never have missed it otherwise." Truthfully, she wouldn't have gone to Trena's celebration anyway. Toni couldn't stand her. Besides, it was only Trena's fourth child.

Her friend scrubbed at his greying beard and ran a wrinkled hand over his drawn face. "You have a job for me?" He cut to the chase. This was why she'd contacted him. He was always on point.

"Yes. I need you to meet me on Midock to transport an important package to Marn."

"I'm on warehouse clean up, Delle. The boss put me on it as soon as you sent through the information on the Resonators."

"This is more important."

"Marn? Really?" He huffed out a breath, his eyes crinkled as he smiled, deepening the lines around them. "Well, since it's you, of course. I'll hand off here. Deric will manage."

"I wouldn't ask, but it really is urgent." Toni confirmed.

"I'm on my way." He signed off leaving Toni staring at a blank screen. Another five hours before they arrived on Midock. She just hoped she'd get there in time. Closing her eyes, she tried to relax. Instantly, Dan's face popped into her mind. Rubbing at her aching eyes, she dropped to her knees and returned to repairing her immobile partner.

CHAPTER THIRTY-FOUR

"Do not be fooled by the Confederate Prince's exaggerated sense of morality and his play to your emotions. What threat, I ask you? Sector Three has every right to enforce the protection of their own borders. Are we suggesting each Sector no longer has the right to defend their own people?"

Toni startled awake, opening her eyes on the live feed still streaming from the summit. Sparks exploded in her neck. She clutched at the spasming muscle and groaned. Her other hand jolted against cold metal. Khegh. She'd fallen asleep while working on the C-bot. She pulled her hand out of his insides and tugged white hair from her eyes, only realizing her hand was covered in lubricant when hair stuck to her fingers. "Who the khegh is that?"

"Senator Kalzee'tiam," Zach answered.

"Who?"

"Vice-President Ramo's nemesis."

"Nemesis, Zach?"

"Seems fitting."

Toni had to agree. She examined the man on the screen. A bone thin, pale face amplified the man's judgmental sneer.

He raised his head so that he appeared to be staring down his nose into the camera. "Praying to long-dead gods for assistance—is he serious? We have not been attacked. There is no evidence of Ascendancy armies waiting for Sector Two to fall so they can attack us. Prince Chrismatt is asking us to send *our* soldiers to *their* borders to fight an army whose only goal is to strengthen and protect their own lines against the Confederate conspiracy.

"And make no mistake, if we were to send our troops to aid the Confederacy's imaginary battle, we will weaken our own defenses, freeing the Confederacy to launch an attack on *our* border. Join with them, he pleads! What a subtle way of saying, 'We want access to APE troops from within.' This cannot be borne, this *will not* be borne!"

A rumble grew, bursting forth from the *Blackflame*'s speakers. The view on Toni's screen changed as different cameras panned the audience. Angry whispers and catcalls rose up from the crowd. Many faces shown were downturned or scrunched with teeth bared. Nearly all of them were nodding.

"He seems to be swaying the audience." Zach said.

"Mindless cattle." Toni scoffed. "He's clearly never been out to a border planet. Zach, how far are we from Midock?"

"We shall arrive within five minutes." The scrolling ident on the screen reported Ramo would be up soon.

A reedy voice cried out, amplified suddenly as if a hidden microphone had been turned up, snapping Toni's gaze back to the screen. The vision cut between different angles as the director tried to locate the voice's owner. "If the Ascendancy attack Sector Two, then I say let them. It is not *our* fight. Let both sides weaken themselves, and when their war is over, they will have no desire to take us on. In the meantime, let us strengthen our own borders and build up our own defenses."

Toni rolled her eyes so hard it renewed her dormant headache. *Kheghing fools.*

"The President is not even here today. Is that not the clearest indication we have that he does not support his own Vice-President in this matter?" another voice shouted. The screen flashed around the audience again, as if the cameraman might find the President hiding somewhere amongst the crowd. It was a fair point to raise. Why wasn't the President there? Did Ramo not have his support? The camera stopped on the pale face of the Vice-President.

"Look." Toni muttered. The woman's set expression hid her reaction and Toni had the feeling that said everything. "She's kheghing furious. Do you think the President is ill?"

"I could find out, hack into—"

"Presidential systems? No, Zach. I can't allow that. Besides, you might not get through their security."

"I could."

"Zach!"

"Fine, can I look elsewhere?"

She shook her head. "I don't want to know, Zach."

"Got it, Boss."

The camera had returned to Kalzee'tiam. He was pounding his fist against the podium. "I challenge Vice-President Ramo to make public what evidence she has that proves the Ascendancy intend to attack," he jeered. "I demand she show us the declaration of war. I demand an immediate dismissal of this so-called vote until such evidence is received and reviewed!"

"We should probably look into 'Tiam in relation to the threat against the Vice-President," Toni mused. Had Zaambuka's obsession with Gallian blinded them all to the real killer?

"I can start a search."

"Do it, Zach. How is Doctor Telksh going with that antidote."

"He is currently asleep on your workbench. His machine is active."

"Right. I suppose that's a good thing." Toni peered over her shoulder at the closed door.

"They are awake."

"What are they—you know what? I don't care." Toni slumped back into her chair. "I'm tired, Zach."

"You should sleep."

She groaned and scrubbed at her stinging eyes. "I can't. I have to fix Mate. We're nearly there. I can't go without him, Zach." She eyed the silent C-bot, the panel in his side wide open.

"You may have to, Boss."

"I can't search for the assassin on my own."

"The smugglers?"

"We're coming with you." Dan lounged in the doorway. Toni assumed it was because he couldn't stand upright without assistance.

"No."

"Toni—"

"You'll be a liability. You're injured and besides, this is my job."

His sigh filled the cockpit. She refused to be swayed. The view through the main screen exploded into stars as they fell out of forcedspace. Midock swelled in the center of the screen. "Do you know anything about Balandez?" she queried, capitulating a little.

Dan fell into the seat beside her. "He'll head high."

"How do you know?"

"It's what I would do," Berni announced entering the room.

"That's comforting." Toni muttered. Both smugglers glared at her. She ignored them.

"He's a loner," Dan added.

"Speaking from experience? I'm actually serious. Have either of you ever met Balandez?"

"Hearsay only."

"Go ahead." She'd take any information she could get her hands on.

"There'll be eyes everywhere inside the Great Hall, security everywhere and they know about the threat on the Vice-President's life, right? Security are hyperaware, searching for anyone moving on their own. He'll have cover or a disguise, probably infiltrate in a group." Berni certainly sounded knowledgeable. Toni wondered if she could trust anything the woman said.

"By now, he'll have dug in somewhere," Dan added.

"Concealed?"

"Probably. He won't emerge until he's ready to act. Which means he'll need line of sight," he said.

"Hence up high."

"Right. He won't be able to reach the floor. Too secure. Don't even bother going inside the hall," Berni said.

Toni nodded. That was actually good advice—Zaambuka's teams would be everywhere. Toni's mission was to keep the Vice-President alive. She'd never get to Ramo's side in time. Would she be better off going after the assassin? "Zach, get me the agents on the ground."

"Be careful. Balandez is a shadowlink. You won't see him coming. And he's deadly—best in the biz," Dan warned.

"Worried about me?"

There was no answer. She refused to look at Dan's face.

"Don't turn your back, even for an instant."

It was advice she wished she had years ago. A lesson she wished she'd never had to learn the hard way.

CHAPTER THIRTY-FIVE

Black lines in the maroon plush pile flashed before her eyes as Toni raced along the upper floor of the Great Hall. An almost overpowering tangy scent of flowers tickled her nose, hiding any clue the potential assassin may have left behind. In the corridor, she could hear the Vice-President begin her speech. Time was running out.

"Every concern raised here must be respected and honored. Today I will address your arguments and hope that when the time comes, your decision will be made with an informed mind and confidence in your choice."

Zach's updates kept popping up on Toni's glasses display.

Zach: The smugglers are one floor below you. Agent Nar is a floor below them. Doctor Telksh is pacing.

"Not happy, I take it?"

Zach: I believe the word is frustrated. He reports the antidote is not yet complete but it should be any moment now. He's asking if Agent Nar will be ready to transport it to Marn."

Toni kicked open the door leading to a room with a balcony overlooking the Great Hall. Each room she searched looked identical to the one before. Her eyes scanned over the theatre chairs, the table for dining and across every dark corner as she ran forward. Nothing. She flicked the curtains aside to confirm the balcony was assassin-free. It took seconds to be happy the area was clear. At the balcony edge, she peered down at the floor of the Great Hall. The head of security's report said the Vice-President had a personal bodyguard. They didn't say who. She glanced quickly at the stage. Enough to see the woman standing at the podium. Toni examined the floor, searching for movement. Every chair was filled. The back of the hall appeared to be barricaded with what looked like a transparent shield. *Ha!* Media trapped like Sain fish in a bowl. Her gaze darted over the Mixitt horseshoe shape of the stage, allowing senators from all thirty-five original member races to sit at the semi-circular table. The sixty-five newer APE members—from the human settlements—sat behind them on a raised circular platform.

Toni glanced up. *Woah.* The ceiling's arching braces soared over them like giant waves. Probably symbolizing the fluidity of nature or some other such fancy notion. Balconies on the dozen floors overlooked the hall. It was a truly beautiful room, and one in which hid an assassin. *Keep moving.* Toni raced out, returning to the corridor and into the next room.

The speaking woman's voice rose. "This is a unique opportunity, one we will not see again in this generation, perhaps in any generation. A chance to change the life of every being living in our two Sectors today.

"The economic and financial benefits that come with aligning with the Confederacy, a Sector as strong as our own, are unparalleled. A Sector whose strengths lie in their comprehensive health services and strong governmental support systems. It is our mission, it *must* be our mission, to protect the systems, planets, and governments under our care, but also our people. We can do that together. As we did over three hundred years ago when the first human transports entered our sector. We were not afraid of an alliance then and we should not be afraid now. Humans fleeing their own world's destruction, a violent aggressive people and a people with their own culture and traditions, and we did not turn them away. Now, humans are some of our most productive members of the APE and a valued voice on the Senate."

The group cheered. Toni snorted. The woman was a good speaker, of that there was no doubt. But Ramo was a fool for ignoring the threat to her life. Toni cleared the next room. Once more, she checked the balcony and then leaned over the edge, hunting for unusual movement.

The Vice-President was resplendent in her white gown. Toni sniffed, shaking her head. Bet it was heavy and probably itched like khegh. The high neck and full train too ostentatious. Of course, it was tame compared to some of the ceremonial outfits Toni could see. Toni shoved the curtain aside and ran back out to the corridor.

Ramo's voice had a musical quality that slithered beneath Toni's skin. She could almost hear a beat, a ticking clock. "We have another chance to strengthen our borders and enrich our discoveries. Sector Three is ruled by a dictatorship, not content to remain safely behind their own borders. The Ascendancy's desire to expand and dominate means every world and every life is in danger of falling to their bloodlust."

Another update appeared before Toni's eyes.

Zach: The smugglers report no sign.

Toni froze in the wide corridor—too many damned rooms. "Zach, you said security searched every floor?"

Zach: Yes, Boss.

Am I wasting my time?

Ramo's voice softened. "We, the APE, have a duty to protect our worlds and our children. The Confederacy has a duty to protect *their* worlds and *their* children. Together, our goals are the same—to save every individual from a life of slavery at the hands of an enemy who will stop at nothing to destroy us."

There was a long pause. Toni bolted to the next room.

"I understand and respect the points raised by Senators Corini and Vlashma, and in particular that of Senator Kalzee'tiam. But I ask you, how can we, as a government entrusted with the protection of the people, elected to serve the people, afford to sit back and wait for the Ascendancy to attack?"

Nothing here. In Toni's head, the clock ticked faster.

"Signing a treaty of Peace with the United Planets Confederacy is not a declaration of war against the Ascendancy, as some in this room would have you believe, but just what it is—a declaration of peace, the offer of an alliance with a people and a government very much like our own.

Nothing.

"We share a common goal, and that goal can be strengthened by each other's support. The lessons of both Sectors will serve to benefit all peoples, and will create a vast pool of experience from which we can draw upon to combat the inequities facing both of our societies, and not, as Senator Kalzee'tiam would have you believe, each other."

Again empty.

"But how can we align ourselves with another Sector and another government, when our own leaders operate from a private and secretive agenda? Today I was informed of some very distressing news. One of our own people, a senator in this very room, has betrayed us to the very enemy we are discussing here today. Despite my instinct to deny the accusation, I was provided with proof."

Khegh it. As the Great Hall erupted in a wall of sheer noise, Toni ran to the balcony edge. Pushing aside the curtain, she stared down at the podium. The Vice-President's inflammatory remarks were going to get her killed. It was the perfect opportunity for the assassin to strike. Security officers in the crowd raced forward, clearly thinking the same thing. They were forced to push back the surging senators demanding Ramo explain.

Toni's eyes sprang wide. *Zaambuka here?* Her boss stood at the Vice-President's side. His tanned face had paled significantly. Toni could see him edge closer to Ramo, his lips moving rapidly. Trying to convince her to leave, no doubt. It didn't appear he was getting through to her though. His hand fell to his weapon. For a split second, the curling in Toni's gut told her *he* was the assassin. Her hand, the one holding her pistol, raised in his direction. She lowered it, sucking in a sharp breath. If he was there to kill Ramo, he'd have done it already. When had she lost faith in him? *When I stared at him in Gallian's face.* Her gaze flew to all of the balconies she could see. Not a single curtain moved. Where was Balandez?

He had to be here somewhere. Toni could taste the coming attack in the air.

Ramo raised her hands to draw the room's attention before continuing. At first she shouted to be heard, but quickly dropped her volume back as the room silenced, everyone anxious to hear what her report would entail.

"Through a lengthy and confidential investigation, it has been discovered members of this very Senate have been dealing with parties working against our interests." Her voice strengthened with every word.

Move! Toni's breath puffed from her mouth, her sides aching from her stop start race. "Zach?"

> Zach: Nothing, Boss. Agent Nar is heading to the floor.

Toni ran for the next room.

"For individual wealth to be considered so advantageous that these conspirators would consider their actions above reproach is simply beyond my scope of comprehension. These deals have been made to prevent an alliance being formed. Without an alliance, the probability that the APE or the Confederacy alone can defend against attack is hampered, if not made impossible. By undermining this peace process, they ensure the Ascendancy will win against us all." Ramo's voice became sharp, cutting a swathe through the thick silence.

Empty.

"If this is not a pre-emptive strike by the Ascendancy, I do not know what is. Surely, this is the evidence you have called for, evidence that demonstrates the Ascendancy is conspiring with our own people to force our submission. We must act now. We must act to prevent war."

There was a long pause. *Shenghi, what a fool.* Zaambuka had his hands full with her. *Focus on the mission.* A whisper of movement caught Toni's eye. Leaning out over the balcony edge, she stared at the curtain two rooms across. A breeze? There was no further ripple. *That one!* She pulled back, heart thudding. If she was wrong... She sprinted for the room. The time ticking in Toni's head stopped.

"There's no defining mark ..." The Vice-President cut off in a scream. Below, the hall became a pit of noise. Toni couldn't spare it any attention. She ducked the swinging right hook and danced out of reach, watching the crazed man warily. The assassin gripped a bowcaster in his left hand and lashed out with it again. The noise it made when the projectile fired still rang in her ears. *Did I knock his aim enough to save the Vice-President?*

He turned on her the moment she hit him, wild-eyed and roaring with anger. The shadowlink's skin blurred and blinked from the color of the curtain to gray shale blending into the shadows of the darkened room. Ready as she was, the strength of his blows still caught her by surprise. She struggled to remain conscious after that first punch and was still shaking her head to clear away the stars that hampered her vision.

She blocked the next attack and tried to snatch the weapon from his hands, her chin stinging where the edge had struck. Blood dripped onto her shirt.

The assassin struck her across the face again, smashing her shades and slamming the bowcaster down onto her wrist with enough force that Toni heard a bone snap before she felt it. She screamed. Her voice blended in with the noise from the main hall, her pistol falling from lifeless fingers. The assassin kicked her weapon across the room.

Toni just avoided another fist, clutching her damaged wrist close to her chest. She kicked out. The bowcaster flew from the assassin's hand over the balcony ledge into the crowd below. She spared a thought for everyone standing beneath and hoped no one would be struck. Gasping, she sidestepped the man's angry charge, throwing out her other arm. It connected with his throat. Colors rippled across his skin. He gagged and coughed.

Desperate to find anything she could use to her advantage, she risked taking her eyes off him for precious seconds to locate her pistol, spotting it half-hidden under the curtain near the balcony's ledge. It might have been a world away from her current position. She lashed out with her good hand, grabbing the assassin's forearm as he charged again and dragged him around to drive her elbow into his ribs. He grunted.

Khegh! She couldn't stop the half-gasped scream that tore from her throat. Excruciating pain raced up her bad arm. Her vision blurred. She staggered drunkenly, her breath rasping. More shouts, a cacophony of moving chairs and bodies running drowned out any call for calm. The assassin rose to his knees. The crazed look in his eyes told her he would kill her. He leapt at her from his knees, his body stretching impossibly long.

She twisted and came up under him, jamming her knee into his face. He doubled over, sucking in air, his skin snapping back with an audible pop. She hooked her foot around his leg and pushed at his chest. He fell hard. She dove on her fallen pistol, spun and fired. The assassin dropped, sightless eyes staring straight at her.

She waited for him to sit up, the pistol in her hand trembling. When he didn't move, she dropped to her knees.

Deep breathing allowed her to push the pain of her hand back as she stumbled toward the body. Searching it thoroughly, she wiped her left hand absently along her chin. It came away a bloody red. The chaotic sounds from the hall were starting to fall in volume.

Khegh. Her fingers found a piece of plastipaper in the assassin's top shirt pocket. *Dumb, very dumb.* Written in a fine type were the orders detailing Vice-President Ramo's assassination—signed by Senator Kalzee'tiam. She slammed her hand against it to prevent self-wiping.

A little too convenient. Gallian set 'Tiam up. That meant he assumed Balandez would be caught. The evidence pointed only to Kalzee'tiam ... which meant ...

Damn!

She raced to the curtain and thrust it aside, searching the crowd. Senators, aides, and assistants were surrounded by security. The only people moving were the journalists and holo-crews who had escaped their barrier and filmed the bedlam. Vice-President Ramo and Antonio Zaambuka huddled behind the podium. *Why hasn't he moved her to a secure location?*

Gallian's plans crystallized in Toni's mind. For 'Tiam to be taken down, the assassin had to fail, but the Vice-President still had to die in order to trigger the Resonator attacks.

There had to be a second assassin.

She scanned the crowd. *Where?* One man moved determinedly toward the dais, His black beard did not detract from his fierce expression. He emitted a howl and easily slipped past the security block that shielded the stage.

Dalmith!

The giant man vaulted onto the dais, leaping impossibly high above the closest ring of security. A palm-sized pistol appeared in his left hand.

Toni raised her gun in her bad hand and fired.

She missed.

Dalmith didn't.

The Vice-President flew back from Zaambuka's push. Zaambuka fell to his knees, his own pistol lax in his useless hand. His chest bloomed with a red stain that spread rapidly.

No!

Amidst the chaos and runaway security, Dalmith took aim at the Vice-President. Striding forward, he bared his teeth in glee.

Toni steadied her aim. Gritting her teeth through the pain, she fired again. The sounds of two shots echoed throughout the hall.

CHAPTER THIRTY-SIX

Toni gaped, her heart in her throat, expecting the Vice-President to fall. She didn't. A red stain appeared on Dalmith's chest. He fell forward onto the stage floor, dead before he hit the boards.

The Vice-President knelt beside Zaambuka and began tearing at her skirt. Toni caught the movement of Zaambuka's head in her direction. She nodded to him, unsure if he could see her, and pushed back the balcony curtain. "Zach, call the—" *Khegh it, my shades!* She found the shattered glass against the wall. *Useless.*

Toni raced back out through the corridor anxious to get downstairs and to Zaambuka's side.

Pushing and shoving, her arm throbbing with every footfall, Toni made her way through the Great Hall floor in record time.

Medics appeared as Toni reached the stage, rushing straight to Zaambuka's side. Toni changed focus. "Madam? Vice-President?" It was a struggle not to stare at her boss while he was being worked on. *He'll survive. He has too!*

"No, I won't leave."

"Madam Vice-President," Toni snapped, fury rumbling deep in her aching chest. She pushed into the woman's face. Zaambuka had been shot protecting her. How dare Ramo insist on staying out in the open. The Vice-President backed away, her eyes impossibly wide. Toni cradled her damaged wrist to her chest. Her priority had to be the Vice-President's safety and she was seconds from drawing her pistol to enforce her order. *I'm shouting at a distraught woman who'd just survived an assassination attempt.* Today was not Toni's best day.

Beside them, medics knelt over Zaambuka's body. Urgency filled their voices as they spoke of applying pressure and inserting tubes. Toni couldn't look at them. She couldn't bear to see her boss lying so pale and still. Her stomach churned, both from shock and pain, her mind in turmoil. She wanted to grab Zaambuka and demand that he not die. She also wanted to confront him about his relationship with Gallian. She pushed the noise away, knowing she had to pull it together and focus. Zaambuka would want it that way. But when he survived, and he would survive, they were going to have an important talk. Her awareness returned to Ramo as she realized there could still be a danger.

Everywhere Toni's gaze fell, there were too many people moving, too many unknowns she could not account for. The buzz of voices drowned out the chatter of the medics only three paces away. Toni wouldn't hear anyone approaching. She had to get the Vice-President out of here.

"Madam Vice-President. If you don't start moving toward your quarters immediately, I will shoot you. Don't think that I won't."

Alarm fought with the leftover fear on the Vice-President's face. She glanced down at Zaambuka's still body. "Yes, yes, of course." With a final order to the medics to inform her of any developments, Cat Ramo allowed Toni to usher her from the hall.

Every part of Toni ached, and the throbbing in her wrist threatened to derail her concentration. But as soon as she stepped into the Vice-President's rooms, her mental acuity snapped back into place. Demanding the woman remain near the door with her two bodyguards, Toni and the third bodyguard, a big-shouldered hulk with close-set eyes, searched the temporary apartment thoroughly. When Toni was satisfied the rooms were clear, she gestured for the guards to escort the Vice-President inside. Ramo was pale and visibly shaking. Blood speckled her white senatorial robes.

Toni snapped her fingers at the bodyguard standing at the door. "Get her a drink." She desperately wished she could have one herself. Following him to the table, Toni stared at his hands so intently the bottle trembled. Amber liquid splattered the table around the glass.

Zaambuka had been shot—might even be dead. She recalled his face, frozen in annoyance, the day he arrested her. The choice he'd given her and of his implied belief in her abilities. Ever since that day, he'd believed in her and trusted her to get the job done. She couldn't, wouldn't let him down. She choked on a hysterical laugh and pushed the image of him covered in his own blood from her mind. *Concentrate!*

Vice-President Ramo was frozen in the center of the room. She stared blankly at the wall and rubbed her hands together. Toni directed her to an armchair and pressed the glass into her hands. "Get me a blanket and a medic," she hissed to the other bodyguard. He snapped her a salute and raced from the room. Turning back to the pale woman, Toni prompted, "Drink this, Madam Vice-President."

"What?" The woman looked up but her eyes didn't focus. Tears glistened in the corners.

"Madam Vice-President," Toni coaxed again, kneeling beside the woman. After a moment, Ramo looked Toni in the eye.

"Who are you?"

"Agent Toni Delle, Madam Vice-President."

"The missing agent?" The trembling woman's gaze flew to Toni's wrist. "Oh, you're injured. We must call a medic."

"On their way, Madam," Toni confirmed.

"Citriss, my assistant? Where is she? I need her here."

"Madam Vice-President, we must limit—"

"I need her." It appeared Ramo's strength had returned with her anger. She sat up and glared at Toni. "I completely vouch for her, she has been my friend and confidante for years—longer than she has worked for me, Agent. I assure you, I will be perfectly safe."

Toni eyed the remaining bodyguards. They nodded. One spoke, "She has been cleared, Agent. By Commander Zaambuka himself."

"When the other guard returns, send for her," Toni ordered. He acknowledged and told the man next to him to remain outside the suite to guard the door. He then took up a position on the inside. Toni squawked as the Vice-President grabbed her arm.

Ramo released her quickly and raised her hands. "Oh, I'm sorry, Agent. Please forgive me."

"Can I help you, Vice-President?" Toni asked through clenched teeth, tears threatened with the sudden agony. She blinked them away as her arm throbbed.

"You have to send someone after the President. He must be put into protective custody until a formal inquiry can be launched against him."

"Ant will ..." Toni broke off with a choked gasp. Zaambuka couldn't do anything, might not do anything ever again. Her chest tightened with unshed emotion. *He will be fine. They'll patch him up as good as new.* The Vice-President herself had kept him alive until the medics reached his side. *Wait...* "The President? He is the one you were investigating?"

"Yes. His reclusiveness was merely a sham. He was taking money! And he—"

"Madam Vice-President, the assassin carried instructions signed by Senator Kalzee'tiam. But I don't believe he—"

"What? 'Tiam too? Well, that will come as a surprise to nobody."

"Madam Vice-President—"

"'Tiam must be taken into custody too."

Toni pinched the bridge of her nose. The woman was too shaken, she wasn't going to listen to logic. Toni had no way of convincing her Gallian was behind it all, certainly not without proof. "Madam Vice-President, you need to contact your security council and General—"

Ramo shook her head. "I cannot be involved in the investigation, nor can my people participate. It must be a PST initiative or the Senate will think this is a coup."

Toni had no idea who the next in command was at the PST. "Madam Vice-President, you need—"

"Agent Delle, I am authorizing you to act on the Commander's behalf while he is indisposed."

Shenghi! Toni stared at the woman as her mouth dropped. On the edge of exhaustion, with her arm echoing the beat in her head, she couldn't possibly take over as head of the PST. It was ludicrous. But the Vice-President held her gaze. *Shenghi, she is serious!*

Heaving a sigh, Toni demanded a communication unit from Ramo's bodyguard. As she spoke into the device, a confident knock rapped against the door. Toni's stare shot to the closed barrier. She checked Ramo could not be seen, and drew her weapon. The bodyguard opened the door on her nod.

Two women entered. The one in the medic's uniform was stopped at the threshold. The other moved swiftly past. Toni sprang up. "What?"

"She's cleared."

"Cit?" The Vice-President held out her hand and the woman raced to Ramo's side, brushing blond hair out of her face as she knelt down. Toni holstered her weapon and returned to her call. The medic hovered just out of Toni's reach. When Toni realized she was there, she waved the girl to attend the Vice-President first. The call connected, and Mary Jeller answered.

"Yes, Agent Delle?" The woman's voice was soft and wobbled slightly. She must have been briefed on the earlier events. Probably the whole galaxy had heard by now.

"Mary, we must put aside our issues and—"

"Of course, Agent Delle, what do you need? I've been watching the holo-newscasts. Have you heard anything about Commander Zaambuka's condition?"

Haltingly, Toni told the woman what happened. She didn't have an update on Zaambuka, but would ensure Jeller was added to the emergency contact notification list.

Mary cleared her throat. "What can I do?"

"Can you organize a conference call with the department heads? Put it through to this unit number?" Toni's eyes ached.

"Of course, Agent Delle. Give me five minutes. I will contact you shortly."

With a heavy heart, Toni moved onto her next call. Without her shades, Zach and Mate would have no idea what was going on. They'd be frantic.

"Boss, what happened? Are you—?"

"Zach," she interrupted. "Are Mate's systems back up?"

"Yes, Boss. The reinstall of his backups are complete."

"Send him to my location immediately."

Instead of his usual litany of complaints or a bombardment of questions, he acknowledged and not even a second later, reported Mate was on his way. "Zach, any word on Nar?"

"Last time I saw him on camera, he was headed toward the rear of the Great Hall."

"Zach, find him." Dalmith had come from that direction—he wouldn't have got past Nar unless . . . "Send medics to Nar's last known location immediately. What about the smugglers?"

"Disappeared from the surveillance cameras."

"Khegh it."

"Boss ... Security reports finding Agent Nar's body next to the reporters' enclosure."

Toni screwed her eyes shut on her tears. *Shenghi.*

At a loss for something to do, she stared blankly at the wall until the medic reappeared at her side and coaxed her to sit down.

While she worked on Toni's wrist, Toni called to the Vice-President's assistant. "Ma'am, Citriss?"

"Yes, Agent?"

"Can you liaise with Zaambuka's personal assistant, Mary Jeller, and keep her apprised of any news on his condition?"

"Of course, Agent, anything we hear."

At the trill of the communicator, Toni forced herself to her feet. Head heavy and thoughts sluggish, she felt numb, as though she'd been drugged except the medic had not administered anything. Assuring the medic she would return, Toni stepped into the corridor to brief the heads of the PST's various departments: General Trasken of the STCT, the Leader of the Defenders, Peta Milterne, and the head of the Sentinels service, Maline Sesh. The three remained silent while Toni spoke. She advised them of the Vice-President's order. "I don't accept her command. These are your teams and you are the most qualified to make any decisions relating to them."

"As the agent on the ground, what is your current situation?" General Trasken asked.

Toni strengthened her voice. "The priority is to find and contain the President. Ramo is insistent she has proof of his collusion with the Ascendancy. Kalzee'tiam has been taken into custody here. An investigation into all claims must be conducted. The Senate can sort it all out later. I have the Vice-President under my personal protection here on Midock, but I'm injured. I need a team to take over her detail."

Peta Milterne spoke, her tone troubled. "My Sentinels will protect the Vice-President, Agent."

"The Defenders will apprehend the President," Maline Sesh added. "We will send a joint team of Sentinels and Defenders to Midock to isolate, interview, and escort the remaining parliament and the Sector Two visitors to a secured location."

"What do you require from the STCT, Agent?" the General asked. "We are already assisting Agent Nar's teams with the Resonator raids across the Sector."

Khegh it! "Sir, Nar is dead. He died in the service of the Vice-President."

"I'm sorry to hear that, Agent Delle. Agent Nar was a good man."

Milterne and Sesh signed off, leaving Toni to speak with the General privately. "General, I know your teams are spread thin, and while I appreciate all that you were doing to assist Agent Nar, I have intel regarding an attack on Marn."

"We just received intelligence on factional in-fighting on Marn. But how did you—"

"One of the factions on Marn call themselves The Underground. They have access to a poison and plan to contaminate the water reservoirs."

The General was silent for a moment then he swore vehemently. "Marn supplies all the STCT contracts."

Toni sucked in a startled breath. "Shenghi! I knew about the supply to the Sector's army, but I didn't realize they supplied the PST too."

"It's a recent contract."

"That's why Marn's the target," Toni said. "General, I have the antidote here on Midock. The man who manufactured the poison for the terrorists created it. I have him in my custody. As soon as Milterne's Sentinels arrive—"

"Agent Delle, you cannot wait for them. Marn is an ongoing threat. We must have access to that antidote immediately in the event that our teams do not regain control."

Toni clenched her eyes shut and pinched the skin at the top of her nose. The General was right. She couldn't wait. And she trusted only one to keep the Vice-President secure in her absence. Her heart cried out at the thought of leaving without him at her side. "I will meet your teams on Marn," she said and signed off.

Irregular footfalls indicated Mate's approach. It sounded like he was favoring one leg.

Within seconds, her arms were full of her partner. She buried her face in his fur and wrapped her arms around his sides, hugging him as tightly as her broken wrist allowed.

"You are injured?" Mate asked.

"I'm fine, or I will be. How are your legs?"

"They are functional."

Rubbing his head, her chest constricted until it was almost impossible to breathe. She choked out, "I have a mission for you."

"Boss, I will not—"

"Mate, I am ordering you. I need you to stay here with the Vice-President. Do not leave her side. Full protection detail until I return."

"Boss?" The C-bot sounded pained by her request. Toni's hands shook where she clutched his side. For the first time, their separation would be at her behest. It felt like betrayal. Somehow she would have to find the strength to go on without him. At least she would have Zach.

"Mate, I need you to do this."

He lowered his head.

"I know you don't like it, but I need you here. Sentinels are on their way, but I have to get to Marn. I need to know she's safe."

"Yes, Boss."

With tears in her eyes Toni re-entered the Vice-President's suite and introduced her partner to his new charge.

CHAPTER THIRTY-SEVEN

A young STCT officer greeted her at the base of the *Blackflame*'s ramp. "This hoverjeep will take us to the frontline." He looked like every other soldier she could see standing guard at the doors, vehicles, and around Marn's primary landing dock. Bright eyes, clean-shaven face, crisp military salute and all. "Agent Delle, I am to brief you on the situation at the dam."

"Situation?" Toni slid into the vehicle and the STCT driver took off at top speed. She grabbed onto the rear seat with her bad hand, sending a shock of pain up her arm. Though her injury had been treated by the medics on Midock, the recently reknitted bones were exceedingly tender. She carried the precious vial Telksh had handed her strapped to her side, secure beneath the sling keeping her injured arm pinned to her chest.

A biting wind whipped her hair around like a live electrical line. Tugging the strands out of her eyes, her thoughts drifted back to her departure from Midock. She hadn't been able to look at Mate after her goodbye. The silence inside the *Blackflame* had been palpable. "Where are the smugglers?"

"They have not returned." Zach admitted, his voice soft as if he too was feeling Mate's loss. That Dan and Berni had taken the opportunity to disappear was barely a blip on Toni's radar. Of course Dan had left. It was what he did. She didn't expect she'd ever see him again.

Her thoughts returned to the scenery speeding past, ignoring the chasm inside her chest through long practice. A glance at the empty seat beside her reminded Toni of Mate's absence. *I'm all alone here.* The further they traveled from the dock, the stronger the feeling of being too exposed. She couldn't control the trembling of her hands or how frequently her head turned, searching for dangers she was afraid she wouldn't see in time.

The young officer leaned close to be heard above the whistling wind. "The Underground launched their attack on Nesine City the very moment Vice-President Ramo was targeted."

Toni stared out over the deserted city streets. She counted too many bodies, damage from Resonator fire everywhere she looked. "Where are we headed?"

"Dtrellingham Dam. It's the largest on Marn. The Underground forces have barricaded themselves inside the central control room of the dam's powerhouse. We're attempting to breach their shields. Somehow, they got their hands on a railgun and have prevented us flying over the Dam to drop behind their lines. They're threatening to dismantle the filtration generators and release the poison into the dam's reservoir. The Dtrellingham Dam reservoir is fed by the planet's water table, and has links to the six largest dams on this continent. If the water here is tainted, it will affect everything. The process plants will be forced to shut down. The longer they're inoperative, the more worlds will be affected by the lack of supply."

The thought was horrifying. "I have the antidote," Toni shouted as they sped through the city.

"That's why we have to get you on location, Agent."

Toni knew from Zach's earlier briefing that there were over six thousand dams and water filtration plants across the planet. Marn was a world dedicated to the storage and packaging of clean drinking water, and supplied not only the STCT and the Sector's military troops, but many desert worlds as well as worlds suffering the effects of severe drought. Millions of people would be affected by a lack of clean drinking water. There would be deaths all over the Sector before new supplies could be organized and distributed. If the terrorists infected the underground water table, she hoped Telksh was right and the small amount of antidote she carried would be enough to reverse the effects. Her heart thundered at the sense of urgency, frustrated at her inability to do anything but wait until they arrived.

The officer continued, raising his voice to be heard above the sounds of rapid gun fire. "Over four hundred square miles, the dam contains thirty-two million acre-feet of water. The control center in the heart of the Dam provides electricity to the main powerhouse. It's a fifty-story building situated just in front of the shields that keep the water contained." They passed more bodies, Underground terrorists in their dark purple uniforms and masks and the black of Marn's security forces. They arrived just as Marn's two suns were beginning to set. An eerie green dusk lit the building standing sentinel before them, casting long shadows that crawled toward the STCT encampment.

Toni was sent directly to the officer in charge. Her mouth dropped open. "General?"

Trasken himself was in command. He looked Toni up and down. His pinpoint stare immediately put her on edge.

"Sir?"

"Agent, sit rep?"

"Sir, the poison is a manmade toxin called Genmiktok. I have the creator of the poison in custody and the antidote in my possession." She retrieved the small case strapped to her side and tried to hand it to the General, but he wouldn't take it. His thin lips pressed together. He ran a hand through cropped silver hair. Toni's blood ran cold.

"Agent, we have a situation here and it appears it is one you are uniquely qualified to handle."

"Sir?" She was only here to transport the antidote and had assumed her part in the operation would be concluded once she handed over the vial. The way the General was looking at her made her instantly aware of her small stature. The bad feeling in her gut intensified.

General Trasken led her into a makeshift situation room. Over a large table-monitor was a three-dimensional schematic of the powerhouse. A hand-drawn path was highlighted below the current powerhouse's conduits. *Oh shenghi, more air ducts.*

"Agent, the earliest pipework systems are not on any known schematics. Orbital scans found us a way in. We have a path into the main control chamber where the Underground terrorists are holed up. You can see our problem."

Yes, Toni could see it. In four locations on the plan, the conduits dropped to less than two feet wide, barely more than Toni's own shoulder width. It would be a kheghing tight squeeze, as well as extremely claustrophobic for the person infiltrating the powerhouse. They'd have to be small and wiry, and also flexible—the last conduit line before the exit point on the lower level of the powerhouse twisted into a dog-leg sharper than Mate's hind legs. *Mate could have fit if I hadn't kheghing left him behind!* Once again, her decision making when on her own proved disastrous. This time it would lead to millions of deaths.

"Agent, all of my men are too large. We were preparing to send for one of our most junior tech officers when you arrived."

Nausea swirled in her belly. "You want me to climb in there." It wasn't a question. She couldn't do it, not with her wrist strapped to her body as it was. She'd have to remove the sling. All she'd be left with was the thick compression bandage, and maybe if she was lucky, a brace to support her inner wrist. She'd need her hand and fingers free for the crawl. A mission without Mate. Her mind froze. She stared blankly at the map.

"Agent Delle."

Toni startled back, her gaze shooting up to the General's face. His right eye twitched, but he said nothing more. Toni sucked in a deep breath and nodded. She was the only one who *could* do this.

It was immediately obvious she'd be unable to wear any of the STCT's protection gear. To remain as flexible and thin as she could, she stripped down to just her long-sleeved shirt and trousers. She had an ear comm, her shades, and her small pistol tucked into her boot. At least she had Zach on text display and the general in her ear, so she was not entirely alone. *As good as, though.* She carried the vial of antidote in a sleeve strapped inside the brace on her bad wrist.

"We cannot confirm enemy numbers," the General said as they stood outside the incursion point. He was as apologetic as she'd ever seen him. "My men believe we can force visual contact within two hours."

"Obviously we cannot wait that long." Her stomach churned. She'd be alone and without protection. But she had to do this. She *would* do this.

"You should have an easy run of it until you reach the first cross-section."

Having loaded the schematics to her glasses earlier so she wouldn't lose her way in the endless run of tunnels, she agreed with his assessment that the first cross-section would be her first true test of agility.

"Good luck, Agent," the General said.

Toni stepped over the lip of the cutaway conduit and ducked inside. She gulped at the endless blackness before her. Setting her glasses to night vision, the tunnel appeared in green and shades of gray. "Agent?" The General's voice sounded in her ear comm loud and clear.

"I hear you, General."

"Good luck."

Toni dropped to her hands and knees, wincing at the pressure applied to her recently repaired wrist, and hobbled her way along the first length of tunnel. In moments, she was surrounded by ghostly green walls. The first bend was a tight fit. She scraped skin off her shoulders as she pulled herself up and twisted sharply. It took all of her strength to haul her body up the steep incline to the next twist. The comm in her ear gave a sharp squeal and then fell silent. Her glasses fritzed. All she could see was black. "Hello, General?" she whispered. "General? Zach?" There was no answer.

She was on her own.

CHAPTER THIRTY-EIGHT

I can't do this!

She didn't know where she was. She couldn't see. The scent of cold metal saturated her senses. She gasped, searching for air she couldn't find. Her body trembled violently, jarring her arm and sending sparks of pain shooting through her frame.

Toni flashed to a memory—long ago, blinded by Colten's flashbang, Mate had led her to safety. She closed her eyes, blocking out the blackness entombing her and focused on her memory of the C-bot's voice. *"Take one step at a time—I am here."* She jammed her back against the wall and shuffled upward, imagining Mate's fur beneath her fingertips and his voice in her ears. Eventually, she opened her eyes. One step at a time.

She could do this.

Hearing Mate, at other times Zach, Toni climbed silently, contorting her way through what felt like miles of metal tunnels. She wasn't unfit—not at all—but these tunnels were a maze. If she wasn't claustrophobic before, when she got out of here she would be. Her breathing was heavy, sucking in stale air, tasting dust and grit. The scent of chemicals and water was growing stronger.

Squeezing up and over another joint, she scraped her knees. Dear gods, her knees and elbows would be rubbed raw by the end of this journey. *Is there even an end?* Fearing she would be stuck down here forever, she was close to talking aloud just to create some noise. Though she was puffing and sweating from her exertions, she was also freezing. Her nose and fingers were icy cold, and her nose kept dripping. Her constant sniffing and panting was surely too loud, and ... *Wait ... what was that?*

A barely audible metallic ping sounded somewhere up ahead.

She crept closer to the sound. It was constant now, and growing louder.

In moments, the light around her grew bright enough to blind her. She froze, waiting impatiently for her eyes to adjust. The end of the conduit lay just ahead.

According to her memory of the plans, she should exit out into a small storeroom. This was the moment of most danger. Would she be heard or seen while trying to open the sealed vent? *Oh, khegh it!* She eyed the vent unhappily. The diagonal corners were barely wider than her shoulders. Thank goodness for her boyish hips. The rails of the screen were a finger width apart, giving her a clear view into the room beyond. Luck was with her—the room was empty.

Toni set to work on the clasps holding the screen to the wall. The STCT had given her military grade acid-oil to burn through the bolts. Watching it work its magic and dissolve the catches was a joy to behold. She'd have to get a supply of her own—it would've come in handy back on Uxt. In minutes, the bolts were gone. She held the vent screen in place with just her fingers. *This is it.* Taking a deep breath, she wriggled right up to the screen and popped it loose with a gentle push. The grate emitted a soft sucking noise as it came away. She edged the screen forward and listened carefully. There was no movement from the room beyond and, more importantly, no shouts of alarm.

Shuffling forward, she lowered the screen and slipped from the vent. Her earpiece burst with static as her listeners came back online. "Agent? Agent!" Her shades remained black.

"General. I'm in," she whispered, her body sagging with relief.

"Sit rep?" The General's voice became clear over the rest of the chatter.

She crouched, waiting for someone to come running. A quick glance showed boxes and stationary items stacked haphazardly on rickety shelves.

Removing her inoperable shades, she pulled her pistol from her ankle and tiptoed to the door. There was a faint murmur of voices outside. Cracking the door ajar, she checked the corridor. Seeing only an empty hall, she ducked out of the store room and crept toward the sound. A number of purple-clad men were gathered in a large, open space. Behind them sat three shield generators, humming loud enough to send a vibration through the floor back to where Toni stood. Every so often it let out a sharp ping. *Aha. That's why no one heard my entry.*

By the sound of it, the terrorists were arguing about time. Toni couldn't make out the exact words over the generators. She backed away slowly. Her mission was to get the entrance open, not deal with the Underground by herself. Following the path General Trasken's men talked her through, she crept toward the powerhouse's exit. There was a man guarding the gate. One well-placed shot took him down.

The voice in her earpiece gave her instructions to disable the outside shields and in seconds she was surrounded by the insertion squad. She held still as they thundered past, content to let the men do their jobs. All she had to do now was find a safe spot to hole up. The creak of an unoiled hinge snapped her head around. *What was that?*

Holding her weapon tightly in her wrong hand, she headed down the opposite end of the tunnel, following the signs leading to the water filtration access tunnel. The shadow of a man crossed the wall in front of her. "General? I have sight of an unknown at the filtration hub."

The General grumbled and then shouted a muffled order. His voice came online a second later. "Hold, Agent. I'm sending two men back."

Toni wasn't going to hang about. This man was down here alone for a reason. She crept forward and poked her head into the room beyond.

The filtration hub was a giant pool of water with a thin metal walkway over the center. A shield shimmered mere inches above the pool. The walkway had a box-like machine right in the center that ran down beneath the walkway and under the water to the pool's edge. A crisp, fresh smell tinged with something pungent—like oily chemicals—filled her nose. The hair on her arms rose making her skin tingle. That must be the shield preventing access to the water below. Power lines and tubes covered every wall, like the roots of a tree stretching down into the pool.

The man was on the walkway, a bag at his feet. He knelt beside the machine, fiddling with the insides.

Toni burst into the room. "Freeze!" she shouted. "Stop what you're doing and step away from the machine." The masked man bolted to his feet at the sound of her voice and snatched up his bag. Toni fired at him. The shot flew over his head and exploded against the wall, just missing one of the power lines. He took off for the far end of the pool.

Toni chased after him. As the terrorist approached the wall, he fired at the power lines. The conduits appeared to travel the entire length of the room, all the way under the pool back to the shield generator. *He's still trying to disable it!* Toni hit the walkway a split second before two STCT officers burst into the hub. As soon as they spotted the terrorist, they began shooting. Shots exploded against the wall in front of the terrorist, driving him back toward Toni. Breathing hard, she fired several times, each shot missing as the walkway beneath her feet swayed. One shot hit close to the terrorist's head, forcing him to the floor.

Raising his own weapon, he fired—not at Toni, but at the wall. The shield below the walkway sparked and then dissolved. *Shenghi!*

The man rolled to his feet, tearing open the bag. Toni ran faster. Her feet pounded the metal walkway, but she was too late. He found what he was looking for and dove toward the edge of the pool. Her next shot hit the terrorist square in the back. He stumbled forward and tumbled into the water. Toni's blood turned to ice.

"No!" she cried. Spinning to the soldiers, she shouted, "Get those pumps off now!" She dove after the terrorist, hitting the water hard, and dragged the limp body toward the edge, thrusting the dead weight up into the STCT soldier's hands. "Find the vial," she panted, treading water and watching the soldier search.

He held aloft a small vial. "Empty."

Toni focused her gaze on the water. It was turning a sickly green, spreading out in a growing circle. "Xendia!" Without wasting another second, heart pounding out the words *too late* in her ears, Toni tore open the bandage around her wrist, dumping the contents of the vial into the water, swirling it around with her hands.

"Are we in time?" the soldier asked.

"I don't know."

The water began to change again, fading slowly back to its original crystal-clear blue. Relief flooded through her as she gasped, "I think so."

CHAPTER THIRTY-NINE

Pale pink was a horrendous color. Toni actually asked the nurse outside about it. Apparently, the trauma center's management felt the color aided in the creation of a calm environment and helped encourage patients to accept their diagnosis and submit themselves fully to the demands of the center's staff nurses. In reality, she told Toni, the color drove the staff crazy and the patients into fits of despair.

Everywhere Toni looked, she found pink—the walls, the ceiling, even the drapes preventing the harsh glare from the early morning sun reaching the beds were pink. Different shades, different textures, but all terribly pink. *Xendia, even his bloody hospital gown is pink.*

Zaambuka groaned and shifted on the bed. *Finally!* She'd been sitting in the hardest, most uncomfortable chair in existence for hours, waiting for him to wake, trying to figure out how to ask him about Gallian. Her report on the Marn project was on the tablet in her hand. She couldn't put it down.

Fortunately for Zaambuka, the laser bolt had impacted his shoulder and burned down his side. His crisp white bandages didn't show any sign of blood. The nurse told Toni he was lucky—if the beam hit any lower, he'd be in a morgue.

The injured man groaned again. The door popped open and his nurse appeared. She ignored Toni, as she had the last four times she'd come in, and puttered around his bed, straightening already straight lines and checking his screens. Her nametag called her Delin and her uniform was the first non-pink Toni had seen. Faded, untailored, well-worn—but a refreshing blue.

"Excuse me, Commander Zaambuka? The President has requested a short visit."

He stirred and his eyes peeled open, blinking stupidly at the nurse. *How rude.* Toni had been sitting here for hours and he didn't even notice her. The cheerful smile Nurse Delin bestowed on Zaambuka got under Toni's skin. Toni's left eye started to twitch. She rubbed at it and the movement seemed to get Zaambuka's attention. His gray gaze fell on her face, widening slightly before the door opened again. A delicate floral fragrance preceded Cat Ramo into the room. Catching sight of Toni, the woman froze. Reluctantly, Toni climbed to her feet. Ramo waved Toni to sit back down. "Stay, Agent. Please. I was briefed on your success on Marn. Well done."

Toni nodded, taking the praise stoically.

Cat Ramo's simple yellow shift muted her regal presence. Her dark hair flowed gently around her shoulders. She focused on the bed. "Commander Zaambuka?"

"You look tired, Madam Vice-President." Zaambuka attempted to sit up, but the flattened pillows at his back made that difficult. Nurse Delin hurried around Ramo to raise the bed and adjust his attached tubes and lines. Toni didn't move. Her fingers tightened around the tablet.

Ramo fiddled with his pillows as the nurse checked his screens again. After a moment, the beautiful woman held up a wrapped package. "I am tired, but you look a lot better than you did a few days ago. I brought you a gift."

"You didn't need to do that," he muttered. A red flush rose on his skin. The sight would have normally amused Toni, but Gallian's face—the mirror of Zaambuka's—wouldn't leave her mind. Though her boss's gaze didn't return to Toni, she had the impression he was well aware of her attention. He took the small package from Ramo's hand and thanked her for her thoughtfulness.

Nurse Delin stopped at the end of the bed and made a show of adjusting Zaambuka's blankets. She glanced at Ramo, in no obvious hurry to leave.

"Thank you, Nurse," Ramo said. "If you could please give us a minute? Unless, of course, Commander Zaambuka still requires your attention?"

The blue-clad woman hesitated but one look at Toni's face and she quickly left the room, though she lingered in the doorway as the door closed.

Zaambuka unwrapped the gift. He stared at it straight-faced. "A tie?"

"This one I picked myself," Ramo insisted.

Toni suppressed a laugh as Zaambuka held the tie aloft. It was pink.

Snorting, he dropped it on top of the mobile table beside his bed. His gaze fell to Toni again. She returned his stare.

Ramo coughed delicately. "An emergency meeting was convened last night. Initiated by the majority Senate who reluctantly agreed to return after the events of, well ... you know."

"What? I must say, I am surprised they returned. Was a decision reached?" Zaambuka shifted, wincing as he struggled to find a more comfortable position.

"Yes." Ramo smiled, leaning forward to hike his pillows higher. "After it became clear Senator Kalzee'tiam paid that assassin to ..." She broke off, seemingly unable to finish. Taking a deep breath, she continued. "To kill me, a number of Senators came forward with the results of their own investigations into the President, and the money he was laundering. With these reports, and the one you gave me, a vote of no confidence was called."

Toni shook her head. *Politicians. Couldn't they see 'Tiam had been set up?*

During the week Zaambuka had been in intensive care Toni had met with the three department heads of the PST.

General Trasken told her that without proof 'Tiam would be held accountable and that they were investigating the links between the President and 'Tiam. The suggestion was that he had conspired with the President to assassinate Ramo.

Ramo continued. "During the same session, they tabled a suggestion that the APE should have a new leader, one to work directly with the leader of the Confederacy to formalize the alliance between our two Sectors. They voted on that too. It passed."

Toni had been wondering when Ramo would get around to telling him. She personally thought it was all too rapid, but no one cared what she thought.

"I was elected by a unanimous vote. I assume I've been offered the role out of sympathy," Ramo said unassumingly. "However, I plan to take advantage of the new powers I've been bestowed for as long as I can, to get the process underway."

A smile quirked Zaambuka's lips. "Congratulations. Then they also voted for the alliance?"

Ramo smiled again. "Yes, effective immediately," she said. "There will be a great deal more discussion, of course—legal proceedings to be raised against the ex-President, details to sort out, but now that this decision has been made, things should flow more smoothly."

Toni smirked. An alliance with the Confederacy would be anything but smooth. However, she was sure Ramo was up to the challenge.

"Congratulations on your new position, Madam President." Zaambuka touched Ramo's wrist. The woman's pale skin flushed. Ramo took his hand in both of hers.

"Please, call me Cat. You saved my life."

"I hear you saved mine as well."

Toni swallowed a groan. *Give me a break.*

Ramo withdrew her hands. "Kalzee'tiam's supporters are in disarray. Did Agent Delle tell you?" she asked, looking at Toni. "Senator Kalzee'tiam has been arrested."

He glanced at Toni. "Not yet. I—" The door flung open and the nosy nurse rushed back in.

"Madam President!" she gasped.

Toni jumped to her feet. "What is it?"

Nurse Delin moved straight to the wall and activated the viewscreen, changing the channel and standing back.

"—found this morning. I repeat, the former President's body has been found this morning. After the impeachment notice, the office was sealed pending investigation into the former President's conduct. The staff here are obviously extremely upset; we have been unable to speak with anyone. We understand Tessa Dutton, the President's personal assistant, found the former President's body and has been hospitalized for shock."

Shenghi. Gallian's cleaning house.

Ramo stared at Zaambuka, her eyes wide. Her hand covered her mouth. Zaambuka's lips tightened. Toni's gaze returned to the news anchor.

"Are there any indications of foul play, Shell?"

The reporter shook her head. "No, Miena. We have spoken to the lead investigators at the scene, and we understand a note was found next to the body."

"Do you know what it said?" The well-dressed anchor straightened, her eyes lit at the scent of scandal.

The reporter nodded. "Sources say that the note accepts full responsibility for the assassination attempt on then Vice-President, now President Ramo. Of course, investigators were quick to point out that this—"

Ramo gestured for the nurse to turn the screen off. Her security team would no doubt appear at any moment to hustle her away. She turned to Zaambuka. "Suicide?"

"Apparently."

Toni knew it wasn't. She suspected Zaambuka knew too. With the former President accepting full responsibility for the attempt on Ramo's life, any official inquiry into the assassination plot would end. With the change in government, perhaps no investigation would take place at all. She wondered if that was a coincidence.

Gallian's plan had backfired. The Senate was more united now than ever. If it *was* Gallian's plan.

After a long pause, Zaambuka made an obvious attempt to change the subject. "Have they given you an official title yet?"

Oh, come on!

Ramo grimaced. "Yes. Chief of Universal Unity, Head of the Allied Planets Executive Senate, and Joint President of the new Allied Planets United Confederacy."

She should be embarrassed. It's ridiculous.

"That's quite a mouthful."

"Well, as I said before, I would like you to call me Cat, if you would, Ant," she said, touching his arm.

He broke out coughing. Letting Ramo hike his pillow higher, he smothered his next cough against his shoulder to avoid hacking into her ear.

He took a deep breath. "Ant?" he echoed.

Ramo's face pinked and she let loose a giggle that Toni thought completely inappropriate. "Yes, if I may call you that? Agent Delle said that's what your friends and family call you."

Toni stilled. *Here it comes.*

"Family? I don't—"

"Well, she didn't say family exactly. She mentioned your brother."

Zaambuka's jaw dropped open. His eyes snapped to Toni. She held his stare.

Yes. I know.

EPILOGUE

"She's late."

Toni eyed the C-bot beneath the table. Mate lay at her feet; his head resting on top of her boot. "I know."

"It's not like her."

"I know." She tapped the edge of her empty glass, her third in as many hours. Jas had never been this late before. A chill kissed Toni's neck, sending a shiver over her body. Something was wrong. Scratching her shoulder, she ran through all the reasons Jas might have to excuse her tardiness. It was a short list.

Leaning back, she glanced around the noisy bar. Their latest haunt was hopping with many unfamiliar faces. The perfect game pool. So where was her friend?

The twin scents of body odor and sweat threatened suffocation. Toni twitched as three dock workers passed her chair. She needed a new drink to bury her nose in.

Music once again burst through the bar's speakers, thumping with a beat she felt low in her belly. Toni caught the eye of the man at the bar. Human of Asian descent.

Cute. Dark eyes, sensual lips, high cheek bones. It was an attractive package. He would do as a nice distraction. She flashed him a smile. His eyes darted away instantly; his entire body stiffening as he turned his back on her. *Whatever.* She waved a hand at the barwoman and was acknowledged with a nod. Running a finger along the side of her shades Toni signaled Zach. His text bloomed onto her display.

Zach: Do you want me to send Cos a message?

"Yeah, could you? I'm getting a bad feeling."

While she waited for the CII to get back to her, she scanned the room again. Two women were engaged in an intense conversation at the table in the far corner. The blonde leaned into the smaller woman's body, her face furious. The petite woman straightened her shoulders and pushed up, her hands moving as quickly as her mouth. Ouch, lovers' quarrel. Toni's eyes skittered past them and locked onto a pair of dark eyes staring directly at her.

No.

Mate picked up on her tension immediately. His head came out from under the table. A growl reverberated deep in his chest.

Toni flung back her chair. It landed with a crash behind her, turning every head, including Asian hottie at the bar. *Too late, cutie.* Before she could take more than two steps, Daniel Colten stood in front of her. He held up a hand but it was the look in his eyes that stopped her from pushing past him.

"We need to talk."

*

On the border of Confederacy space, the Ascendancy's attack fleet opened fire.

THE END

Acknowledgements

I'd like to thank the following people who helped *White Fire* become what it is - so much fun.

Anthony, Cathy and Bernadette - you know why.

Linh, Margo and Carolyn for reading it over and over, and for your CP & Beta-ery goodness! Every time I received an email from you my writing became better. You are just fabulous. Keep on keeping on. I can't wait to read your words soon.

Mum and Dad who read it time and again, and didn't sigh too much when I said I had another version.

Kit Carstairs, Stuart MacDonald, Marissa Fuller, Kate Foster, Joel Naoum and Libby Turner - You make my words sing! Thank you for everything.

Helen for believing.

Gerry for loving me and for listening to my doubts, changes, thoughts, edits and for being made to read it! (And for the printer! Oh, how I love thee.)

I love you all so much. Thank you!

www.ingramcontent.com/pod-product-compliance
Lightning Source LLC
Chambersburg PA
CBHW032057180726
48284CB00002B/331